The questions begin...

"I'm Detective Hawthorne," he said, unnecessarily. "I need to speak to"—he looked down at a notebook he'd flipped open—"Mrs. Nik—, Nik—"

"I'm Mrs. Nikolopatos," I said. "Please call me Georgie." *It's about time the cops got here*, I thought.

"Mrs.—uh, Georgie."

"Yes?"

"I'm looking into the death of Domenic DiTomasso, sometimes known as Big Dom."

"I'm not sure how I can help you." This guy was definitely scary. I guess that's a good thing in law enforcement.

"We understand that you and Mr."—he consulted the notebook again—"Morgan found the body."

"Yes, Keith was giving me a ride to the spa on Valentine Island when we found him."

"You were just motoring on by and saw a floating body?" His tone was skeptical. My hackles rose.

"That's right."

"And you went over to investigate?"

"Yes."

"Why did you disturb the body?"

I took a deep breath and refused to be baited. I'd seen enough winter reruns of cop shows to know that he was trying to throw me off balance and get me to admit to something. For God's sake, was I a suspect?

Feta Attraction

Susannah Hardy

BERKLEY PRIME CRIME, NEW YORK

THE BERKLEY PUBLISHING GROUP
Published by the Penguin Group
Penguin Group (USA) LLC
375 Hudson Street, New York, New York 10014

USA • Canada • UK • Ireland • Australia • New Zealand • India • South Africa • China

penguin.com

A Penguin Random House Company

FETA ATTRACTION

A Berkley Prime Crime Book / published by arrangement with the author

For information, address: The Berkley Publishing Group,
a division of Penguin Group (USA) LLC,
375 Hudson Street, New York, New York 10014.

ISBN: 978-0-425-27165-0

PUBLISHING HISTORY
Berkley Prime Crime mass-market / January 2015

PRINTED IN THE UNITED STATES OF AMERICA

10 9 8 7 6 5 4 3 2 1

Cover illustration by Bill Bruning.
Cover art: *Broken plate* © Pavel Ignatov/Shutterstock.
Cover design by Diane Kolsky.
Interior text design by Kelly Lipovich.

*For Mike and Will, because this book,
and every book, is for you.*

*And in memory of Gary Stacy and
William Appleby, Jr., two extraordinary teachers
who inspired me to write, and without whom
this book would never have come to be.*

ACKNOWLEDGMENTS

To Mike and Will (yes, you get a dedication *and* an acknowledgment), thank you for supporting me every step of the way, and for making the sacrifices of eating out, going to the movies, or going fishing when I needed time alone to write. You are my greatest loves, now and always.

To Vivienne Lynge, who made me know it was possible to write a book and finish it. I raise my fruity girlie drink in your direction.

To Casey Wyatt, Sugar Jamison/Ginger Jamison, Katy Lee, PJ Sharon, Regina Kyle, T.L. Costa, Gail Chianese, Jamie K. Schmidt, and the rest of the ladies and gentlemen of the world's most dangerous writers' group, the Connecticut Chapter of Romance Writers of America (CTRWA), for their unwavering friendship. Come to think of it, you all deserve a toast with a fruity girlie drink as well.

Acknowledgments

To Jesse Hayworth, Lucy Burdette/Roberta Isleib, Kristan Higgins, Thea Devine, and Laura Bradford/Elizabeth Lynn Casey, for their invaluable advice on breaking into and navigating the publishing world. Thank you, ladies, for everything, from the bottom of my heart. I hope I can pay it forward someday.

To my agent extraordinaire, John Talbot, and my fabulous editor, Michelle Vega, for taking a chance on a newbie and for making this book so much better than I ever thought it could be.

And to Laurie Paro. She'll know why.

The secret of happiness is freedom. The secret of freedom is courage.

—THUCYDIDES, ANCIENT GREEK HISTORIAN, 460 B.C.–404 B.C.

◈ ONE ◈

When you marry a gay man, it shouldn't come as a surprise when he leaves you.

I stuck a clean spoon into the vat of Greek tomato sauce I'd been stirring, gave it a taste, and added another handful of oregano and a pinch of cinnamon. The Bonaparte House kitchen staff bustled around me, but I barely noticed them.

This wasn't the first time my husband had gone off for a day or two. He usually headed over the border to Montreal, an easy drive across the St. Lawrence River by way of the international bridge from Bonaparte Bay, New York.

But this time felt . . . different. I couldn't say why. Call it intuition, a gut feeling, whatever. This time, I wondered whether he'd left me for good. For another man.

"Etty-six!" My mother-in-law, Sophie Nikolopatos, brought me out of my thoughts and back to the present. The last dinner of the night had just left the kitchen. Sophie rose from her chair, a pained expression on her elfin face, and limped out of the kitchen toward the central staircase leading to our living quarters on the second floor. She beckoned me to follow. As though I didn't have a couple of hours of work left to do tonight, even after we closed. Managing this place meant sixteen-hour workdays, all summer long. I shut off the burner and complied.

"Have you heard from Spiro yet, Georgie?" she demanded, out of earshot of the busboy and servers.

"Not since the night before last."

Sophie extended a wad of loose papers toward me with one hand and patted her apron pocket, which was bulging with most of the night's cash receipts, with the other. "We had a good night. Many lamb specials."

I nodded and took the paperwork. It had been a real struggle to get her to accept credit cards, and Sophie still resisted the computerized ordering and payment system I'd installed a few years ago. She kept track of the business by hand and memory. I usually just tossed the stuff when she wasn't looking.

"No thanks to that no-good son of mine," she said. "Close up for me, dear, will you? I want to go upstairs."

"Of course." I closed up every night, and opened up every morning, and handled pretty much everything else too. Sophie owned the place but was more or less a figurehead. Spiro was the spoiled, lazy heir to the kingdom. I loved them both—Sophie like the mother I didn't have, and Spiro . . . Well, I don't know what we were to each other, really. Cohabiting co-parents, perhaps, to our daughter, Callista. I felt a pang of loneliness as I thought about my beautiful girl, even though I knew she was safe and happy visiting her great-aunt in Greece.

Sophie's eyes narrowed. "You sick? You're not talking much."

Sick? No. But I'd been stewing all day. If Spiro divorced me, I'd not only be out of a marriage. I'd be out of a job. After twenty years, I didn't know how to do anything else. And I didn't want to. This restaurant, with the living quarters upstairs, was my home.

But it wouldn't do to bother Sophie. She had enough to worry about. "I'm fine." I mustered up a smile for her. "Go on, now. I'll finish here."

"I can't believe he no call his mother."

Depending on what he was doing, I could. "Don't worry. I'll track him down. Good night, *Mana*."

Her face relaxed, and she smiled back at me. "*Kali nichta*, dear. You a good girl." She patted my cheek, in a gesture that meant she loved me. In her own slightly skewed way.

A door slammed in the kitchen, followed by the unmistakable sound of china hitting the tile floor and shattering. Sophie spun on the heels of her immaculate white walking shoes and hustled back the way we'd come, cursing in Greek. Our dishwasher, Russ Riley, was in for a tongue-lashing. Breaking china was pretty close to stealing, in her book. I had to work to keep up.

"Sophie, Sophie, Sophie! Where are you, my darling?"

I smelled him before I saw him. Domenic "Big Dom" DiTomasso leaned up against the stainless steel prep counter as the overhead fan blew a wind of stale cigar smoke my way. His dark trousers were held up with a black leather belt

3

positioned under the overhang of his considerable belly. His snowy dress shirt was open at the neck, revealing a pile of thick salt-and-pepper hair curling up and over the collar.

Sophie trotted into the kitchen, the limp forgotten. Her eyes flashed.

"Why do you come here, Domenic, and mess up my etty-six? Don't you have your own etty-six?"

Big Dom owned the Sailor's Rest, a restaurant a couple of doors down from the Bonaparte House. His place was our main competition. Once at the beginning of the season, once at the end of the season, and periodically in between for the last few years, Big Dom approached Sophie with an offer to buy her out. She refused, holding out for more money or because she just didn't want to sell to Big Dom; I was never sure.

"You beautiful creature," he purred, a three-hundred-pound kitten in cuff links.

"Please leave my restaurant, Domenic. You are frightening my customers away." She smiled, though. Her eyes weren't flashing anger, as I'd thought. She was . . . flirting with him?

"Sophie, your customers are already leaving. Come out and have a drink with me."

"I don't think so," she said loftily. She smoothed her cap of auburn-dyed curls with one hand, looked at her nails, and cut her big dark eyes back at him.

"A woman like you should not be working. You should be spoiled and pampered. Let me buy this place. Then you can take your family and go back to your beautiful island. I will come with you and keep you warm in the winter." He grinned suggestively.

4

She ignored that last bit, and I shuddered at the thought of living, even part of the year, in any kind of proximity to him. Of course, whether I would be spending any more winters in Greece remained to be seen.

"How much?" The offer had never been enough before, but I guess she couldn't resist hearing it again.

He leaned forward and put his big tanned face close to her ear. *Damn!* I was roosted over by the massive Victorian sideboard that served us the waitress station, and I couldn't hear what he was saying.

"Pah!" She practically spat at him. "Get out of here, Domenic!" She let loose with a tsunami of Greek that even I, who had a pretty good command of the language after all these years, could only partially decipher. One phrase I caught would translate loosely into English as "horse's genitals."

He laughed and made a courtly bow, no small feat for a man of his proportions.

"You haven't seen the last of me, my goddess." He turned and swept out of the kitchen with another slam of the door.

"That man is a—a menace!" she shouted after him. "I'm gonna put him out of business. You wait and see!" She turned and stormed off upstairs.

After the last of our employees had left, I locked the front doors, shut down the exterior lights, and headed into my office. I sank into my sumptuous down-filled chair and ottoman, ridiculously expensive but so worth it. I poured myself a glass of Cabernet—frankly, I've never cared for the Greek *retsina*, which tastes like a pine tree. My feet ached and a deep fatigue settled into my muscles as I willed myself to relax.

I booted up my laptop, scrolling through my in-box and hoping for a message from Callista. I deleted all the ads for Viagra, a little bit wistfully just the same. It had been a long time since I'd had any romance in my life. The missive from a deposed Nigerian prince also went to the recycle bin.

I sipped my wine and set it back on its coaster on my desk. A message caught my eye. The address field read "Sender Unknown," but the subject line was "Georgie—Urjent." *Crappy spammy speller,* I thought, and clicked on the message. Too late, I realized my mistake. Hopefully my computer hadn't just become infected with a virus or worm.

FIND IT AND BRING IT TO ME OR YOU'LL BE SORRY.

Huh? I shrugged and hit the *delete* key.

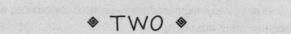

❖ TWO ❖

I woke to bright sunlight flickering through the leaves and branches of the huge old hickory tree outside my bedroom window. A cool breeze off the river billowed the sheer pale curtains into the room, and I instinctively pulled the comforter up around my neck with a shiver. August days are hot here in the North Country, but nights and mornings are cool and afford a nice excuse to stay in bed a bit longer. The alarm clock radio wouldn't go off for a few more minutes.

"Damn!" I threw off the covers and jumped up, an adrenaline surge allowing me to brave the chill, and ran through my little sitting area to the attached bathroom. I turned on the hot tap full blast and waited for it to warm up, which could take several minutes in this old pile of rocks. I couldn't believe I had forgotten that, weeks ago, Spiro had arranged for *Ghost Squad* to come and investigate the house and restaurant for paranormal activity. The cast and crew of the television show would have full run of the place all afternoon and through the night, and I hadn't picked up my rooms; nor would I have time to do it properly before they got here. Not that I was a huge slob, but having a dozen or more people poking around my private living spaces would require some tidying up.

I threw off the oversized T-shirt I had slept in and stepped into the steaming shower. At least I could absolve myself of guilt for not attempting the Pilates DVD I'd bought in Watertown, the closest city to Bonaparte Bay, last week. My intentions had been excellent. But the shrink-wrap was still intact.

No sense dwelling on that now. My core could wait. I soaped up with some luscious almond-smelling creamy stuff and breathed in a big lungful of the scent. I shampooed, rinsed, and stepped out onto my plushy bathmat, grabbed the towel from the European-style towel heater, and dried off.

Fifteen minutes later I was dressed and had shoved all the visible loose clutter into the emptiest drawer I could find. I'd have to come back upstairs in a couple of hours and see whether I could straighten out the closet. Those *Ghost Squad* members were forever opening doors and sticking equipment into enclosed spaces.

No sooner had I gotten downstairs and into the kitchen, hair still damp, than Sophie accosted me. For some reason that crazy e-mail from last night popped into my head. *Bring what to who? Or whom*, I mentally corrected.

"Where is he? I need to talk to him," she demanded.

"I still haven't seen him, Sophie." I dumped a premeasured foil packet of coffee into the Bunn machine and flipped the switch. I retrieved two thick china mugs from a shelf and added a good slug of cream—the real stuff that we whipped up fresh every night for the desserts—to each. This was one of the reasons I needed that Pilates DVD.

Sophie was more insistent than usual regarding Spiro's whereabouts, making me instantly suspicious. "What's so important?"

Her face softened. "Never mind. Just let me know when you see him."

"Have you checked his room?" The coffeemaker spluttered and I removed the carafe, sticking the coffee cups one by one under the stream of hot liquid. I replaced the pot and congratulated myself for not spilling any during these maneuvers. Just one of my many skills, honed after years in the restaurant business. I handed a cup to Sophie and took a sip out of my own.

"Not there. And he don't answer his cell phone."

I looked out the back door into the employee parking lot. Dolly, our cook, was stepping out of her metallic green Ford LTD. "The Mercedes is still gone." A bubble of anger formed in my gut, mixed with the hot coffee, and expanded. It was damned inconsiderate of Spiro to just ditch us for so long without so much as a phone call. This had to end. *Maybe it's already ended—for you,* a voice piped up inside my head.

Well, when he did turn up, I was going to let him have it. Not that I hadn't done it before, and not that it ever did any good.

Dolly came in and set a platter of assorted pastries on the counter. "Help yourself," she said. "I stopped at Kelsey's

Bakery on the way in." Dolly had worked for us longer than I'd been here, thirty years or more. Her hair was blond and teased up in a high nest into which she'd inserted a sparkly butterfly barrette. Her real name was Norma, but the story was that she'd seen Dolly Parton play at the state fair one summer and had been inspired to change her name. It suited her. She got herself a cup of coffee and sat down for her morning gossip with Sophie.

I lifted the plastic dome and grabbed a cheese Danish off the tray, then went to my office. I put the pastry on a napkin and sat down at my desk. If Spiro divorced me and I had to leave, where would I go? I'd miss this place, with its beautiful natural woodwork and shining floors and the flood of bright sunlight through the bank of tall windows overlooking the little garden I'd set up for the employees to take their breaks.

No time for wallowing, I thought. I checked my to-do list, feeling in control for the first time that morning. Number 1: Update Menu Copy. That entry had been on my to-do list since the beginning of the season, I noted, feeling out of control again. But it needed to be done today before the ghost hunters got here. I took the top menu from the stack on my desk and pulled out the paper insert containing the history of the Bonaparte House.

WELCOME TO BONAPARTE BAY AND
THE HISTORIC BONAPARTE HOUSE!

Well, that much could stay. *Bonaparte Bay is located on the picturesque American shore of the St. Lawrence River in the heart of the Thousand Islands. The St. Lawrence connects Lake Ontario and the rest of the Great Lakes to the west with the Atlantic Ocean to the east. Thousands of ships pass through these waters every year.*

I bit into the Danish and sucked some sticky frosting from my fingers without thinking, then wiped them on my apron. My ever-present bottle of hand sanitizer sat accusingly a few inches away and I pumped a dollop into my hand.

The Bonaparte House was built around 1822, although the records are sketchy. This native fieldstone mansion, built as a two-story octegon (I circled that with a blue pen) *with a large cupola adorning its crown in the style of Orson Fowler* (Okay, that language could be modernized. And I should say who Orson Fowler was. I think I knew once, but I'd long since forgotten), *is the oldest surviving building in Bonaparte Bay. Local legend says that the house was intended for Napoleon when his escape from exile was accomplished. Of course, Napoleon never did escape, and he never lived here.*

In the last century, Vasilios "Basil" Nikolopatos settled in the Thousand Islands, which reminded him of the landscape of Greece. He bought the Bonaparte House and transformed it into a restaurant serving the delicious foods of his native land. Basil died years ago, but his wife, Sophie, and son, Spiro, continue to operate the Bonaparte House for your enjoyment today.

Spiro had left me off the menu when he'd prepared it this spring. If I'd bothered to review the back copy instead of just the menu selections then, I might have known he was up to something. I opened up my laptop and plugged in the flash drive Spiro had left on my desk, found the document containing the menu, and edited it. I added "daughter-in-law, Georgie" between Sophie's and Spiro's names. *Ha*. I made the other necessary changes, executed a spell-check, then printed off a hundred copies of the inserts and stacked them beside the menu folders to be assembled later.

I logged into my e-mail account. There was a note from my friend Eileen asking whether we could get together this week. She must have man trouble again. *Join the club,* I thought.

What the hell? There was another message from an unidentified sender. I couldn't help myself and clicked it open.

WHY DON'T YOU ANSWER? FIND IT AND BRING IT TO ME, OR YOU'LL BE SORRY.

Well, that was helpful. If somebody wanted something from me, the least he or she could do would be to tell me what it was and where I should deliver it. A knock sounded at the door. I looked up, startled, then took a sip of coffee to collect myself. "Hi, Russ. You're here early this morning. Come on in." My pulse slowed, but I still felt jumpy.

Russ Riley was Dolly's son, our dishwasher and general gofer. He was a beefy five feet eight, not quite fat, but he probably would be in a few years. The tail of his long black mullet brushed his waist. He'd tied a red bandanna around his forehead in lieu of a hairnet, which he said cramped his style. His hands were shoved in the pockets of his cutoffs.

"Ma said I should bring this in to you." He looked down

at his Croc-clad feet, then back up. I'd often suspected he might have a bit of a crush on me. He filled my cup from the coffee carafe, then turned and left.

I called out a thank-you and read the e-mail again. If it was a threat, it wasn't very . . . threatening. Should I go to the police? What would I tell them? I sighed in relief as I realized someone must be playing a joke on me. That was what it had to be, though I had no idea who would do such a thing. The e-mail was so vague, so nonspecific, I just couldn't take it seriously. Still, I left it in my in-box. Administrative work finished, I shut down the computer and headed back to the kitchen.

The faint, not unpleasant scent of bleach wafted up to my nostrils as I donned an apron, fresh from the laundry service, and tied it around my waist. Giving my hands a good scrub at the sink, I dried them on a clean towel, put on some gloves, and got to work.

A bowl of lemons sat in front of me, their bright yellow skins making a lovely contrast to the gray stainless steel of the prep counter. I smiled and began to rub the fruit with a fine grater. The process required a light touch; press too hard and I'd have the bitter white pith as well as the fragrant outer peel. A familiar sense of peace washed over me as I cooked. This was my element; this was my art. This I could control. I scraped the zest into a container of fat, silky chicken breasts, and added the juice of the lemons and some olive oil. A bit of sea salt, a few grinds of freshly cracked black pepper, a handful of fresh herbs, and a stir completed the prep for today's lunch special: Greek Chicken with Lemon and Thyme.

Next to me, Dolly peeled and sliced potatoes and onions for the accompanying side dish, and we worked in companionable silence, each of us in her own zone. I covered and refrigerated the meat. With a simple salad of grape tomatoes, cucumbers, feta cheese, and fresh ribbons of basil, all drizzled with olive oil, we were good to go.

Some of the dishes we served were complicated. Pastitsio and moussaka, though undeniably delicious, required hours to produce. My favorite recipes were like today's, though. Simple, and making use of local ingredients whenever possible. The growing season this far north is short, but the produce is fresh and flavorful, and I bought it whenever I could.

A few hours later the lunch rush was over, and Russ, Dolly, and I had completed the daily cleanup and prep work for tomorrow. I put a film of plastic wrap over the leftover cooked meat, which would become a lovely chicken salad with green grapes and toasted walnuts tomorrow, and handed it to Russ. He toted it over to the walk-in cooler.

"Can I stay and help?" Russ removed the bandanna from his head, stuck it in his back pocket, and donned a baseball cap sporting a chain saw manufacturer's logo. I figured he was hoping for an in-person glimpse of *Ghost Squad*'s lone female investigator, a buxom young woman who always seemed to be dressed in a tight, low-cut tank top even when the rest of the crew wore sweatshirts.

"Thanks, Russ, but they've told us we all have to leave so we don't influence the investigation," I said, giving my hands a scrub at the dishwashing sink.

"Do you think this place is haunted?" His big open face

was uneasy as he took off his apron and tossed it in the laundry bin.

"I can tell you that I've lived here for a lot of years and I've never heard or seen anything that makes me think that."

"But Spiro has. He said he heard noises, and got creepy feelings like he was being watched. I think I might have heard something the other day," he added.

"We'll have to see what they find."

Speaking of Spiro, the inconsiderate darling still hadn't shown up or bothered to call. Sophie and I had both tried to contact him several times, but his phone went straight to voice mail. I hoped he was having a good time, wherever he was, because when he got back he was going to have some 'splainin' to do. Whether he'd left me for good or was just off on an extra-long joyride, I was angry with him.

And angrier with myself for not having prepared an exit plan.

Adding to that, I now had to do the interviews with the *Ghost Squad* people myself. What I wanted to do was spend the whole evening relaxing at the spa on Valentine Island, where I'd begged my best girlfriend, Liza, to find me a room. This would be a rare treat in the height of the tourist season.

I headed upstairs and stopped at the door to Spiro's room. Could he have left a note? It seemed unlikely, but I put my key in the lock—couldn't remember the last time I'd done that, or wanted to! The door opened without my turning the key. *Strange.* Being moderately paranoid, Spiro always locked his door.

I surveyed the room. He'd decorated the twelve-by-fifteen-foot space tastefully, though it certainly wasn't to my taste. Chocolate brown walls complemented the original wide plank floorboards, sanded and polished to a glowing honey finish. A few scuffs in the wood over by one of the walls, but that was to be expected in a place this age. Pale blue drapes and some shiny chrome accessories, no fingerprints dulling the surfaces, gave the room a minimalist, modern feel. Nothing was out of place; nor had I expected it would be.

The blue and cream spread covering the king-sized bed was wrinkle free, and the graphic chocolate and vanilla throw pillows were arranged with precision. Hard to tell whether the bed had been slept in. He was such a neatnik, he never left his room without making the bed. I checked the closet—he wouldn't be embarrassed when the *Ghost Squad* checked out his room—but his Louis Vuitton luggage was still there, and it didn't look as though he'd taken anything else with him.

The small table he used as a desk was clean and bare except for a lamp and an unlabeled manila file folder, which I opened. The top pages appeared to be photocopies of historical research about the Bonapartes, but I didn't go any farther. Spiro was convinced Napoleon was Greek, not Italian or French. He was fascinated by the Bonapartes and had been researching the house for years.

That knot of anger in my stomach twisted and re-formed in a different pattern. Why did I continue to allow him to blow off his responsibilities? And why did I continue to clean up the messes he left behind? Only a few months ago, the answer would have been simple—our daughter. But Cal was grown now, off on her own.

I took one last look around. He never, ever went anywhere, including the toilet, without his cell phone, yet there
it was, lying on the night table. I picked it up and stuck it in
my pocket, intending to look at his call records later on.
He'd be ripped when he came back and found it missing. I
smiled at the thought.

A commotion caused me to pull back a curtain and look
outside. Three big black vans with "NYPI" emblazoned on
the side were parked in front of the restaurant. *Ghost Squad*
had arrived.

I descended the stairs and nearly tripped over a thick
orange extension cord. During my short absence, Sophie
had greeted the team from the New York Paranormal Insti-
tute, then left with Dolly, who would drive Sophie to her
cousin's to spend the night. I'd seen the show on cable a few
times and knew that for the two main investigators, the
paranormal was their sideline—during the day they were
electricians or contractors or something. *Hmm,* I thought.
*Maybe I can get them to fix that broken light switch in the
bathroom.*

"I'm Jerry, from NYPI." A studly guy with a shiny bald
head pumped my hand.

"Georgie. I'm one of the owners here." Well, my name
wasn't on the deed, never would be now, but it was way too
complicated a situation to explain on camera.

"Where can we sit down and do the interview?"

I led him and Gary, the other investigator, out to a table
in front of the fireplace in the main dining room, while the
crew set up the video and audio equipment around us. I
cleared off the napkin dispenser, salt and pepper shakers,

and the small Neofitou vase filled with red carnations, moving everything to table six. I made a mental note to order more vases. The little black-and-gold beauties tended to disappear into coat pockets and oversized handbags as free souvenirs.

Gary switched on a microphone. "Your husband called us saying he's been hearing noises at night—knocking, shuffling, voices, that sort of thing?"

"Yes, he has mentioned that to me and to other people here at the restaurant."

"How about you? Have you ever heard or seen anything strange?"

"This is an old house. Who knows what's in the walls? I'm not sure I want to know, to tell the truth. I've heard noises at night, but nothing that scared me."

This was so not my thing.

"I see Napoleon's portrait here over the fireplace." Jerry nodded toward the huge oil painting that presided over the room, and the camera operator panned upward. "We understand that this house was built for him."

"That's the legend. A group of French exiles built it hoping to rescue him from Elba, hide him here, and plan out his return to power in France."

"Has there ever been any activity associated with the portrait? We sometimes find that to be the case."

"Again, I don't have personal knowledge of any 'activity.' My husband would be the one to ask, but he . . . was called away unexpectedly."

"Napoleon never lived here."

I guessed this had to be dumbed down for television. "That's right."

"Do you know if anyone ever died in this house?"

Not yet, I thought darkly. "Not to my knowledge, no, but as I said, it's a two-hundred-year-old house and it's certainly possible."

"We're going to set up our equipment and see if we can help you out here."

I wasn't aware we needed help. But they seemed like decent guys and free advertising was nothing to be sneezed at. It was all over town that we were being investigated. We were booked solid with reservations through the next three weekends.

"Here's my cell number in case you need to reach me." I handed him a business card.

On a whim, I returned to Spiro's room and grabbed the manila folder. I shoved it into the outer pocket of my overnight bag—a Target special. I did not share my husband's designer tastes. There might be nothing interesting to read over at Liza's. Maybe Spiro had left a clue as to where he'd gone.

I walked the half block down to the Theresa Street docks and called the water taxi to take me to Valentine Island. Twenty minutes later, the afternoon sun was dipping lower on the horizon, and I was still waiting. I opened the folder and read the headline of the top newspaper article. "Joseph Bonaparte, Once King of Spain, Was North Country Resident." Before I could read further, a friendly toot-toot of a small boat horn made me look up.

"Waiting for me?"

I smiled down into the soft gray eyes of my friend Keith Morgan.

"My whole life." I batted my eyes at him, then felt ridiculous. I was no good at flirting. And I shouldn't be flirting with Keith anyway.

He grinned and put a hand to his chest. "Be still my heart."

"The water taxi hasn't shown up, and I'm supposed to spend the night pampering myself at Liza's."

"Want a lift? I'm just out for a little cruise. It's such a nice day. I can even offer you a drink."

"You are the absolute best."

He looked up at me, his face serious, the sun behind him turning his hair into a golden halo.

Hello! I thought, wishing I could take it back. He was a great-looking guy, and if my situation weren't so complicated, we might have made some sense together. As it was, something was missing and I didn't know what it was. I was pretty sure the problem was me. I had no idea how normal couples acted in real relationships.

"You'd better mean that." He tied off his boat, a gleaming teak and mahogany antique with the words "Chris-Craft" stenciled on the hull, then reached up onto the dock and grabbed my bag. He stowed it down by his feet, not that that would keep it dry if we got sprayed by something bigger—or faster—than us. A laker blew its horn off in the distance. The football-field-length freight boats that sailed the Great Lakes and made their way out to sea via the main shipping channel of the St. Lawrence Seaway could capsize a small boat if the drivers weren't careful.

Keith took my hand and bent his head to kiss it lightly. Why'd he have to do that?

"You're looking lovely tonight, Georgiana."

Yes, I thought, I'd worn my most glamorous "I Heart Thousand Islands" sweatshirt just for the occasion. And scrunchied my unstyled hair into an elegant ponytail to boot. If he was trying to win me over, calling me by my god-awful given name was not the way to go about it.

He dropped my hand and reached into the cooler sitting next to him, pulling out two icy Canadian beers and opening each with a deft twist. He wiped the condensation off one with the tail of his shirt and handed it to me.

"Have time to go for a ride with me before I drop you off? I was just going to tool around for a while, then head home."

I considered his offer. "I guess I've got time for that." Liza lived at the spa and wouldn't care what time I got there, and since she owned the place, the Jacuzzi, kitchen, and wine cellar were always open.

Keith set down his beer and pulled back on the throttle, expertly maneuvering away from the dock and out into the water. The drone of the motor rumbled through me and dissipated the tension of the day as we glided down the river coast, past beautifully landscaped Victorian mansions neighbored by small cottages. As we passed Yale's Skull and Bones society retreat, which was, inexplicably, rather dilapidated, I asked whether Keith had seen Spiro around town lately.

"I've been working over at Liza's all day." Keith was one of the few locals who worked year-round. He had a small business on the east end of town where he restored antique boats and provided storage services in the off-season. Last winter he'd gone to Vermont and taken a two-week class from a master woodworker to learn how to make furniture using only hand tools. He had a talent for it and had sold several pieces to summer residents, with many more on order.

Keith waited for me to go on.

"He left the house and didn't take his cell phone with him, and we haven't heard from him."

"That's not so unusual, is it?"

Everybody knew about Spiro and his little . . . indiscretions.

"No, of course not." We were nearing the Devil's Oven, a cave on the edge of an island where a locally famous river pirate once hid out during the War of 1812. Next weekend the town would celebrate Pirate Days, and I had an enormous amount of work to do to prepare for the influx of tourists. "It feels off to me, you know? He's been gone longer than he ever has before. Maybe I'm just angry about him ditching me when the TV crew got here."

He didn't say anything, but maneuvered around an object bobbing just ahead. I was surprised as we passed it. It was a half-full bottle of Ouzo, the same brand we carried at the Bonaparte House. It drifted toward the island, then floated into the mouth of the cave, where it disappeared.

I glanced over at the Oven and could feel my forehead furrowing. "What's that?" I squinted at the sun-dappled water. Something didn't look right.

"What?" Keith cut the motor.

I pointed. "Over there." I stared as we drifted closer. "That's a person!"

Protruding from the cave entrance and floating on the surface of the water was an arm.

Keith turned the motor back on and throttled up slowly toward the floating form, which undulated gently.

"Get closer," I ordered. "Whoever that is could still be alive." I stood up on the deck and prepared to dive into the water.

Keith put a hand on my shoulder to restrain me. "Let me do it," he said.

I considered my swimming skills—surprisingly poor considering I'd lived my entire life on the water. "I'll call nine-one-one." The call would summon either the local police, who owned a speedboat, or the Coast Guard, which maintained a small station a short way upstream. I took a deep breath to calm myself.

We were near the body now and Keith stepped over the side into water up to his knees, his back toward me.

"Nine-one-one, what is your emergency?" The voice was scratchy and kept cutting in and out. Cell phone service could be unreliable in this area.

"Nine-one-one, what is your emergency?" the dispatcher repeated, less patiently this time. I recognized the voice of Cindy Dumont.

"Cindy, it's Georgie from the Bonaparte House. I'm calling from a boat." Best not to say it was Keith's boat. It would be all over the Bay before she even called in the emergency personnel that I was out with him—not that people wouldn't find out soon enough anyway. "There's a body floating at the mouth of the Devil's Oven."

This got her attention. "Really?" I could practically see

Susannah Hardy

her sitting up straighter. "Who is it?" Cindy asked, her voice almost gleeful.

"I don't know. The body's facedown. It's wearing a suit coat so it must be a guy."

"Well, roll him over and find out. It'll be easy since he's in the water."

Sensitivity had never been her strong suit. "Cindy, just call this in to Rick over at the police station."

"Oh, okay, but call me back when you find out who it is."

"I'll do that." I'd do no such thing. She'd find out soon enough since she and Rick's wife, Joanie, played bingo every Saturday at the American Legion and were thick as thieves.

I ended the call and turned back toward Keith. He'd managed to turn the body faceup, but I still couldn't see much.

"Keith, can I help? Is he still alive?" I didn't see how that was possible.

"No." His face was grim. "He's dead. Been dead for a few hours, I'd say. And there's a dent in his skull."

A thought struck me then, hard. My husband was missing. I stopped breathing. Just like the guy in the water. *Spiro.*

◆ THREE ◆

"It isn't . . ." I couldn't bring myself to finish the sentence. Spiro and I had our differences of opinion (like every hour of every day), but I wouldn't want to see him dead. Sophie would be devastated. Cal—my poor angel Callista—would be crushed. I guessed I'd miss him too.

"Honey," Keith said. "It's not Spiro. It's Big Dom."

"Big Dom?" I asked stupidly. A wave of relief washed over me even as my head began to spin.

Keith sloshed aside and I could see the body, black suit, black open-necked shirt, with enough wet gold around his neck, left wrist, and pinky that that might have been what sunk him.

"Georgie? Georgie! Did you hear me? It's Big Dom." I shook my head as Keith waded over and put his arm around me, turning me away from the cave and toward the shore. "Don't look anymore, okay?"

I nodded and rested my head on his shoulder. I heard the whine of a motor and could see Chief Rick Moriarty and Deputy Tim Arquette taking this opportunity to run the BBPD police boat at full speed. Smiles dropped from their faces as they approached.

"Keith, whatcha got there?" Rick blustered, now on official police business.

"It's Big Dom. We were out for a ride and saw him floating out of the Oven. We came over to see if we could help. But I'm afraid it's too late."

He held me a little closer. I let him do it, even though it felt . . . funny. Sort of okay, but almost wrong. Which was of course ridiculous, considering my marital situation.

"We'll handle it from here," Rick said. "Timmy, call up Greta over at the hospital and tell her we've got a stiff coming in to the morgue. Then get over here and give me a hand getting him into the zipper bag. He's wet and he's gonna be slippery."

"Rick, I'm taking Georgie over to the spa. If you need statements or anything, let me know."

He waved us away dismissively. "You two go on, now. We've got this under control." He pulled out his phone.

"Yes, Joanie, I called you as soon as I knew. Now, don't be that way or I won't tell you . . ."

We motored on up the river. Big Dom had been eighty-sixed.

Fifteen minutes later Keith had delivered me like a FedEx package to my friend Liza Grant. I was nicely ensconced in a big, rose-colored velvet chair with my feet up and a Henry VIII–sized goblet of red wine in my hand. Liza sat in a matching chair next to me, serenely waiting for me to talk when I was ready. She was the most calm and centered person I knew, and her presence was so comforting, it took only a few sips of the gorgeous ruby liquid to bring back my voice.

"He was dead, Li, dead and floating on the water." The scene repeated in my head like the skipping Shaun Cassidy LP I had for some reason saved from my junior high years and stored away in the back of my closet at the Bonaparte House.

"There was nothing you could have done. You need to focus on something else and let it go."

"And Spiro is gone again— of course, it isn't the first time, but this time I'm worried. I don't know why. And I've got ghost hunters in my house. What if they find something?" I didn't believe in ghosts but my anxiety level was rising again. I took a big gulp of the wine. Yikes! What if they found the Shaun Cassidy record? Now, that would be embarrassing.

"There is energy at the Bonaparte House, but there are no earthbound human spirits." Liza could be a little scary sometimes. What the heck did that mean?

"Well, that's comforting, I guess."

"Here, have something to eat." She passed me an antique silver platter loaded with plump green grapes, a soft goat cheese, and a warm, fragrant loaf of sliced French bread. Where had she gotten a fresh baguette at eight thirty at night on an island when I knew the cook had gone home hours ago? The sight of the luscious vittles reminded me that in my rush to leave the restaurant and get out of the way of the investigators, I had neglected to eat dinner. I spread some cheese onto a piece of bread with a mother-of-pearl-handled knife, scarfed it down, and ate another. I recognized the cheese as a local artisanal variety that was made by gray-bearded throwbacks over at the communal farm at Rossie (which we locals pronounced with the accent on the second syllable—"Raw-SEE") a few miles away. They'd been there since the seventies and apparently weren't going anywhere.

"Have you heard from Cal? How is she doing in Greece?" Her attempt to distract me was obvious, and I appreciated it.

"I got an e-mail a couple of days ago. She says the archaeological dig is a lot of physical work, but she's having a wonderful time. She's dating a Greek boy Sophie's sister set her up with."

"You must miss her."

"I do. We e-mail and talk on the phone a few times a week, but it isn't the same as having her with me." I sighed. "I know she's happy, so I try to be happy for her."

"I had Keith over here today working in the boathouse. He's looking well." Liza handed me a plate of rich-looking, dark chocolate truffles dusted in cocoa powder. I popped a whole one into my mouth and let it melt luxuriously on my tongue, savoring the creamy, sweet-bitter taste as long as I could before I swallowed.

"Yes, I guess so." I didn't want to talk about Keith.

"Are you seeing much of him?"

I sucked in another truffle. At this rate the whole plate would be gone in ten minutes and I'd need a glucose meter and an insulin injection.

"Well, I've been to his shop to look at his chairs, and we have coffee down at the Express-o Bean every once in a while, if that's what you mean." The name wasn't a clever sobriquet indicating a place where you could get a quick cup of strong coffee. North Country business owners were often rather bad spellers and even worse pronouncers.

"Mm-hmm." Her expertly tweezed eyebrows rose.

"Cindy is going to call everyone in town tomorrow morning about me being out in a boat with him tonight."

"I don't think so."

"What makes you say that?"

"Because it's all over town tonight. Cindy called Midge at the T-Shirt Emporium and Midge called me before you got here. She told me that you and Keith had been doing it in his boat inside the Devil's Oven when you discovered the body. By the way, if you're looking for your black lace thong, it fell overboard, floated away, and got tangled up in Dom's gold chains."

I felt my face heat up with either embarrassment or anger; I wasn't sure which. Like I would ever intentionally wear a piece of underwear in my butt crack! The thought was horrifying . . . wasn't it? I'd have to figure out a way to do some damage control. Sophie was going to have a bird. She might believe me that I had not been having semipublic sex with Keith, but she would be in a state over the insult to "her" reputation that the gossip would cause. Spiro, of course, could do whatever he wanted, whenever he wanted, with anyone he wanted. She could ignore his little dalliances with equanimity, but the rules were quite different for me. A little swell of defiance rose in my chest. *So what? I'm a grown woman.* I reached for another truffle.

"Georgie, I've wanted to talk to you about something for a while. Now seems like a good time."

"Is this something I want to know?"

"You tell me."

"Okay, hit me." I took a deep breath—not much else could go wrong today. Maybe she *would* hit me, I thought, knock me out, and when I came to, it would become clear that this had all been a dream. Zeke, Hunk, and Hickory would be huddled around my bed, Auntie Em and Uncle Henry each holding a hand, Toto leaping up beside me.

"When was the last time you had an affair?"

I aspirated a little of my wine and began to cough. The question caught me off guard. I sighed. "You know I've never had an affair. Don't make me talk about this now." I hated the whiny tone in my voice.

Liza pulled her bare feet up into her chair, the pale pink of her perfectly pedicured toes shining softly in the low light. "Then it's definitely time for one."

I wasn't so sure about that. Love had always pretty much stunk for me. The thought of diving in again held little appeal, and yet, I couldn't deny that there was a tiny, deeply buried longing somewhere inside me.

Liza broke the silence. "Keith's in love with you. Has been for years."

"He's not in love with me. I'm a married woman," I said, although I knew how ridiculous that sounded.

"You are not a married woman. You are a woman with a piece of paper loosely binding you to a man who doesn't love you, cannot love you, will never love you in the way you should be loved."

"We have a daughter."

"A wonderful daughter, yes, a well-adjusted, grown-up-and-moved-away daughter. Having a child together doesn't make a marriage."

"I made my choice to stay with him years ago. It seemed like the right decision at the time, to keep the family intact for Cal." I fingered the stem of the wineglass. "I don't have to tell you that I know all about Spiro."

"I doubt you know all about Spiro."

"What's that supposed to mean?" Silence. "All right, Li, spill it. What do you know? Do you know where he is?"

"No, I don't know where he is."

Ugh. "Again, what *do* you know?"

She sighed. "Take this for what it's worth, but there are rumors around the Bay that Spiro is in trouble."

"What kind of trouble?" I couldn't believe she was giving any credit to whatever this was. Rumors around the Bay were virtually always just that—rumors. They rarely turned out to be true. I had the phantom thong to prove it.

"You know he's been having an affair with Inky."

Inky LaFontaine? He owned Tat-L-Tails, the tattoo parlor on Thompson Street, and had enough body art to open a gallery and enough piercings that he jingled when he walked. I hadn't known about Inky, but I was often out of that particular loop. Fastidious as Spiro was about personal hygiene and grooming, and given his almost pathological fear of needles, this was a surprising relationship.

"Inky's apparently the type to kiss and tell. He's been

spreading it around that Spiro thinks he's found the fortune his father was always talking about being hidden in the Bonaparte House."

I rolled my eyes involuntarily. That old chestnut had been kicked around and bounced off the curbs of the Bay for the last hundred and fifty years. Everyone in town knew the legend that valuables had been hidden in the house for the use of Napoleon when he escaped and took up residence there. It was beyond comprehension that in all that time nobody had ever found anything. The treasure was of some undetermined makeup—some said it was gold bars; some said it was jewelry; others said it was a Stradivarius violin. For fun, I'd been through every inch of the place with Cal when she was little, and I know Spiro had done so more than once, and we'd never found anything more than some dust, cobwebs, and a few resident arachnids up in the oversized cupola. That Liza was giving this story any credence at all was confounding.

"There's no treasure in that house. It's ridiculous."

"Maybe, maybe not, but I'm just telling you that the story is out there."

"The story is always out there. Why is it surfacing now? Spiro hasn't said a word to me about it."

"I don't know, love. I'm just telling you what I heard."

"So what does this have to do with Spiro being in trouble?"

She set her glass on the side table and leaned back in her chair. "The word is that Spiro has gotten himself involved with the SODs."

"The what?" I scanned my brain but couldn't come up with an association.

"The Sons of Demeter. It's a group of farmers who've banded together to try to preserve their agricultural way of life. Mostly it's just a bunch of old guys watching each other's backs so they can grow their pot without legal interference. Lately, though, I hear that some of the members have gotten more aggressive and have been making loans at double-digit rates to people who are in danger of losing their farms, and it looks like they've branched out into offers to the general public."

"Are you saying Spiro owes this group money?" This made no sense. As far as I knew, Spiro had plenty of money—he certainly spent plenty of it—and I hadn't noticed anything unusual in his activity lately. Why would he need to borrow money?

"I'm saying that he was one of the bankers."

"You mean, like a loan shark?"

"Yes. The Sons are apparently missing a pretty good chunk of money—Spiro's capital, plus more—and now Spiro is gone."

"How do you know all this?" Liza came into town only a couple of times a week, yet had far more information than I, who lived right in the middle of it all.

"People have a tendency to tell me things. And no, I don't generally repeat them, if you're worried about me revealing any of our conversations." There was something so reassuring and innately trustworthy about Liza that I could well believe strangers on the street might confide in her.

"Who are these SODs? Anybody I know?"

"At this point I don't have any more information than what I've told you. I'll keep my eyes and ears open, though, and let you know if I find out anything else."

She handed me a teacup containing a warm amber liquid, which she had prepared while we'd been talking. "This is my special, gentle pain relief and detoxification infusion." I was a bit fuzzy due to the effects of the wine, but it came to me. "You mean, like a hangover preventer?"

"If you want to call it that," she said, with just the slightest testy edge to her voice. I sometimes forgot that this was how she made her living, pampering and detoxifying people. I ought to be more sensitive. "I've given you the Clover Room, since I remember that's your favorite."

"I thought you were booked for the rest of the summer. How's that room available?"

"It developed a sudden air-conditioning problem and its rather famous occupant couldn't take the heat. I've moved her and her entourage over to the Waldorf Suite, which I hadn't planned to use until it was redecorated this fall." She rose elegantly. "Come, now, time for beddy-bye."

I followed her up the fantastically carved dark wood staircase and down a long wallpapered hallway lit with flickering, candle-type electric sconces. The thickly padded carpet runner was bordered on each side by a strip of glowing, polished wood floor, the kind that could be found only in these huge Victorian homes.

We stopped at a heavy dark door carved with a four-leaf clover. The skeleton key was in the lock, and Liza turned it. The door swung open. The walls were the color of a field of lavender in the French countryside. A satiny white comforter covered the bed, which contained a pile of soft pillows in every conceivable shape. A crystal lamp with a silk shade edged in crystal beads glowed and shimmered on the small writing desk. My small overnight bag had been unpacked by some unseen attendant. My reverie slammed shut like a front door in a windstorm when I realized I had brought only an XXL shirt clearanced from the T-Shirt Emporium to sleep in. Not that anyone would see me in my jammies, of course, but somebody had been through my clothes and had handled the pathetic garment. Embarrassing.

"Good night. I'll get you up early, but not too early, for breakfast. I know you have to work tomorrow so I've scheduled the water taxi to be here at nine o'clock sharp."

"Night, Li. Thanks for everything."

"That's what friends are for."

She turned at the doorway and said, firmly but not at all unkindly, "By the way, your 'pajamas' were unacceptable for this establishment. Or for any self-respecting woman, for that matter, whether or not she has a companion at night. I've replaced them with something more suitable."

The door closed and I turned to the closet, where I found a pink silk nightie hanging on a matching padded hanger. It was lovely, but it seemed like a waste to wear this when no one would see it. Had I even shaved this morning?

I used the toidy and brushed my teeth. The toothpaste tube was marked with the Valentine Island logo, the contents another of Liza's concoctions, judging by the unusual herbal taste.

What the hell, I thought. Not that I had any choice. My

nightshirt was gone. It was either the negligee or my birth-day suit. I stripped and slipped the fluid fabric over my head. It ran down my body like a soft shower and settled down around my ankles. Was that a matching wrap on the adjacent hanger? Yes, of course it was. I put it on and did a twirl, the skirts flaring out around me. The only thing this outfit needed, I decided, was a pair of kitten-heeled mules with marabou feathers and I would look just like Barbara Stan-wyck in one of her femme fatale roles. Except, I noticed, examining myself in the cheval mirror, that I needed to get my roots done. And that Pilates DVD would definitely improve things. *All in all, though, not too bad,* I thought, being kind to myself. I took off the wrapper and hung it back up on the padded satin hanger. Where I normally would have just flopped into bed and yanked up the covers, this time I neatly turned down the coverlet, lay down, and pulled the downy warmth up around me. The air-conditioning was working just fine, I noted.

I felt like someone else—someone I'd maybe like to meet again sometime—and fell asleep, dead body, treasure, and amorous boat-builders forgotten.

❖ FOUR ❖

I woke the next morning to a gentle, melodious chiming coming from a small box on the bedside table. "The time is seven thirty a.m.," a mellifluous female voice intoned. I drew back the covers and slid off the bed with a lovely swishy sound. I dressed, now wishing I'd brought something a little nicer than jeans and a T-shirt, took one last appreciative look around the Clover Room, and closed the door behind me.

Back at the Bonaparte House I opened the kitchen door to a blast of country music. Russ came in behind me lugging a box of organic romaine lettuce and tomatoes he'd just picked up from the Rossie hippies. He set the box delicately on the stainless steel counter. It had taken a long time to train him not to slam the boxes down, bruising the produce within. "Treat the veggies like beagle puppies, Russ," I'd told him, and he got it after about a hundred reminders.

"Mornin'," he grunted. He must have been out late carousing. Easy enough to do that in Bonaparte Bay.

"Good morning, Russ."

"I made you a cup of coffee, just the way you like it—cream and lots of sugar," chimed a voice from behind the prep counter.

"Hi, Dolly. Thanks so much." I'd already had a cup of delicious brew at the spa, but those little pink bone-china cups, so thin you could see a transparent rosy glow through them if you held them up to the light, did not hold anywhere near enough to fortify me for the morning. I accepted the cup gratefully and took a sip.

"It's my birthday today."

"Happy Birthday! Any big plans?"

"Well, I have to work tonight." She looked at me expectantly.

I considered. "Why don't you get the prep work done and then take the afternoon off? You can come back in around four o'clock and leave early tonight." I'd have to run down to Kinney's, the drugstore on the corner, and get her a birthday card and a bottle of Shania Twain's perfume. Starlight, it was called.

"Thanks, boss!" She smiled, picked up a giant chef's knife, and went back to chopping onions at a pace that always left me concerned for the future of her fingers. For whatever reason, she didn't like to use the food processor and would just chop, chop, chop all morning until a giant mound of vegetables was reduced to the appropriate-sized cookable pieces. At least the worker's comp insurance premiums were paid up.

I didn't honestly think that Dolly thought she was putting one over on me by telling me it was her birthday. She just enjoyed celebrating her birthday twice a year, once in the summer so her coworkers could share in the gift giving, and once in late November when she was actually born. The summer date tended to change around a bit, so as not to fall on her day off. Sophie and I always played along, not wanting to spoil her fun.

Hmmm, where is Sophie? I thought.

"Dolly, Russ, have you seen Sophie?"

"She called and asked me to have Russ go pick her up at her cousin's about ten," Dolly said.

I turned to Russ. "Finish up putting away the produce, pull out the tomato sauce I made yesterday, and then head out. Better take Sophie's Lincoln, so she'll be comfortable," I said. "And no smoking in the car," I added.

"I ain't smoking anymore," he said, puffing out his chest just a bit.

"That's terrific, Russ. I'm proud of you. Quitting must have been tough."

"It wasn't so bad. I'm dipping now."

I looked at Russ. There was a distinct unnatural bulge in his lower lip. Ick.

"No spitting in the Lincoln, then. Or out the window, either," I added. "Get rid of it before you get in the car." The thought of a big brown glob of tobacco juice blown by the morning breeze along the side of Sophie's immaculate white land yacht was enough to turn my stomach.

I took my coffee and walked through the hallway, down into the main dining rooms. There were three rooms we used to seat guests: two that had originally been parlors separated by beautifully grained native chestnut pocket doors, and the third the home's original dining room, which now served as the bar area. The other downstairs room had been the library, and was now my office. All four rooms were of a moderate size, and felt intimate despite their soaring twelve-foot ceilings. Because the house was octagonal, which was thought to promote the flow of good energy back in the days the place was built—a kind of French Empire feng shui—the rooms were a bit oddly shaped.

Sophie had decorated the tall narrow windows with heavy blue velvet drapes. Shiny gold ropes ending in long, fringy tassels tied them back. They were awfully formal, and a bit gaudy if you asked me, but the guests seemed to like them all right. One winter while she was in Greece and Cal was still in school, I had ripped out the carpet and had the underlying wood floors refinished, which lightened and modernized the whole place. Sophie hadn't been happy when she found out, but the floors were spectacular and were nearly always the first things customers commented on when they walked in. Second were the white marble fireplaces that graced each room, relics of the days when houses did not have central heating. The walls were still white with a stenciled blue Greek key border around the top. If it were my place, really my place, I'd paint everything red.

I toured around all the rooms and noted with satisfaction and relief that the ghost hunters from the night before did not seem to have disturbed anything or left any equipment lying around. I straightened up some of the oak chairs that were out of place, but otherwise everything looked pretty good. I'd have to see how the upstairs fared later.

I returned to my office and sat down at the desk. My laptop whirred to life as I pressed the *power* button and pulled up the file I'd made last year containing my notes and plans for Pirate Days, which would start soon. For two weekends in August, the Bay celebrated a two-hundred-year-old skirmish between some river pirates and British soldiers stationed on the Canadian side.

For the last decade or so a group of rebel reenactors had been sailing across the river and invading the village. They traipsed around in full pirate regalia, brandishing swords and large mustaches for the amusement of the tourists, many of whom dressed up as pirates themselves. There was music, dancing, magic shows, human chess games, and a whole lot of drinking.

Sophie initially thought her establishment was too sophisticated to allow the rowdies in, but eventually she realized that Big Dom was sucking in cash by the boatload by opening up his bar, and she followed suit. "It's only for two weekends," she said, counting tens and twenties as she spoke.

We would have seafood specials all week, with discounts on rum cocktails as well. I'd found a recipe for a lovely rum cake, which we'd serve with a big dollop of vanilla ice cream. The waitstaff could dress up (no big billowy sleeves, though, to drag across the entrees; some cleavage would be okay) and I'd allow them to be pert and saucy with the customers to increase their tips.

I made some notes and e-mailed the next day's orders to

our suppliers. In the background Dolly was singing "Stand By Your Man" along with Tammy Wynette. Dolly was horribly off-key but passionate. She loved the classic country station on the satellite radio. By this time she would have finished slicing the eggplant for the moussaka. Next would be the half bushel of heirloom Baldwin apples to be peeled and cooked into a chunky applesauce, redolent of cinnamon, nutmeg, and clove, dark and syrupy with cooked brown sugar. It would make a perfect accompaniment to tonight's American special of pork tenderloin medallions sautéed in butter and sweet onions.

I began to sort through the mail, which Russ had brought in and dropped into the wire mesh basket that served as my in-box. The circulars and flyers went into the recycling box without a second look. A couple of bills that would need to go to the accountant to pay. My personal bank statement and my retirement account statement, neither of which was likely to inspire more than the basic satisfaction that they existed. I had a decent nest egg saved from my manager's salary, but I wished there were more. If I had to start over somewhere on my own, I would need a stake.

I set those aside and reached for a note from the ghost hunters saying they would contact me in a few days, after they reviewed the material they had recorded. Next in the stack was a white number ten envelope with no return address, no stamp, and no postal cancelation. The envelope was addressed to "Georgie," with no surname and no address, in odd blocky handwriting I did not recognize.

I took a swig of my still-warm-enough coffee, and opened the envelope. A single piece of lined notebook paper fell out. The edges were yellowed and frayed as though the paper had been sitting around in bright sunlight for a few years. Printed in the same strangely square lettering was:

BRING IT TO ME AND I WON'T HERT HIM.
WAIT FOR INSTRUCTIONS.

What the hell? As if vague, misspelled e-mails weren't enough. Him? Who was "him"? I sat up straighter. Spiro. Could he have been . . . kidnapped? The thought was ridiculous, yet it was starting to make some sense in light of his disappearance and the fact that he didn't have his cell phone. Liza had said he might be mixed up in something shady. But this was Bonaparte Bay, for Pete's sake, not New York City three hundred and fifty miles to the south. Not that we didn't have our share of petty crime, being so close to the Canadian border. But people just didn't get kidnapped around here.

People don't get murdered, either, a voice piped up from somewhere in my brain. My thoughts turned back to Big Dom. Nobody had said anything about murder. It had looked like an accident to my untrained eye. He'd been drinking, most likely out on a boat. He'd fallen and hit his head, then toppled overboard. *But if that's true, where's the boat?* I frowned. If he'd been alone, the boat should have been found nearby if he'd dropped the anchor, or farther downriver if he hadn't. And if there'd been somebody with him, why hadn't his companion come forward? Well, maybe he—or she—had, and I just hadn't heard about it. Liza might have, though, and I made a mental note to call her later.

43

As for Spiro, all evidence pointed to the fact that he was off somewhere and had either forgotten his phone or was planning to buy a new one and had just left the old one here. He'd always come back before, and I was pretty sure he would this time as well. The e-mails and the note I'd just read still felt like somebody's idea of a bad joke, though who would be sending me such things was still an unanswered question. I couldn't think of anyone who might have a grudge against me.

But first things first. It was time to start looking for Spiro. I reached for my purse to retrieve his phone. Maybe there was something in his call records or voice mails that could tell me something. The landline rang. I turned, banging my knee on the side of the desk. An ugly bruise would no doubt grace my knee by nightfall.

"Bonaparte House, this is Georgie."

"Mrs. Nik-Nik—" The voice faltered.

"Just call me Georgie. What can I do for you?" Whoever this was, I needed to get rid of him so I could look at Spiro's phone and decide whether I needed to go to the police. State police, I amended. The local cops were more or less good guys, but they were a lot better at busting up bar fights than investigating real crimes.

"This is Captain Jack Conway from the Coast Guard station," he said in a smooth baritone, apparently relieved of the burden of attempting to pronounce my name.

"Yes? Would you like a reservation for this evening?" I picked up a pen and tapped it impatiently on the desk.

"No. I would like to come by and speak to you later this morning, if I may. It's about the body you and Mr. Morgan found yesterday." The voice was beautiful, deep, and oddly compelling. I felt a little flutter in my stomach and wondered what the rest of that package would look like. I was more or less married, for now, but not dead. I sighed when I realized the caller would no doubt have a face for radio. And I had much more important things to be thinking about right now.

"I suppose that would be all right, but it might be a waste of your time. All I saw was Big Dom floating there on the water. I don't know any more than that."

"Please, ma'am, I just need to ask you a few questions."

"Can you come by in a half hour or so and make it short? I'm sorry, but I have an enormous number of things to do."

"I'll be there soon, and I'll keep it brief." He hung up

Coast Guard? Why would the Coast Guard be calling me about this? Wouldn't the state troopers be investigating Big Dom's death? Well, maybe he'd tell me when he got here.

I reached for the letter again, a knot forming in my gut. A little bell dinged, signifying that I had a new e-mail. I set the cell phone on the desk, then turned to my laptop and double-clicked on the mail icon. The screen flashed up large, angry-looking letters:

BRING IT TO ME AND I WON'T HERT HIM. WAIT FOR INSTRUCTIONS.

This was starting to feel less and less like a joke.

"Georgie? Are you in here?" a voice warbled from the doorway. "Are you all right, dear? You're white as a sheet."

I closed my laptop quickly and turned toward the voice. "Nothing to worry about, Sophie. I just banged my knee on the desk and it hurts."

"Would you like for me to get you ice?"

"No, no, I'll be fine." I took a deep breath and attempted to compose myself. Sophie was sharp and perceptive, sometimes eerily so. I didn't want to alarm her until I had more information.

"Have you heard from Spiro? He still no answer his phone."

"Uh, he's just gone off again. You know he likes to do that." Sophie frowned. "I imagine we'll hear something today." Was my nose growing? I hated to lie to her but what was there to tell? I had nothing.

She looked at me expectantly.

What? Oh, of course. She'd heard about Big Dom. I sighed and took a deep breath.

"Yes, I found him. Keith Morgan gave me a ride to Liza's spa on the island last night. We noticed the body and tried to save Dom, but it was too late."

She continued to stare.

"I am not having an affair with Keith and there was no black thong near the body," I spat out, and felt deflated. As though I'd just been through a grueling interrogation session in some downtown precinct room with a detective in shirtsleeves asking tough questions, smoke rings floating through the air.

She watched me, hawklike, and apparently decided I was telling the truth.

"Let me know when you hear from Spiro." She turned and left the room.

◈ FIVE ◈

I reopened the e-mail. The sender's name was hidden, just as before, and while I'm fairly proficient with the computer and handle much of my day-to-day business that way, figuring out who the sender was would be beyond me. I saved it in a new folder and looked at the white envelope again. It had apparently been hand-delivered, probably this morning while I was over at Liza's. Seemed like overkill in light of the e-mail with the same message.

I went back out to the kitchen and asked Dolly whether she had seen who delivered the envelope.

"Nope," she said, the rhinestone butterfly fluttering in her hair as she expertly peeled one long, shiny red ribbon from an apple and plopped the denuded fruit into a pot of lemon juice and water to keep it from browning. "It was under the door when I got here this morning. I put it on your desk."

"Did you and Russ come in together this morning?"

"No, we drove separate." Of course, she'd been hoping to get to leave early so they'd each brought their own cars. "He came in after me."

Dead end.

"Thanks, Dolly. Let me know if any more deliveries come in."

I had just returned the envelope to my desk and locked it in the top drawer when Dolly buzzed me on the intercom. "Georgie, there's somebody here to see you. I wish he was here to see me," she said. I could almost see her waggling her eyebrows.

Coast Guard guy, I thought.

"Ask him if he wants a drink, and send him to my office, please."

"Coffee, tea, or me?" I heard before she took her finger off the intercom button.

A couple of minutes later a tall figure filled the door-frame. "I decided on the coffee," the voice from the phone call drawled. "I'm Captain Jack Conway from the Coast Guard station. You must be Georgie?"

He was wearing tan khakis that could have used a hot iron, a brown leather belt, and a faded Ralph Lauren polo shirt in a pinkish shade that on most men would have been an unfortunate fashion choice, but he carried it off. He offered a large, strong hand and I took it. A little tingle ran up my arm. "Captain Jack? Really?"

"Really. I'm hoping for a promotion soon, for many reasons." He was about my age, with some rather cute crinkles around a pair of intensely blue eyes.

"I can imagine. Uh, can I have my hand back?"

"For now." The little crinkles appeared again, and he dropped my hand.

A charmer, and damned good-looking. If I hadn't been so preoccupied with the events of the last day and a half, I might have enjoyed this little repartee more, but I had no patience for it now. "Captain, my staff will be arriving soon and we'll be opening for lunch, so if we could make this quick?"

"Call me Jack."

"All right, Jack, what is it you'd like to know? As I said, I only got a very brief glimpse of Big Dom, and I don't know what I could tell you."

"You were out for a ride with Keith Morgan last night."

"Yes, the water taxi didn't show up and he offered me a ride to Valentine Island, where I spent the night at the spa."

"So you got in the boat and drove toward the spa. Did you make any stops?"

"No."

"Meet anyone along the way?"

I thought. "I don't remember any other passenger boats on the water, though there might have been one or two. There was a laker off in the distance, too far away for me to read the name."

"Who saw the body first?"

"I did. I pointed it out and Keith pulled the boat over toward the cave. I stayed in the boat while he waded out to him. Keith rolled him over to see if there was any chance to save Dom, but he was already dead."

"Did you notice anything about the body?"

"I could see it was Big Dom. He was wearing a black suit and a lot of gold rings and chains."

"Could you see his face?"

"I tried not to look." I thought for a moment. "His face was all discolored." I shuddered. "And he'd hit his head on something."

"Was there anything near the body, anything floating?"

Had news of the black thong reached the Coast Guard station too? "No, I don't remember anything like that." I held my breath.

No trace of amusement crossed his face. My breath came out in a whoosh.

"Then what happened?"

"I called nine-one-one. Rick and Tim from the village police came and sent us away. Keith took me to the spa. I spent the evening there, and returned this morning."

He studied me for a moment. "I think that's all I need for now. If you think of anything more, give me a call."

He rose and handed me an official-looking card. "Goodbye, Georgie. I wish we could have met under nicer circumstances." He took my hand again and looked down at me.

I felt strangely uncomfortable, yet as though I'd known this man a long time. Weird. "I'll call if I remember anything more."

He left by the kitchen door, and I admired the view of his khakis from the back. Hopefully Dolly let him go without too much of a fuss.

It was three o'clock before I got another break. The place was packed with tourists for lunch, most of whom wanted to know what the ghost hunters had found. Two ladies wearing a lot of twinkly beads and long swingy skirts claimed to be "sensitive" and asked, after a couple of tours around the three dining rooms and the restrooms, whether they could go upstairs and attempt to connect with the spirits inhabiting the house. I respectfully declined. I completed the work schedules for the following week, finalized the menus for Pirate Days, called in the payroll, and had enough other work to do that I was able to put the strange notes out of my mind for a while at least.

I e-mailed Cal in Greece that I loved her and to be careful, and to please check in with me by e-mail or phone every day. She'd roll her eyes at that, but she'd comply. I didn't necessarily believe that anybody could get to her over there, but some caution on her part couldn't hurt.

I grabbed a glass of ice water from the kitchen and headed upstairs.

I looked into Spiro's room. Still no sign of him. I opened my door. The ghost hunters must have been conscientious there as well, because I didn't notice anything amiss. I opened my closet door and was relieved to see that they had apparently not delved too far back into that terrestrial black hole—the Shaun Cassidy record was as I had left it, covered with an old quilt and guarded by more than a few oversized dust bunnies. My small bag remained on the floor near the bathroom where I had dropped it unceremoniously this morning. Unpacking would have to wait for later.

I went into the bathroom and washed my face with warm water and ran a brush through my hair. When I came back out, I sucked in a breath. Sophie was sitting in my armchair.

"Sophie, you gave me a start," I said. Despite her claims

of constant pain and infirmity, she could move like a cat when she wanted to.

"There is still no word from Spiro."

"No." There was no word directly from Spiro—only from his kidnapper. Maybe. *Is it kidnapping if the victim is a grown man?* I wondered.

"It is time to start looking for him."

"I've already started, Sophie."

"He is not answering his cell phone." Because it was sitting on my desk under a pile of papers where I had left it. I needed to look at that ASAP, but had gotten sidetracked with the Coast Guard guy and the influx of customers.

"Georgie, I'm worried."

"I know. Me too." He was a pain in the ass and not any kind of husband to me, but he was a good father to Cal and I did love him. As a friend. A friend I liked to annoy every once in a while just for the heck of it, but a friend nonetheless.

"Please try to find him." Her eyes were imploring and looked straight into mine.

"Sophie, is he in some kind of trouble that you know about?" I had the feeling she was not telling me something.

She hesitated, apparently trying to decide how much, if anything, to reveal. "There is money missing from our accounts."

She and Spiro had both names on their local accounts, but to my knowledge they didn't keep huge amounts in them, preferring instead to keep most of their assets in cash to avoid paying taxes.

"How much money are we talking about?"

"Twenty-three thousand dollars." It was probably more, but still, that was a substantial sum she was admitting to.

"When was the money withdrawn?"

"I don't know. I need you to find out."

"Have you looked at the bank statement?"

"I call the accountant, but he said he didn't have it. He looked on last month's paper and the money was there."

"That means he withdrew it sometime in the last couple of weeks. I'll check online for you tonight."

"Thank you, Georgie. You are a good girl." Spiro and Cal were her reason for living. I hoped I rated in there somewhere too.

"I'll find him." I had no idea how to go about doing that. The smartest thing, of course, would be to take my suspicions to the police. First, though, I needed to look at that phone. If there was nothing more sinister than Spiro off on a shopping spree, I did not want to get the authorities involved. Under the best of circumstances, living in a village like Bonaparte Bay was like living in a fishbowl. I wouldn't subject Sophie to the resultant gossip if I could help it.

We descended the stairs and she headed for the kitchen. I went into my office and shuffled the papers around.

I opened up all the desk drawers, a rising sense of foreboding speeding up my movements. I got down on my hands and knees and looked under the desk, then pawed through the trash can. I felt around in my purse, and in every pocket. Spiro's cell phone was gone.

◆ SIX ◆

I left Sophie supervising Russ and Dolly in the kitchen and took a walk down Theresa Street toward the docks. Midge was setting out racks of bright-colored clothes in front of the T-Shirt Emporium. She called out to me, but I merely waved and smiled as I went by. I did not want to be answering any questions about anything.

Before I left I put in a phone call to the state police. The dispatcher said that someone would call me back when the cruisers came back in from their rounds. Standard operating procedure in a village this size. My thoughts returned to the missing cell phone. There had been exactly five people in the Bonaparte House this morning, including me. I could think of no reason Sophie, Dolly, or Russ would snoop in my office. As far as I knew, I was the only one who'd seen the phone, so how would they know what to look for even if they did snoop? That left the Coast Guard guy. What had he called himself? Captain Jack. While he was charming me and I'd been staring at his broad chest and wondering what kind of six-pack he had under that shirt, could he have somehow found and pocketed the phone?

I passed the Sailor's Rest. A sign on the front door indicated that the restaurant was "Closed for Remodeling."

Would the Rest open again at all this summer now that Big Dom was dead? Sophie would certainly be happy if it didn't. I wouldn't put it past her to put her own sign underneath the "Closed" sign that read, "Try the Bonaparte House!" with an arrow pointing up the street. I did feel some sympathy for the staff, who wouldn't be able to get in enough weeks to receive their winter unemployment checks if the place didn't reopen. Big Dom hadn't been married—at least there was no wife in town—but he might have had some grown kids. Hopefully the heirs would get the place up and running again as soon as possible, or do the right thing by the employees. I supposed we might take a couple on at the Bonaparte House, but we certainly couldn't accommodate everyone.

I continued on down past the Express-o Bean and debated stopping in for a cappuccino, but decided against it. I crossed Theresa Street at the Thompson Street intersection (virtually no traffic at this time of the morning) and walked the few yards to the Tat-L-Tails Tattoo Salon.

The door was open and I walked in to the music of some tuned door chimes. Jim Morrison stared down at me, shirtless, druggy, and sexy, from a poster on the wall to my left. Tie-dyed T-shirts and leather vests hung on a rack underneath. The other wall was covered with pictures of diverse tattooed body parts, designs that could be chosen or samples of Inky's work, and a framed New York State tattooing license issued to Ignatius LaFontaine. The front display case was filled with bongs and pipes and clips and rings and chains of varying size and some other hardware whose use I could not identify, nor did I want to. I was bent over, examining one particularly baffling item through the glass, when someone came through a set of swinging saloon-style doors.

"Can I help you?" a voice said.

I stood up and just missed banging my head on the counter. The air was thick with the scent of some kind of heady incense, or possibly something less legal. It was making me a bit dizzy. "Hi," I said. "I'm Georgie, from the Bonaparte House." I held out my hand.

He took my hand with his own exceptionally colorful one and looked at me, his big brown eyes wary. "I know who you are."

"You're Inky, right?"

"Yes." He was covered from the neck down in tattoos, thankfully none on his face, although some sort of tentacle did reach up behind one ear, winding its way into the black stubble of his shaved head. It was fascinating, and I found myself wondering what sort of creature was on the other end.

"Inky, have you heard from Spiro in the last couple of days? He hasn't come home and I'm worried about him."

He tensed up, causing the little silver rings in his eyebrows to clink together. "Spiro who? Why should I know?"

"Inky, I know that you two are seeing each other. I don't mind, honestly. It's fine." *Mostly fine.*

He visibly relaxed, letting out a sigh. "I've been so

worried too! I haven't heard from him in days!" he said animatedly, the words coming so quickly there was a time delay while my brain caught up to my ears. "He calls me every day at least twice whether we see each other or not!"

"How long have you been seeing him?"

"Oh, a couple of months."

A couple of months? The gossip machine in this town works overtime and I was just hearing about this now? I needed to start paying more attention to what was going on around me.

"He came in for a tat in June and it was just lust at first sight."

Good Lord. Spiro had gotten himself inked? Last I knew, he had a debilitating fear of needles. I couldn't help myself. "What kind of tattoo did he get?"

"We decided on a small tiger's head for his first tat, since he was kind of nervous about the whole needle-slash-permanency thing, and he's such a passionate pussycat, you know? I did a nice job, if I do say so myself. You haven't seen it?"

"Errr, no."

"Oh, right. Well, I guess maybe you wouldn't since it's on his—"

"Stop!" I wanted to cover my ears and sing "La-la-la" till he had finished speaking. This was too, too much information.

I framed my next words carefully. "You two are so close, I bet you talk about everything?"

"Oh, yes, everything."

"So, what's going on with him?"

"Well, he's been very excited lately, and I don't mean just by me!" He winked and I nodded, resisting the urge to roll my eyes. Inky seemed like a nice guy and I could feel myself warming up to him. He was quite good-looking, with tanned skin—at least, the part that wasn't inked looked tan—and a buff physique. He wasn't the intense type I would have expected Spiro to take up with. But really. What did I know?

"What had him so excited?"

"He'd found it. I mean, I never saw it but he said he knew where it was, and it was going to make him super rich. I've heard stories since I was a kid about some kind of treasure in that house, and now it's true!"

Here was this story again. If there was something valuable in that house, it would have been found by now. It was just a legend. Still, I had to ask. "What did he find, Inky?"

"That's just it—I don't know and it's killing me! Spiro promised to tell me what it was as soon as he cleared up some business. We were planning to go away in October for a long weekend to this adorable bed-and-breakfast I know in Vermont, and he invited me to come to Greece this winter. I'm hoping he might propose. Unless I propose myself . . ."

Hmmm, I could think of one rather large impediment to their getting married. Namely me. And was he planning to keep Inky at the house in Greece? We'd all be one big happy family, wouldn't we? Maybe we could get our own reality show. "Did he say where he'd found it?"

"No, just that it was in the house somewhere. 'Hidden in plain sight,' was what he said."

That wasn't much help. "What was the business he had to take care of?"

"Oh, I don't know. But it did seem to be bothering him, if you want to know the truth."

"Do you have any idea where he might be? Did he mention going away somewhere?"

"I don't know where he is. I assumed it had something to do with the thing he found. I miss him," he said.

I fished around in my purse and came up with a business card. I peeled off a sticky mint and an errant hair that had attached themselves to it and handed the card to Inky.

"Call me if you hear anything."

"I will. Say, I'm not busy. Want a tattoo? I'll give you a discount since we're practically family and all."

"I'll think about it, Inky."

"You do that. Bye bye!" He waved as I exited the store with a merry tinkling of the door chimes.

I retraced my steps toward home. The aroma of the Express-o Bean, though, pulled me in like a tractor beam and I was powerless to resist. "Large cappuccino, extra shot of espresso, shot of vanilla, shot of caramel, extra foam."

"For here or to go?" The barista was a tiny waif I hadn't seen before, most likely a student from the community college in Canton or Watertown, with blue hair worn super short in back and long over one heavily lined eye.

I considered. "To go."

"Comin' up," she said. I'd expected her to be surly, but in fact she was quite friendly. The girl performed some kind of magic gestures and produced a good-sized paper cup with a travel lid and a small cardboard sleeve to serve as a hand-hold.

"Taste it," she urged.

I slurped some up through the little hole in the top. It was exceptional. "Perfect." I smiled at her.

"Three fifty." She smiled back.

I handed her a twenty. She rang it in and reached into the register for change. I glanced down and saw the tip cup on the counter—"TIPS NEEDED TO BUY BOOKS FOR CLARKSON NEXT SEMESTER—PLEASE HELP. THANKS! VANESSA."

"Are you Vanessa?" I asked.

"Sure am." I had to stop judging people by how they looked. A very high math SAT score was required to get into Clarkson University. I was impressed.

I dropped the change from the twenty into her cup. I remembered all too well what it had been like to be poor and on scholarship. If she was working here for the summer instead of tanning on her daddy's boat, she needed the money.

"Good luck at Clarkson, Vanessa. Come see me at the Bonaparte House if you want to wait tables next summer. I've got a full staff right now, but I'll put you on full-time next summer. You'll make a lot more in tips than you will here, though you can keep this job in the mornings if you can handle both."

"Wow, thanks." She beamed.

I carried my steaming cup back outside and headed up the gentle hill on LeRay Street toward Riverfront Park. The park was on the site of one of the huge wooden hotels that had dotted the coast at the turn of the century, every one of which had burned to the ground despite being located right on the water.

I climbed the steps to the pavilion and exited on the other side, passed a few rusty metal trays on poles with grates that served as barbecue grills, sidestepped a few protruding rocks, and plunked myself and my purse down on a bench on a granite bluff overlooking the river. The late-afternoon sun was nearly blinding as it reflected off the surface of the water. I didn't have a lot of time before I had to get back to the restaurant for the lunch rush.

I tasted the coffee. Delicious. A snowy white seagull bobbed up to me looking for food, but I had regrettably forgotten to buy a muffin. "Sorry, fella," I said to him. I considered giving him the linty mint I'd found in my purse earlier, but decided it might choke him. Better hungry than dead.

I replayed my conversation with Inky as I watched a sailboat go by. I'd have to think about my becoming part of a polygamous multi-gender harem later. His story corroborated what Liza had told me. Having raised a teenager, my truth-o-meter was pretty sensitive. I was fairly sure Inky wasn't lying. He didn't seem to know anything about whatever business Spiro was mixed up in, only that something had to be "taken care of." He apparently believed that Spiro had found something at the house and that it was valuable. "Hidden in plain sight" wasn't much of a clue, but it was all I had to go on. Maybe it was time to take a look around the house again.

And what was the name of that group of farmers Liza had told me about—the SOBs? Or was it SODs? I'd have to see what I could find out about them as well. They didn't sound like nice people. I would give the state police the information and let them follow up when they got around to calling me. But it would kill Sophie if it came out that Spiro was involved in an organization like that.

A hand touched my shoulder, jerking me out of my thoughts. A little coffee slopped out of the cup and onto my lap. Fortunately the liquid had cooled and I was only damp, not burned.

"Hi, Georgie."

I turned but the hand stayed put, giving my shoulder a little caress in the process.

"Oh, hi, Keith."

"Sorry if I startled you. I saw you leave the Bean and I thought I'd come up and see how you're doing. Oh, you spilled some coffee—was that my fault?"

"Don't worry about it. I'm fine."

"I have some extra napkins." He sat down next to me and pulled some out of his pocket. Briefly I wondered whether he would attempt some dabbing at the coffee in my lap, but he merely handed the wad to me.

I accepted the napkins and proceeded to blot.

"So, are you okay? It was sure a shock to find Big Dom. I'm so sorry you had to see him like that."

"Do the police know what happened yet?"

"Word on the street is that he was murdered."

"Murdered?" I had wanted to believe it was an accident. I couldn't recall a murder, ever, in all the time I'd lived here. Well, there was that time that Louise Brodie brained her husband, Duane, with a slow cooker full of butternut squash because he blew off her mother's Thanksgiving dinner to go deer hunting. But murder changed everything.

"Why would anyone want to murder Big Dom?" He was no doubt involved in some kind of shady dealings, but I'd never heard anything worse than that he was skimming money off the business, which I think everybody did. Except me.

"The rumor is that it's the Watertown mob, but that's always the first assumption when there's an Italian guy involved. For once, Rick seems to be keeping the investigation confidential."

"How did you find out?"

"I saw Sherry this morning at the diner and she told me the coroner is calling it murder." Sherry Harper was a nurse and had probably been called in to assist the medical examiner before he took the body back to Watertown for the autopsy. Our little hospital wasn't equipped for forensics. "The ME told her that his initial impression was that Dom was hit over the head with a blunt instrument, then died of a gunshot wound before he was dumped in the water. That's why he was floating when we found him—he didn't take water into his lungs because he wasn't breathing."

I shivered as the picture of his floating corpse, that ugly welt impressed on his head, popped back into my brain. Keith put his arm around me. "It's gonna be okay, honey."

I looked up at him and he smiled down at me, our faces close. The breeze was lifting his blond hair and I could see that, unlike Big Dom and his Trumpish comb-over, Keith was genetically blessed with the hairline of a boy. A little stubble on his chin and jaw showed he either hadn't shaved yet this morning or had a fast-growing beard. His eyes were soft and his lips were slightly parted.

He's going to kiss me, I thought, momentarily panicked but a bit thrilled at the same time. It had been a long time since anyone had kissed me. Why not Keith? He was my friend. I could trust him. He was a great-looking guy. *If he wants to kiss me, I'll let him,* I decided. *I could do a whole lot worse.* A laker glided by in the distance, and let out a blast of its horn. *What if you can do better?* a little voice in my mind piped up. According to Liza, Keith was in love with me. We were sitting on a park bench in full view of anybody who happened to walk or boat by. In light of recent rumors about us, somehow this didn't seem like a good idea. I might have a crumbling, sham marriage and be about to be thrown out of my home and job, but I wasn't ready for this. I wriggled out of his embrace and stood up, walking over to the nearby trash can to dispose of the damp handful of napkins and empty coffee cup I was still holding.

"I should be getting back to the restaurant," I said.

"Bye, Georgie." He was smiling but it seemed a bit forced. Was he disappointed about the thwarted smooch?

"Bye, Keith." I started toward the pavilion, then turned back as I remembered something I'd wanted to ask him before being distracted.

"Keith, any idea why the Coast Guard would be investigating Big Dom's murder?"

"The Coast Guard?" His face clouded. "That's the state police's jurisdiction."

"Some Coast Guard guy came around earlier asking me some questions."

"What kind of questions?"

"Just about what we saw, that sort of thing. He wasn't there long. He didn't call you?"

"No."

"Well, I imagine he will."

"What was his name? I know quite a few of the guys at the station."

"Jack, uh . . . Captain Jack somebody, you know, like the Billy Joel song? Or those Johnny Depp movies? I have his card back at the restaurant somewhere."

"I don't think I know any Jack stationed here. Do me a favor and look for that card, will you? I'm interested to find out what this is all about."

"I'll call you if I find it. Bye again, Keith."

"Bye again, honey." He grinned.

The restaurant was bustling when I returned. Sophie was in her usual cushioned chair, feet outstretched on a footstool, right by the cash register. Dolly chopped away at a mound of carrots destined for either the salad or tonight's vegetable side. Russ, the long tail of his dark hair swinging across the AC/DC logo on his T-shirt, emerged from the walk-in cooler carrying a box of lettuce to be cleaned and shredded.

"One of them white envelopes got shoved under the kitchen door a while ago," Dolly said. "I looked out the window but whoever left it was gone by the time I got there. It's on your desk."

My heart rose up in my throat. Sophie perked up and turned toward me expectantly. "Just an invoice from one of the suppliers," I offered. This seemed to satisfy Sophie, but she continued to watch me. Damn, but she could make me uncomfortable, and I hadn't even done anything to deserve it. Except almost kiss somebody, and that didn't count.

I passed through the hallway and into my office. There

was the white envelope glaring up at me. I decided to avoid it for now by listening to the answering machine, which was flashing red. A couple of people had called in for reservations and the ghost hunters were asking when they could meet with me to film the "reveal" of their findings. I called them back first and told them to come in anytime. I'd pull the pocket doors on one of the dining rooms and they could do the filming there without being too disruptive to business in the other two rooms. Although, now that I considered it, the customers would flock in if they knew that a television show was being filmed only a few yards away. Well, after the filming, I'd open the doors so everybody could get a peek at the cast and crew.

I booted up my laptop and opened my e-mail. No surprises here, thank goodness, just the promised note from Cal saying that today was her day off and she was going boating with Sakis, the boy she'd been seeing, and then going back to his family's home for dinner. I sent her back a quick reply again telling her to be careful and that I hoped she'd had fun, since with the time delay her day's activities had already happened.

I pulled up Sophie's bank account information on the screen, and printed it off. Sophie had given me access to the accounts when Spiro proved to have no aptitude for monitoring them. I reviewed the statement again. Yes, twenty-three thousand dollars had been withdrawn from Spiro and Sophie's joint money market account late last week.

I steeled myself and opened the white envelope. Inside was a sheet of the same yellowed paper with the blocky letters. What was it with this guy? Or girl, I amended, just to be PC. One e-mail or one letter would have been sufficient.

I STILL HAVE HIM. FIND IT AND BRING IT TOMOROW NITE TO THE DEVIL'S OVEN. PUT IT IN THE BASKIT HANGING INSIDE THE DOOR. COME ALONE. DON'T TELL ANYONE OR I WILL KILL HIM.

My stomach clenched. Kill him? Suddenly, my theory that this was a joke seemed naïve and stupid. And what was "it"? If he, whoever he was, had Spiro, then he must have the money already, so it couldn't be that. And the writer of these notes had never actually said he was holding Spiro, as opposed to someone else. The only other thing I could think of was the so-called treasure that Spiro had supposedly found. How the hell was I supposed to bring it when I didn't even know what it was, not to mention where? And I didn't have a boat, so how would I get to an island out in the middle of the river if I couldn't tell anybody? The Bay was no longer insulated from murder—Big Dom had been killed just a couple of days ago. A lump of panic rose up and choked me. Could there be a connection?

I looked through the piles one more time and found the card after a minute or two. Underneath a raised seal, "Jack Conway, Cpt" was embossed in blue letters. "United States Coast Guard" and a phone number completed the information. Looked legitimate enough. But according to Keith, the Coast Guard wouldn't have any reason or jurisdiction to be investigating Big Dom. Now that I thought about it, the guy hadn't been wearing a uniform, either. Anybody could get business cards printed up, or make them at home on the computer. I fingered the edge of the card and thought.

The intercom buzzed. It was Sophie. "Those ghost guys are here."

I took another deep breath. "I'm on my way."

I led the crew in through the kitchen door. They followed me with their sound equipment, some large portable lighting fixtures, and several cameras. I directed them to the front dining room, which was empty because we'd seated all the customers in the other two rooms. I didn't think anybody would mind waiting for a seat tonight. We moved a table in front of the fireplace. Napoleon stared down at us from his portrait, hand stuck in the front of his coat. The crew set up a laptop and some microphones on the table underneath the emperor and attached all kinds of cords and wires.

In a surprisingly short time, they had finished. A woman came toward me wielding a hairbrush and a makeup tray. I hoped I looked presentable.

We sat down, Jerry and Gary on one side of the table and me on the other. I willed my racing heart to slow down.

"We're on in five, four, three, two, and action!"

◆ SEVEN ◆

"We've finished our investigation here at the Bonaparte House in Bonaparte Bay, New York," Jerry said, turning toward me. "Now, your husband claims that he has lived here every spring and summer for his whole life and that he has had many instances of hearing noises that seem to come from behind walls. He has also felt like he was being watched. And there are reports of staff people here at the restaurant having similar experiences."

Gary continued. "We set up our equipment and spent most of the night to see if we could document any paranormal activity. You yourself have never had any experiences, right?"

"Right."

"First off, I can tell you that this is a very unusual house, from an architectural point of view," Gary said. "As you know, and as our audience can see from our exterior shots, the house is octagonal with two stories, a basement, and a very large cupola on top, all connected by this magnificent circular staircase." The camera panned over to the center of the building.

"Yes." I nodded. "My understanding is that there were a lot of octagonal houses built in the nineteenth century. The design was supposed to give more usable space for the amount of building materials, though it made for some odd-shaped rooms. Because of improved air circulation, it was supposed to promote health and well-being."

Jerry nodded. "We've done some research. You are correct about the Orson Fowler architectural movement. However, this house predates Orson Fowler by several decades. It might have been an unacknowledged inspiration to him, although there is no record that he ever ventured this far north into New York State. This was not one of his houses. The Fowler houses were built of wood or masonry."

Gary took over. "The Bonaparte House is built of solid limestone blocks. We often find increased paranormal activity in areas where limestone is present, but we don't know why. The building materials, together with the odd interior construction and staircase, give this house some interesting acoustics, which might account for the noises. There was, however, a tradition of octagonal buildings in Europe at the time, and since this house was built by Europeans, that is likely the source of the architecture."

If this was true, I was going to have to update the house's history on the menu inserts again. Come to think of it, I'd never verified any of that information.

"I'd like to show you what we found," Jerry said.

"Okay, I guess I'm ready." Was it possible they had found something? I wouldn't say I was a disbeliever, exactly, but any "proof" of paranormal activity would have to be pretty compelling to convince me.

"First, we set up cameras in various places all over the house and restaurant. Here is some of the footage we took." Gary pointed to the laptop screen. "This is taken right here in the main dining room. If you'll watch, you'll see some orb movement, which takes place just about where we are sitting."

"Orb movement?" I watched the screen and saw small white circles dancing around in front of the fireplace and around Napoleon's head.

"Orbs are balls of light that sometimes appear, either to the naked eye or just in photographs, in places with paranormal activity," Jerry piped in. "They are spherical concentrations of energy, without any sort of consciousness or intent. They can also be dust illuminated by our lights and cameras."

That theory would certainly get my vote. I wasn't crazy about the idea of orbs flying around my house at night, landing on me as I slept. Yikes.

"The next area we'd like you to look at is in the cupola area. The view from up there, by the way, is spectacular."

"Yes. With eight windows facing in every direction, we can see for miles, well into the countryside and across the river into Canada," I said.

A pair of what appeared to be junior investigators sat in the highest point of the house, one in an old midcentury-style armchair that Sophie had never been able to part with, it having belonged to her dead husband. The other guy sat in one of my dining room chairs that they must have dragged upstairs. The investigators got up and walked around, picking up some of the old books, theatrically blowing off the dust and looking at the covers. Some of Cal's old toys were up there too. An anorexically thin bespectacled guy picked up a stuffed purple dinosaur and dangled it over the edge of the railing.

"How much will you pay me to drop him?" he clowned around. If the toy fell, it would drop three full stories, maybe four if they could aim him just right for the basement and avoid him bouncing off the railings below. This didn't bother me much, as that talking critter was extremely annoying, but Cal had loved him and I felt defensive for her.

"I love you!" the toy said in its goofy cartoon voice as the dangler squeezed his tummy.

"I love you too!" The other guy cracked up. He picked up something from the table facing the upriver window and said, "I'll tell you what. I'll give you fifty bucks if you drop him down into the basement and then drop this on him."

"Hey, man, what is that thing anyway?"

"Dude, I don't have any idea." He fiddled with the round end, which spun around with an audible whizzing sound like the chamber of a gun being spun in a game of Russian roulette. "Looks like a telescope. Heavy. It's too dark to look through it, though."

I supposed this was just an act they put on for the show, but it wasn't funny to me. I continued to stare at the screen, as Gary broke in. "Here's what we wanted you to see. Watch over in this corner here."

I didn't see anything at first, but when the tape was replayed, an amorphous shadow drifted past the window.

"We don't know what that is, if anything. There haven't been any reports of apparitions here, have there?"

"No."

"Despite many hours of tape shot all through this building, that is the only thing of interest we caught on video."

Fine by me. Looked like a plain old shadow. Could have been cast by anything, and I'd be willing to bet it wasn't paranormal. I breathed a little sigh of relief. This interview needed to be over, and soon. I had way too many things to think about.

"Next we'll listen to the EVPs."

"EVPs?"

"Electronic voice phenomena," Gary explained. "Sometimes spirits communicate with us in ways that are not audible when they are happening, but they can be picked up by our recording equipment."

"Oh." I wished they'd hurry up. My foot started to jiggle, but I pressed my heel to the floor to stop it.

"Here we had our equipment set up in the staircase area," Jerry went on. "We had several hours of audio to go through. We found something interesting."

Gary pointed to the laptop screen, which was bisected by a white line. "Watch and listen."

A crackly recording ensued and I could see the noise following the line on the screen. There was a spike and some kind of muffled sound. I couldn't make it out.

"Did you hear that? I'll play it again."

I leaned forward and listened again. I shivered. The words were faint but audible. *Help me. Free.*

My blood ran cold and I imagine I was white as the ghost that apparently lived in my house. I could only hope the footage had been doctored for television and they would let me in on the joke later.

"What do you think it's saying?" Jerry prompted.

I swallowed hard. "It sounds like, 'Help me. Free.'" My voice was not much more than a whisper.

"That's what we heard too."

"Based on the evidence we've been able to capture with our recording equipment," Jerry said, "I honestly believe that you've got some paranormal activity going on here."

Gary put a reassuring hand on my arm. "I know this is surprising, but we don't think there is any reason for you, your family, your staff, or your customers to be worried. We think that whatever is here is benign, simply a soul trapped for some reason and asking for help to be set free."

Jerry said, "We asked the spirit to forget his trouble and to look toward the light and pass on from this world. Hopefully, we've been able to help him."

I nodded. I wasn't quite sure what to say to this, so I just said, "Thank you." I hoped I didn't look as dumb and inarticulate as I felt.

Jerry and Gary stood up and I shook their hands in turn.

"Thank you for letting us investigate the Bonaparte House," Jerry said. "If anything else happens, or you feel uncomfortable in any way, just give us a call. We'd also like to talk to your husband about his experiences when he returns."

I hesitated, only for a moment. "I'll ask him to call you when he comes back." *If he comes back,* I thought.

"Again," Gary concluded solicitously, "if we can do anything for you, just get in touch with us." He handed me a DVD in a hard plastic case. "This is a video for you of parts of our investigation."

"I have to say I'm surprised by what you've shown me," I said, regaining some of my composure and recollecting that this was also a free advertising opportunity. "But I do hope you'll come back sometime and enjoy Bonaparte Bay with your families." I smiled. Whether it looked sincere, I'd just have to wait and see. It didn't feel that way.

"We may just do that. Bye, now."

"Cut!" one of the camera operators yelled from somewhere. Almost immediately cords were rolled up and equipment was moved out.

I breathed a sigh of relief. "Guys, feel free to pack up your things and then come back in for a meal, on the house, before you leave for downstate." This would irritate Sophie to no end, but our customers would enjoy it. I opened up both sets of pocket doors to the other dining rooms and instructed the server filling in as hostess tonight to start seating the patrons lined up outside. News travels fast in a village this size, even among tourists.

I closed the door to the relative sanctuary of my office and sat down. I poured myself a glass of red wine even though I was technically still on duty. The delicious liquid coated my throat and moved down my esophagus and into my stomach, where it made a warm and comforting pool in my belly. Some brandy might have been nicer, but I would have had to go to the bar for that. I did not want to see anybody until I had had a chance to unwind a little.

A ghost in my house? Sophie and Spiro's house, I amended. I had to acknowledge the idea that this place had a secret life of its own, independent of the Nikolopatos family. It apparently harbored both a treasure and a ghost, like some creepy hulking edifice in a Victorian gothic novel. I was a bit older than the typical ingénue heroine, I thought ruefully, and I was more or less confident that a cloaked villain was not going to appear on the scene and whisk me away somewhere. Although the way things were headed, I couldn't rule that out.

The intercom buzzed and I started. "Georgie?" Sophie's voice was sharp and accusatory. "Georgie, are you in there?" She was no doubt going to chastise me about the free meals I'd given away. It wouldn't occur to her that the increase in business they had generated would more than make up for some gyros and a few orders of French fries. "Georgie!"

I ignored her.

The telephone rang and I looked at the caller ID. *Keith Morgan.* I took another sip of the wine and picked up the receiver. "Hi, Keith."

"Hi," he said. "Hope I caught you at a good time."

"I've had better days." That was an understatement. "It's good to hear from you," I said, and regretted it. I shouldn't be encouraging him, but the friendly voice was a welcome relief.

"It's good to hear you too." I could almost hear the smile in his voice. "Honey?" I wished he'd stop calling me that. "Have you found that business card? The one from the Coast Guard captain?"

I reached into my pocket and pulled it out, warm and a little wrinkled. I'd intended to call Keith about this earlier, but had been waylaid by the television people.

"Yes, I have it."

"Good. What's the name on the card?"

"Captain Jack Conway, U.S. Coast Guard." I read him the phone number.

"I don't recognize that name at all. I'm going to see what I can find out. As I said before, he would have no reason to be looking into Big Dom's death."

"He wasn't wearing a uniform when he came in." I almost added, "Ask him about the cell phone he somehow stole from my desk," but thought better of it. I wasn't ready to confide in anyone yet about Spiro being taken unless it was the state police, who still hadn't called me back. I didn't want Spiro to be hurt, but I didn't see how I could get him back without professional assistance.

"That might not mean anything. He might have been off duty, although if he was part of some official investigation, you'd think he would have been in uniform."

"That's what I thought too."

The intercom buzzed again. "Georgie!" The voice was shrill and angry.

"I guess that's my cue to go," Keith said.

"I've been avoiding Sophie, but I guess I'm going to have to respond sooner or later, so I may as well get it over with."

There was a slight pause. "Georgie, would you like to come over for a nightcap or a decaf after the restaurant closes tonight?"

"Uh, I'll have to see how things go. Can I call you later and let you know?"

"Sure." He sounded hopeful. "Please say yes."

"I'll call you later. Bye, Keith."

"Bye, honey."

The intercom buzzed for a full three seconds. "Georgie, I'm coming in there right now!"

◈ EIGHT ◈

I slurped down the rest of the wine and stowed the glass under the desk just as Sophie came barging in the door.

"Why you no answer me?" she asked indignantly.

"I was on the phone." *None of your business,* I wanted to add, but refrained. I'd found over the years that the best way to deal with her when her feathers were ruffled was to stay calm, and she would eventually settle down.

"I know," she said blackly. "And I know who you been on the phone with too!"

Something in me snapped. I was tired and it had been one hell of a day. I felt a flash of anger at the thought that she'd been listening in on the kitchen phone.

"I saw his name on that ID caller." That would explain her knowing who I was speaking to, but I still wouldn't put it past her to listen in.

"Are you sleeping with him?" Her hazel eyes flashed.

I took a deep breath to calm myself. I knew this conversation would come someday. "Sophie, I love you. You know that. I've done everything you asked of me and more since I've known you, and I've been happy to do it. Spiro and I loved each other once and we produced a beautiful daughter. But we haven't had a real marriage in years. Callista is a grown woman and understands the . . . situation with her father. If I am having an affair with Keith, or anybody else, it's my business. Okay?" I didn't stand up to her often, and it felt good.

She looked deflated and sighed. "Georgie, I love you too." She dropped the subject of Keith. "Have you heard anything about Spiro yet?"

"I checked the bank statements. He withdrew twenty-three thousand dollars from your account a few days ago, his car is gone, and nobody has seen him since. But you knew that."

She squirmed, almost imperceptibly, but I'd known her long enough to recognize the signs. She was holding something back.

"What else, Sophie?"

She fidgeted for a moment and then said, "There's more money missing."

I thought so. "From where?" I asked, though I was pretty sure I already knew.

"From the cash box."

She kept a metal box full of bundles of cash under some loose floorboards beneath her ornate four-poster bed upstairs. As far as I knew, only Sophie, Spiro, and I were aware of it.

"How much is gone?"

"All of it." She sighed and sank down in the goose down

armchair next to the desk. "All of it," she repeated. "Fifty-six thousand dollars. I don't know what we will live on this winter."

For crying out loud. The woman had piles of money both in U.S. currency and in various bank accounts in Switzerland and Greece, where the cost of living was much, much lower. The—how much would that be?—seventy-nine thousand dollars wouldn't even be a drop in the bucket compared to her net worth. It was of course a considerable amount of money, but she would hardly be eating cat food out of cans next winter as she looked out over the Aegean Sea from her veranda.

"We'll manage." I patted her arm.

"He'd better not be spending it on his—his . . . mimbos!"

Male bimbos. I stifled a laugh. "Is there anything else you haven't told me?"

"No."

That may or may not have been true. She could be secretive when it suited her.

"Have you gotten any letters, or messages, or strange phone calls lately, Sophie?"

Her eyes narrowed. "What do you mean?"

"Just wondering. Anything that might help us find Spiro."

"No."

I thought about my interview with the NYPI team. "Do you believe in ghosts?"

"What did those guys find?" she asked, her voice rising. Was she afraid of the supernatural, or was there something else she didn't want them to uncover?

I tried to be noncommittal, though I had no idea how

she'd react to the news of our being haunted. "Oh, they picked up some noises with their equipment—they couldn't explain it."

"They ate a lot of food and drank a lot of booze," she said petulantly. "That skinny one drank five martinis."

"They brought in a lot of business."

"Maybe, but the show won't be on until after we close for the season, and what good will that do us?"

"Sophie, I should get back to the kitchen. Why don't you go upstairs and lie down for a bit? You look tired." I checked my watch. "I recorded *The Desperate and the Defiant*."

"You know I don't watch that trash," she admonished. I happened to know that she did, most every day, and had figured out how to run the DVR by herself so she wouldn't miss her favorite soap opera. She rose and I stood up to hug her, kicking over my wineglass, which rolled out between us.

She looked down and then back up at me disapprovingly. "Georgie." She shook her head.

Everything seemed to be under control in the kitchen. Our perma-specials, prime rib and lobster, would be joined tonight by my version of Chicken Marengo, said to be Napoleon's favorite dish, now simmering away in a giant pot on the big commercial burners lining the back wall. We Greeked it up by substituting olive oil for the butter, Kalamatas for the traditional black olives, and Metaxa 7 Star for the cognac, and served it with a side of fragrant rice pilaf to soak up the savory tomato-based sauce. Napoleon's original dish featured fried eggs and crayfish in the stew. We made the eggs optional for our guests and added shrimp at the last minute.

I dipped a clean spoon into the clam chowder pot for a quality control test. It was delicious, as always, creamy and full of chunky clams and potatoes. We served New England style here, none of that red Manhattan stuff. Even though it was the middle of summer, evenings got chilly here and the chowder was always a good seller.

I pulled the big latch, opened the walk-in refrigerator, and was greeted by a blast of cold air. Russ started and nearly choked on the fluffy cloud of whipped cream he was spraying from a can into his mouth.

"Russ, I hope you weren't planning to use that for tonight's desserts." We kept the canned stuff for making fancy chocolate milks for children but made hand-whipped heavy cream topping for our desserts.

He swallowed and cleared his throat. "Uh, no. I keep this one aside special. See, I put my name on it." He showed me where he'd conscientiously marked the side with "Russ."

"You're not doing whip-its in here, are you?"

"No, the can's full, see?" He shook it and I could hear the liquid sloshing around inside.

"Keep it that way. And put that can someplace where people aren't going to grab it by mistake."

I realized that I was starving, so I left the walk-in and scooped myself a bowl of the chowder, topped it with a sprinkle of oyster crackers, and went down to the bar for a Diet Coke and a slice of lemon. I carried my small meal into my office and sat down at the desk, arming aside papers to clear a space big enough to set down the tray. I would need to be quick to get back out to the dinner service, since Sophie was still upstairs. I moved my laptop over to the desk's return and swiveled my chair to face it as I booted up.

I called up my e-mail and saw that there was yet another message from my anonymous correspondent. I double-clicked and found the same message as the written note I'd received earlier, still with no identifying information.

I STILL HAVE HIM. FIND IT AND BRING IT TOMOROW NIGHT TO THE DEVIL'S OVEN. PUT IT IN THE BASKIT HANGING INSIDE THE DOOR. COME ALONE. DON'T TELL ANYONE OR I WILL KILL HIM.

I shuddered and took a deep breath. Should I respond to this e-mail somehow? What would I say? *All right, Georgie, think calmly,* I told myself. *What do I know?* According to Inky, Spiro had found the treasure, whatever it was, somewhere in the house. But it could be pretty much anywhere on the grounds. To keep this simple, I'd start by assuming that it was in the house. "Hidden in plain sight." I guessed that would rule out any secret hiding spots like the loose floorboards under Sophie's bed, or hidden wall safes. I looked around my office, which had been Basil's long before I came on the scene.

I scanned the perimeter: bookshelves lined one wall, but I had cleaned and reorganized those shelves of mostly cook-books and mystery novels—I couldn't get enough of either genre and considered myself a junkie—last fall after Sophie and Spiro had left for Greece. There had been nothing out of the ordinary, and I didn't see anything unusual now. A large window on another wall looked out on what was now the employee parking lot but what had been formal gardens in days gone by. Nothing remarkable, just a large philodendron in a blue-and-white Chinese pot atop an antique oak side table. The third wall contained a credenza and filing cabinet with my desk in front of it facing the center of the room. The fourth housed the large door flanked by another dark oak table, which I had managed, uncharacteristically, to keep clear of clutter. I just liked its shape and size and the wooden curlicues gracing each end.

I swiveled back to my laptop and punched in "SODs." Nothing came up except a bunch of ads for fertilizer and some other acronymous organizations that didn't look right. What had Liza said SOD stood for, the group that Spiro was supposedly involved with, the loan sharks? Sons of . . . Demeter, that was it. Being Greek-in-law, I knew that Demeter was the goddess of agriculture. I keyed in "Sons of Demeter" in quotes and was rewarded with nothing, not even a Wikipedia entry. This appeared to be a dead end—not that I'd expected to find the information this easily, but still, it was worth a try. Liza had said she would call me if she learned anything, and I trusted she would. I didn't know anything about loan sharks, other than what I saw on television, but I felt I should be cautious and not ask too many questions myself around town since I had no idea who might be involved with this group.

I shut down the computer and took my now empty bowl and glass back out the kitchen, depositing the dirty dishes into the sink for Russ. Wiping my hands on a clean dinner napkin, I processed some credit card payments and nodded to Dolly, who was now cooking away.

This mysterious treasure seemed to be the crux of the whole mess. If I could find that, maybe I could use it to lure out the bad guy, or guys, get Spiro back, and perhaps by then the police would see fit to contact me. Tomorrow morning I would put in a missing persons report and see whether that sparked any action.

I searched the Victorian sideboard waitress station as I pretended to reorganize its many drawers. I took a turn around the two side dining rooms, nodding to customers and the waitstaff. I was in the front room feeling around inside a large pale green vase when somebody came up behind me.

"Georgie."

I jumped but managed to extricate my arm and steady the teetering vase without breaking either.

"Oh, hi, Sophie." God, how guilty did I sound? And how did she do that, anyway? Normal people cannot move that silently. Vampires or cat-people, maybe, but not humans.

"What are you doing?"

I thought fast. "Somebody called a few minutes ago and said that his son had accidentally dropped a toy car into the vase at lunch today, and just confessed to it now. I thought I'd look for it and return the call. Maybe they'll come back for dinner." That was either inspired or lame; I didn't know which.

She seemed to buy it. "Georgie, I was upstairs and I hear a noise."

"What kind of noise, Sophie?"

"I was in my room resting." Resting while watching her soap.

"And?"

"I hear a noise, like something heavy moving across the floor. Then I heard a—a—" She was frustrated because she couldn't think of the English word. "A groan, like a ghost!"

I pulled out a chair from one of the tables and sat her down. This was getting worse and worse.

"You were lying on your bed when this happened?"

"Yes."

"Where did the noises come from? Both from the same place? Were the noises in your room?"

"Both from the same direction. Not in the room with me. It came from Spiro's room."

"Did you look next door?"

"I thought Spiro had come back, but there was nobody there." She was braver than I would have given her credit for.

Not feeling especially brave myself, I nonetheless said I would go and investigate.

"Take Russ with you!" she insisted.

"Sophie, we've never allowed any of the staff to go upstairs, and I don't think we should start now," I said. "I'll be fine." I hoped. She gave me her hand to help her to her feet and then followed me.

"I will stand at the bottom of the stairs, and you must call out if you need me."

"I will."

◆ NINE ◆

I climbed the stairs to the second floor and walked down the hallway to Spiro's room. I pushed open the door a crack, then all the way. It was undisturbed, the same as the last time I'd been in here. Moving to the center of the room, I listened for a couple of minutes, but didn't hear anything other than the noise of the restaurant downstairs. I tried to open my mind and relax to see whether I could "sense" any presences or anything, but no luck. I didn't think that would work, but was willing to give it a shot. The bathroom and closet were clear.

I continued around counterclockwise to Cal's bedroom, which had been unused for a few months now, then on to mine, neither of which produced anything but silence. No noise, no creepy feelings. I leaned over the banister and waved down at Sophie, who was still standing at the bottom of the spiral. I tried to smile reassuringly. "Be down in just a minute," I said.

I opened Sophie's door and stepped in. She'd done the walls in a busy yellow rose print, and I always felt a little dizzy when I came in here. The repeat of the pattern gave the weird optical illusion that the roses were vibrating. The double bed was covered in a pale yellow Martha Washington spread, its fuzzy, embossed, monochrome pattern just asking to be stroked, its fringy bottom brushing the polished wood floor. No shams or throw pillows, just the spread pulled up over the two pillows and tucked underneath to create a neat roll. A perfect bouquet of a half dozen yellow roses and lacy white baby's breath sat in a crystal vase on the night table. She sent Russ down to the Bay Flower Shoppe a couple of times a week for fresh blooms, counting the change when he returned and requiring him to produce a receipt each time.

Unable to help myself, I peeked in her night table drawer. A pair of reading glasses, a small packet of tissues, the remote control, an unopened chocolate bar. A thick paperback bodice-ripper romance novel to which she would never, ever admit reading. Unfortunately, it was written in Greek, which I did not read well at all, so I couldn't discern the exact type of smut she was indulging in. But there was no mistaking those heaving female breasts and tight male riding britches. She must have had it mailed in a plain brown wrapper, because this book certainly could not be obtained anywhere in the North Country, probably no closer than New York City, a six-hour drive to the south. More likely she got it from her cousin who lived a mile or so up Route 12 during the summer. Marina ran the diner a few doors down and returned to Greece for the winter too.

Feeling guilty for snooping, I replaced the book and

closed the drawer. I lay down on the bed facing the television on the opposite wall, draping my feet over the side so as not to muss the spread too much. I hated bed making. I closed my eyes and listened. Nothing. I got up and smoothed out the indentation my butt had made, then walked over to the wall adjoining Spiro's room. I put my ear up to it. Moved to a different spot. Again, nothing. I rapped on the wall in a few spots, not sure what that would accomplish, but people always did that in movies when they were investigating things. The raps produced consistent sounds no matter where I made them. I looked around the closet and then the bathroom, tidy and immaculate, not even a water spot marring the shiny chrome fixtures. It had always been clear from whom Spiro had inherited his neatness gene.

I closed the door behind me and hurried downstairs. Good thing I hadn't been sucked into another dimension or attacked by something supernatural, because Sophie had left her post and was overseeing the seating of a party of twelve or thirteen in the front dining room. They would be seen through the window from the sidewalk and would give the appearance of a full restaurant, always good for business. Since the Sailor's Rest was shut down and the ghost hunters had been here, we'd had some lucrative days.

Sophie caught my eye and directed Lucy, one of our servers, to take over. She hustled over to me, no trace of her pseudo limp slowing her progress, and gave me a questioning look.

"I couldn't find anything, Sophie. Do you think you might have dozed off and dreamt the noises?"

"No," she insisted. "I no dream this."

"Why don't you call Marina and sleep there again tonight? She'll be good company for you."

"I don't want you to stay here by yourself."

I remembered Keith's invitation to come over for a drink and decided on the spur of the moment to accept it. "Maybe I'll go over to stay with Liza at the spa." It wasn't quite a lie, right? I didn't promise anything.

"All right. I go to Marina's."

"Want me to go and pack you an overnight bag?"

"You come upstairs with me while I do it."

"Sure."

A couple of hours later I trundled her and her suitcase—she'd insisted on bringing the full-sized, hard-sided, baby blue monstrosity, even though she only needed a nightie, a change of clothes, and a toothbrush—into the Lincoln and gave Russ strict instructions to deliver her to Marina and then come straight back, no detours along the way. He'd be gone for a minimum of a half hour, and since we'd had a steady stream of customers all evening, there'd be a huge backup of dirty dishes when he returned. If it got too bad I could pull one of the busboys in, but they always hated that. Before she left, Sophie made me promise to keep all the cash transactions separate, giving me a wink.

I ducked back into my office, flipped open my cell phone, and dialed Keith. He answered on the second ring.

I took a deep breath. "I decided to take you up on that offer for a drink tonight." We were friends, right? Friends could have a drink together.

"Wonderful!" He sounded genuinely happy.

"I'm going to shut down around nine thirty, so I should be able to come by around ten fifteen or so."

"Do you want me to come and pick you up? I'm not sure I like the idea of you being out by yourself with everything that's going on in town."

"No!" That would be the last thing I needed getting back to Sophie. Even though I'd shown some backbone with her earlier, I still planned to be discreet. "It's only a few blocks. I'll walk."

"Okay," he answered, "but call me before you leave. If you're not here five minutes after you call, I'm coming out to look for you."

To tell the truth I wasn't all that crazy about walking over there alone, with a murderer on the loose, but I felt better about it now.

"Talk to you later."

"Bye." I rang off.

I called eighty-six at nine fifteen. The last diners cleared out after lingering too long over their coffees. I oversaw the kitchen and dining room cleanup, shut down the front lights, tallied up the night's receipts (saving one of the cash payments for Sophie to satisfy her lust for the cold, hard green stuff), and hustled the staff out the kitchen door in record time.

I headed upstairs and jumped in the shower. I soaped away the clinging aroma of the Chicken Marengo and shampooed, rinsed, and stepped out. I toweled and combed my hair, giving it a blast with the hair dryer. Makeup? I rarely wore more than some pink-tinted lip gloss, a swipe of sand-colored eye shadow, and some mascara if I had time. I wanted to look like I'd put a little casual effort into my appearance, but not too much so I didn't seem overeager, so I just applied the usual. My hand was shaking and I poked myself in the eye with the mascara wand and had to put some makeup remover on a cotton swab to fix the mess.

At some point during the evening, I'd made a decision, though I couldn't have said when it happened.

If my husband could have a boyfriend, so could I. I wasn't sure whether this qualified as a date, but it was as close as I'd come in ages. It was time for me to move on, and there were a lot worse ways to start off a relationship with a gorgeous guy than as friends.

What to wear? I pulled item after item out of the closet and tossed each onto the bed, finally settling on a slim-fitting, coral V-necked T-shirt, jeans, and a three-quarter-sleeve navy blue cardigan. I put on a matching set of earrings, necklace, and bracelet, all handmade of multicolor, multitextured beads by a jewelry artisan in Clayton, the next town downriver. I smoothed my hair, again wishing I'd made time to get my foil highlights done this week, but it was too late for that. I took a deep breath. There was still time to back out. But I didn't. I dialed Keith's number and left the Bonaparte House.

The night was lit with a cadre of streetlights. The full moon shined bright, illuminating crowds of people in the street, and many more in each of the bar windows I passed. "Hey, baby," a schnockered Canadian with a Gretsky-era hairdo slurred at me from the doorway of Fat Max's. "C'mon in, I'll buy you a drink." I smiled and nodded but kept going. "Come back if you change your mind," he called after me. "You're hot."

Somebody thought I was hot! I was just a teensy bit pleased.

I turned up Caroline Street and walked the block to Keith's boat shop, looking behind me only once or twice. He lived above the shop, which was built over the water so he could work on the boats without pulling them into dry dock. I paused at the street-side door, then summoned enough nerve to ring the bell under the "Morgan Boat Works" sign. He was at the door too quickly to have come downstairs in the seconds since I had buzzed him. Had he been waiting on the stairs for me?

"I am so glad to see you," he said, flashing me a big, radiant smile. He took my hand and led me up the stairs. "Come in, sit down. What would you like? I've got booze or coffee. Whatever you're in the mood for." He gave me a pointed look.

That was a loaded question. I considered. "If it's not too much trouble, I think a decaf with a shot of Bailey's would be great."

"Coming right up." He went to the small galley kitchen and returned a few minutes later with a tray containing two drinks in fancy tall glass cups with handles. He sat down beside me on the ugly but comfortable green plaid couch, close enough that I could feel the heat of his leg through his Levi's but he was not quite touching me. He'd sprayed a tower of whipped cream into each coffee, then drizzled some chocolate syrup over them. A plate of Pepperidge Farm Orange Milanos sat next to the cups. Orange Milanos are a particular weakness of mine.

"Thanks. This is delicious."

"Oh, you know I slaved over these for hours." He took a bite of one of the buttery cookies. "So, how are things going? Any word from Spiro yet?"

"No. You haven't heard anything around town, have you?"

"Nothing other than what Inky is saying."

"What do you know about Inky?"

"Well, I know he's not my type."

He flashed that grin at me. It was beautiful, but I squirmed in my seat, just a little. Maybe this hadn't been such a great idea. Maybe I wasn't ready for this.

Keith took a sip of his drink. "He seems like a decent guy, harmless, talkative. I've never heard anything bad about him, and he's a pretty good tattoo artist."

"How many examples of his work have you seen up close?" I flirted, then was sorry I'd said it. I was so bad at this.

"I see one every day in the shower. Want to give me your opinion of Inky's talent?"

I sucked in some whipped cream from the top of my drink and collected myself. "Uh, maybe later," I said lamely. I was not good at cheating on my gay husband, I realized.

Keith settled back into the couch.

I changed the subject. "What about that Coast Guard guy? Did you find out who he is?"

"I talked to some people I know over at the station." His face darkened. "They say he's on a temporary assignment, but they can't or won't tell me any more than that."

"But he's here to investigate Big Dom's murder?"

"He was here a couple of weeks before Big Dom died."

I took a moment to digest this. "You don't think . . . he killed him, do you?" I had a sinking feeling in my gut. A murderer had been in my office. He'd taken Spiro's cell phone. There had to be a connection, and it couldn't be good.

"I don't know, honey. Rick over at the Bay PD says they're working on some leads now. I don't know if they have any suspects."

"Why would anyone want Big Dom dead?"

"I don't know that, either. Who knows what he was involved in? And if he was mixed up with the Watertown mob, well . . . anything could have happened." He took a sip of his coffee. "So," he asked casually, "who did you get to babysit Sophie tonight? I know she doesn't like to stay alone."

More discomfort. I was in over my head. "She thought she heard a noise upstairs today and was a little freaked out." I hesitated. "I sent her over to Marina's for the night."

He looked at me with interest. "Is that so?" He smiled.

I squirmed. "I'm not afraid to stay alone." In fact I was, but I wasn't going to admit it.

"Of course you're not. But why risk it?" He moved in closer and put his arm around me. "I'm worried about you, Georgie."

"I'll be fine." I swallowed. "I just need to find Spiro, that's all. Then everything will be back to normal."

"Honey, with all due respect, there's nothing normal about your life."

Really? I guess we were an unconventional family unit,

but I'd done my best to make things as normal as possible for Cal, and she'd grown up knowing that we all loved her. So what if her parents weren't in love with each other anymore?

I must have stiffened because he said, "I'm sorry. It's just that I think you're beautiful and smart and funny and a terrific person and you deserve to have a life of your own, apart from the restaurant and apart from Spiro."

I didn't know how to answer this, hardly remembering my life before the Bonaparte House, so I didn't say anything. I glanced up, saw that he was watching me intently, and looked down again. He put his hand on my jaw and turned my face toward his. His eyes were fixed on mine. He leaned toward me and cupped my face with his other hand. I closed my eyes and held my breath. Did I want this or not? I was pretty sure I did.

"Bzzzzzzzzzz!" The theme from *Rocky* blared between us. He pulled away.

"Sorry." He grinned sheepishly and leaned back, reaching into his pocket for his cell phone. "I should have turned this thing off." He looked at the display. "I have to take this call—I'll be right back. Don't go anywhere." He got up and headed for what I thought must be either the bedroom or his home office. I'd been downstairs in the workshop, but I'd never been in Keith's home before.

Relieved and a little disappointed, I tipped my head back on the couch and closed my eyes again. Exhaustion claimed me, and I thought I would just rest for a minute until Keith came back. *I should get going home.* The thought was rather unappealing. I had less than twenty-four hours to find the thing that was hidden in my house and get Spiro back. I'd have to continue the search tonight at the Bonaparte House while I was alone.

When I woke up, the ship's wheel clock on the wall told me that it was five fifteen a.m. I was covered with a striped comforter, faded but warm. A pillow had been placed under my head. I ran my hands down my body in a mild panic and was relieved to find that I was still fully dressed except for my shoes, which were on the floor next to the couch.

"Good morning, Sleeping Beauty," Keith said from the counter that separated the kitchen from the living room. "Hope you slept all right there. I decided not to disturb you."

I sat up and surreptitiously felt the pillow—dry. Thank God there was no drool, but what if I'd snored? I ran my fingers across my scalp to try to smooth down my hair. My neck ached faintly. "What happened?"

"Unfortunately for me, nothing happened." He grinned. "When I came back from my phone call, you were conked out. I figured you'd had a rough couple of days and needed the sleep, so I covered you and went to bed myself."

I got up and joined him at the counter. The sun was coming up and it cast a soft, orangy glow into the room. He had coffee made, and the smell of corned beef hash and eggs wafted in my direction. My stomach growled. "Can I do anything? Butter the toast?" I asked.

"Sure."

We ate together companionably. I saw he liked ketchup on his eggs and made a mental note of the fact, not sure why but it seemed like good information. When we finished I offered to help with the dishes, but he declined, dumping them in the sink. "I know you have a busy day in front of you," he said, and wrapped me in a warm, soft hug.

I returned the hug and we walked toward the door. "Before I go, can I see what you're working on downstairs?"

"Sure, follow me."

We descended the stairs into the boat shop. He led me toward a good-sized boat with a painted white hull and a lot of gleaming teak. "This beauty belongs to Phil Ferris, you know, the SpeedLube guy." SpeedLube shops could be found throughout New York State, and the owner lived in a behemoth of a Gothic Revival mansion on Caledonia Island. "I'm nearly finished with it."

"It's beautiful," I said, and meant it. The small vessel was truly a piece of art.

"Here's the latest chair I'm working on. It's my new design." I followed him over to the shop area, past rows of woodworking tools hanging on pegboard on an interior wall. Most had wooden handles on one end, and metal on the other end in various configurations, but none had power cords. I recognized an array of screwdrivers and . . . What were those? Pointy ends and curlicue shafts—drill bits? I couldn't put a name to anything else and wouldn't know how to use any of these items anyway.

He gestured toward a wooden chair with delicate legs and intricate back spindles. "Go ahead, sit down."

I sat down and the seat felt molded to my own bottom. It was the most comfortable wooden chair I'd ever sat in, bar none. I rubbed my hand on the smooth wooden armrest and marveled at the silky texture of the wood. "It's lovely, truly lovely. Have you sold any of them yet?"

"I have an order for a dozen to match the woodwork in the dining room of one of the big cottages over on Wellesley Island. This is my prototype. I'm going to assembly-line the production as much as is possible with handwork and try to have them done for Christmas. No guarantees," he added with a smile.

"I should go." I stood up and wondered whether he might kiss me good-bye, wondered how I'd feel if he did it. But that moment had passed hours ago and he just gave me another hug.

"Take care of yourself, Georgie. Call me if you need anything."

I exited the shop into the soft morning sunshine. The sky was a gorgeous blue, no clouds at all, and I walked along the river side of the street, enjoying the sparkle of the light on the water. It was still quite early and I felt pretty sure no one I knew would be watching me and speculating on where I'd spent the night. I turned up Theresa Street and put my key in the back door of the Bonaparte House. Too early for Dolly or Russ to be here, so I was alone. The place was gloriously quiet. Peaceful. Here, on a beautiful summer morning, yesterday's talk of a haunting seemed ridiculous.

Feta Attraction

I had work to do, though. That treasure, whatever the heck it was, wasn't going to find itself and bring Spiro back. So he could divorce me. So I could grab him by the neck and shake him. I went upstairs and opened the door to my room. I gasped.

◆ TEN ◆

All the clothes I had left piled on the bed had been tossed on the floor. The dresser drawers had all been pulled out and the contents had been pawed through, as had the closet. A scan of the bathroom showed the medicine cabinet doors open. Even the toilet tank lid had been removed and placed on the tile. I felt so violated I wanted to cry. Who could have done this? And why?

Except deep down I knew why. Somebody, the somebody who had Spiro and was threatening my family, wanted what was in this house and wanted it badly. Blind anger made me fearless. Not caring whether the perpetrator was still there or not, I looked into Spiro's and Cal's rooms, which had suffered the same fate. I wouldn't have time to clean up before Sophie got home, so I just closed the doors and hoped she wouldn't go in.

Sophie's room was also a mess. The nightstand drawer

was on the floor. I replaced the contents and noted that the romance novel was gone. She must have taken it with her to Marina's. A candy bar wrapper was wadded up under the bed, so the searcher must have had a snack. I checked the loose floorboard under the bed—there was the metal lock-box. I shook it and was rewarded with the dull thud of a few days' worth of cash. Whoever had tossed the place had missed that.

It took me nearly an hour, but I put the room back together, including folding up all the clothes and putting them back into the drawers and closet. Fortunately I did her laundry and knew in what order she kept her clothes, so I felt sure she wouldn't notice. Her clutter-free habits made the job pretty simple. I would not be able to say the same for my own room. I used the opportunity to search thoroughly for any other places where valuables might have been stored, but came up empty.

The landline phone rang and I picked it up. "Bonaparte House," I said, pushing my overgrown bangs back from my sweaty forehead. It was getting hot up here.

"Georgie, it's Dolly."

"Hi." *Make it quick,* I willed.

"Listen, Russ ain't coming in today."

Terrific. I mentally listed the jobs that would have to be reassigned. He was scheduled to go out to the farm at Rossie this morning to pick up the fresh vegetables and dairy for the weekend, and Sophie had to be fetched from Marina's. I'd have to put a busboy on dish duty tonight, and they always complained.

"Why not? Is he sick?"

"Uh, no, he ain't sick. Well, maybe a little sick," she added.

"What's wrong, then?"

"He got himself into a scrap down at the Island Road-house last night." The Island Roadhouse was a townie bar out on the road to Redwood, nowhere near an island. A rough place to hang out.

"Is he all right?"

"He got punched in the face and the ribs a few times. I think he got lippy with some of them bikers come in from Bassport for Pirate Days." Bassport was a small city farther north on the river, the crime capital of the North Country. "He's sore and bruised up some and got a pretty good shiner, but I put a steak on it." I was pretty sure I knew where the steak came from. Russ kept a cooler in his car and was famous for sneaking filet mignons and T-bones out under the daily piles of vegetable trimmings he carried to the compost bin behind the restaurant. The Rileys were strictly red-meat people; there was never any chicken or fish missing.

"Will he be in tomorrow?"

"Yeah, I expect so. He ain't gonna look too good, though."

"We'll keep him in the kitchen. Dolly, would you mind coming in an hour early this morning? Of course I'll pay you extra. I need you to go pick up Sophie at Marina's. You know she only likes to ride in her own car, so I'll leave the keys for you. I'll have to go myself out to Sunshine Acres to pick up the fresh food."

"No problem, boss. I got a new George Strait CD. Bet she'd like to listen to that on the way home."

George Strait? I liked him, but whether Sophie had ever

heard of him was doubtful. "I'm sure she will. Tell Russ I hope he feels better. You have your key to the restaurant, right? Bye-bye." Dolly had worked for us for thirty years and was trustworthy—and any little thefts Russ had committed were insignificant in the grand scheme of things.

I left the keys to the Lincoln for Dolly beside her cutting board and hustled out the door. I found my own keys and unlocked the door of my little blue Honda Civic. I loved this car, but didn't drive it much. I was always working during the summer. And up till now I usually spent January and February in Greece, so it sat in Dolly's garage, undriven, during the worst of the winter. A blast of hot, stale air hit me and I fanned the door trying to dissipate it. When it seemed safe, I got in and turned on the AC. I cranked up my *Fabulous Hits of the '80s* CD and exited the parking lot.

I headed north out of town on Route 37. It was still a beautiful morning and I loved to drive, but I did not have time for this trip and that diminished my enjoyment. Old farms with their dilapidated barns and overgrown fields whizzed past, giving way to a few miles of neat Amish farms, their clotheslines pinned with dark trousers and colored shirts flapping in the summer breeze. Farmland was plentiful and inexpensive in the North Country, and the Amish population was growing. I drew closer to a black buggy traveling at a modest clip, put on my signal, and passed carefully so as not to spook the pair of well-matched chestnut horses hitched to the front of the conveyance. I waved and the driver nodded at me from under the brim of his straw hat.

I picked up the pace until I reached the turnoff for Rossie, then pulled off onto the back roads that led toward Black Lake. Eventually a simple, hand-lettered wooden sign reading, "Sunshine Acres—All Welcome Here," appeared.

In the pasture, horses grazed peacefully alongside a herd of boldly patterned black-and-white Holsteins. I'd been here only a handful of times, nearly always sending Russ out for the pickups. It looked the same as I remembered it. Large red wooden barns on either side of the long dirt drive, a two-story rectangular white building that might be living quarters, long hoop houses covered in semi-opaque white plastic off to one side. Fat chickens pecked at the ground amid the spindly legs of dairy goats with low-hanging udders. These goats produced milk for the most delicious feta cheese, which the Sunshine Acres farmers made especially for the Bonaparte House.

I pulled up at the flat patch of dirt that served as a parking lot in front of the store, which was the front third of one of the barns. I opened the heavy door to the clang of a cowbell and was greeted by a spry fellow whose leathery, wrinkled face was set off by a pair of round, wire-rimmed John Denver–style glasses. A grizzly beard reached to just above his belt buckle. I placed him in his mid- to late sixties.

"What can I do for ya?" he asked.

"I'm here to pick up the Bonaparte House order."

"Where's the guy who always comes?" he asked a bit suspiciously. Like this was any of his business.

"He's sick."

"Oh. Well, give me a minute to see if it's ready. You're early," he added, looking out at me over the tops of his glasses.

"I'm shorthanded today at the restaurant, so if you could

check on it, I'd appreciate it." I gave him a smile I hoped would encourage him to speed things up, but he moved unhurriedly through the back door.

While he was gone I admired a large Amish quilt hanging on the wall. The tiny, even stitches fascinated me and I made a mental note that one of these would make a nice gift for myself once the season ended. I scanned the glass-fronted refrigerator and pulled out a bag of cheese curds with today's date written in black marker on the label. Score! Fresh cheese curds were a real treat, not to be found anywhere other than dairy country because they're best the same day they're made. I removed the twist tie from the top of the plastic bag and withdrew a pale yellow blob, which I popped into my mouth. It squeaked against my teeth as I chewed, cheesy and salty.

I replaced the twist tie and set the bag on the counter, placing a big jar of local honey next to it. Sophie's baklava was to die for—light and flaky and dripping with butter, honey, and lots and lots of walnuts. My mouth was watering as I thought of it. I moved the honey closer to the cheese curds and accidentally displaced a pink lined notepad next to the cash register. "Meeting, tonight, usual" was written on the top sheet. The commune must have some kind of loose government, I realized, so they were probably going to discuss business. I slid the pad back over to where it had originally been.

I spied a basket of handmade soaps and selected three— lavender goat's milk, rosewater, and teaberry vanilla—all wrapped up in calico fabric and tied with raffia. Sophie and Dolly could choose one each, and I'd be happy with whichever was left, they all smelled so good. I was a sucker for anything locally produced.

The guy came back out and set a big box of produce and a smaller box of dairy products on the counter. "You're supposed to bring back your boxes," he admonished. "Your boy does it right." He pushed up the sleeves of his red-and-black-plaid flannel shirt, though it must have been close to eighty degrees already.

"Sorry. I'll make sure these get back to you. I'm Georgie, by the way." I extended my hand and he took it in his own, his rough calluses scraping my fingers.

"Hank. Say, you're the owner, right?" He eyed me.

"Yes." Not really.

"What's that other woman's name, the older one whose husband died?"

"Sophie? She's my mother-in-law."

"Sophie." He said it almost reverently. "I've seen her down at the Pancake Heaven. She's a doll."

Yikes. Well, Sophie was a nice-looking senior, I guess. I could picture her flirting with older guys over a stack of flapjacks from her booth at Marina's diner.

"You're married to her son."

"That's right."

"What's he up to these days?"

I didn't answer directly. "Do you know Spiro?" I asked.

"Just in passing. You from around here? What's your maiden name? I might know your people."

"Bartlett."

"You from those Bartletts over toward Redwood?"

"I grew up here in the Bay. Never knew my father."

He looked at me with interest. "What's your mom's name?"

"Shirley. Shirley Bartlett. I haven't seen her in a long time." Not since the day after my high school graduation, when she left town, and left me to fend for myself. But there was no sense dwelling on the past. I wasn't sure why I was giving this man any information. I hadn't talked about my biological family in so long and it felt strange.

He continued to stare at me, fingering his long beard, and I felt uncomfortable. "Uh, I have to get back. Can you ring me up?" After I paid, Hank helped me load my car.

"Don't forget to bring back my boxes," he called after me as my tires kicked up a cloud of dust from the dirt driveway. "The bags too!"

◆ ELEVEN ◆

I hightailed it back to the restaurant. Nobody was around yet so I had to unload everything by myself. A note was stuck on the back door saying that Marina had invited Sophie and Dolly to breakfast at the Pancake Heaven, and they'd be back later. Those three biddies could gossip all morning, so I had some time alone. I put the coffee on and stowed away everything I'd bought at Sunshine Acres, then went to my office to check my messages. No plain white envelopes, thank God, and no e-mails.

The answering machine was blinking, though. I hit the button. Beep. "Uh, hi. This is Jack Conway from the Coast Guard. Remember me? Could you give me a buzz? Thanks." My blood froze. Why was he calling me? No way was I returning that call.

I took a deep breath and headed upstairs with my coffee mug. I opened Spiro's door and surveyed the damage. Briefly

I wondered whether I should even be here, but common sense told me that whoever the intruder had been, he—or she—was long gone. I restored everything to its more or less proper place in short order. For once I was grateful that Spiro was a neatnik and a minimalist like his mother. I checked every possible hiding place and went over the walls, floors, and closet twice, looking for I didn't know what. This break-in should be reported to the police. I knew that. And if the state police ever returned my call, I would. No sense calling the local cops. Like everyone else in Bonaparte Bay, they were preparing for the crowds that would descend during the pirate festival.

I pulled back the curtain at the window and looked out on Theresa Street. It was still early but there were a few tourists sauntering down the street, stopping here and there to look in the windows of the gift shops or examine the racks of sale clothing out on the sidewalks. A line was beginning to form down at the docks in front of the tiny square building that served as the Lady Liberty Boat Tours ticket office. A good day for the tour boats generally meant a good day for the Bonaparte House, and things looked promising. A couple of agile green-shirted deckhands jumped off the *Lady Liberty II*. One used a broom to sweep off the gangplank and the other put up rope railings to keep unwary tourists from falling into the weedy water.

I turned my head and looked in the other direction. I had forgotten how far I could see from this window. My own room looked out over the employee parking lot and our tiny patch of lawn.

There was the Express-o Bean; Sweet'ums, the fudge

and candy shop; the Sailor's Rest, still closed up; and I could see just the corner of Inky's place. I looked down toward Marina's Pancake Heaven and saw a swarm of people exiting the front door in a hurry. A light haze of smoke was emanating from Aunt Jennie, the eight-foot-tall aproned lady whose smiling neon face had graced the Heaven for close to fifty years. Aunt Jennie had some sort of perennial short in her wiring that caused her to periodically sizzle and smoke, not unlike bacon on a too-hot griddle. She'd be okay once she cooled off. I glanced back down at the street and saw Sophie and Dolly heading this way.

I moved away from the window and took one more cursory glance around. My eyes settled on that scuffed spot on the floor over by the wall adjoining Sophie's room. Much as I wanted to ignore it, I couldn't look away, like staring at a zit on somebody's face. It was just so incongruous when everything else around me was so perfect. I couldn't believe Spiro could stand it. Well, if he didn't do it himself, I'd get the floor sanded and treated this fall after we closed down. The downstairs floors needed attention too. I remembered with a pang that if I didn't find what needed to be found, Spiro might not be around to be annoyed by the imperfections. But if I did find him, the floors might not be my problem anymore.

I secured the doors to my and Cal's rooms so the messes inside wouldn't be inadvertently seen, and hustled back downstairs to meet the ladies.

I made it to the kitchen just before Sophie and Dolly came in the back door. Dolly unzipped the gray hoodie she was wearing and hung it on the row of metal hooks installed by the door. Underneath she wore a very tight hot-pink tank top designed for a much younger woman with a few less tummy rolls and a bit less, or at least better contained, cleavage. A huge, shiny yellow-gold crucifix dangled precipitously into the jiggling crevasse between her freckled boobs, drawing attention to the "Baby Girl" logo on the front of the shirt. I was relatively sure she wasn't Catholic, but that was a big, expensive piece of gold if it was real.

"Morning, Dolly. Morning, Sophie." I found it hard to look away from the glitzy Vegas-style mammary show going on over at the prep counter.

"Mornin'," Dolly said as she expertly maneuvered a hairnet over her coiffure, which remained miraculously undisturbed. She opened the walk-in, brought out one of the Sunshine Acres boxes, snapped on a pair of gloves, and went right to work on her pile of vegetables.

"I am going to go lie down for a while," Sophie said. "You can handle everything, right?"

Sure! Georgie can handle everything. "Are you all right, Sophie?" I said with concern.

"I'm tired." She cut her eyes over to Dolly blissfully chopping away, then back to me. "Marina's dog kept me up all night, yip, yip, yip! It make me crazy!" Marina did, as I recall, have one of those microscopic, hyperactive little poodles. Quite cute in small doses but irritating for more than a short time. Sophie was definitely a cat person. We didn't have pets here, but she kept a big, elegant white Persian back in Greece. One of her many other cousins cared for it over the summer until she returned.

"Shall I walk you upstairs?" She apparently wanted to talk to me alone, but didn't want to do it now.

"No, you come up later on if I no come down." She sighed. "You hear any noises last night?"

"Nothing." Not a lie. I hadn't been here.

"Good."

I saw her to the bottom of the stairs and watched her walk up to the second floor. I returned to my office and called in one of the busboys early to replace Russ and adjusted the schedule for the day. I reviewed the specials menu and filed away the receipts and other paperwork that I had left undone last night. I checked my e-mail again. There it was, a message from my anonymous sender. I double-clicked and read the simple message.

DON'T FORGET, TONIGHT, ALONE.

My stomach tightened into a knot. What the hell was I going to do? I had less than twelve hours to find the something, find a boat, learn how to use the boat, get myself to the Devil's Oven at night, deliver whatever it was, and somehow get myself back home to wait for the safe return of Spiro, all without Sophie finding out or getting myself killed.

The phone rang and I let the machine pick it up, too rattled to answer it myself. I heard a click, then: "Georgie, it's Jack Conway again. I'd like to talk to you. Call me back, please." The voice was firm and insistent, but not unfriendly. He didn't sound like a killer, but everybody thought Ted Bundy was a normal guy too. I pressed *delete*.

I went back out to the kitchen. "Dolly, I'm going upstairs."

If there had been anything to find downstairs, I would have found it during my searches yesterday, although it would have been a whole lot easier if I had any idea what I was looking for. I still needed to check my room and Cal's room, and I was running out of time.

"Sure, boss," Dolly croaked back at me, forty years of smoking evident in her voice, her décolletage merrily bouncing in rhythm with her chopping.

"I'll be back down soon. Hold down the fort for me." I turned and started toward the stairs, when a bold knock sounded at the kitchen door. I stopped and heard Dolly call out, "C'mon in, I'm busy here!"

I stepped back into the kitchen. The tall, burly form of a New York State Trooper filled the doorway.

❖ TWELVE ❖

The Trooper stepped inside and the screen door sprang back with a snap behind him. He wore his pressed gray uniform trousers tucked into the tops of his knee-high shiny black boots. He stared down at me and casually removed his mirrored aviator sunglasses, folding them and placing them in his front shirt pocket, under the badge and the nameplate that read "Lt. E. Hawthorne."

"I'm Detective Hawthorne," he said, unnecessarily. "I need to speak to"—he looked down at a notebook he'd flipped open—"Mrs. Nik-Nik—"

"I'm Mrs. Nikolopatos," I said. "Please call me Georgie." *It's about time the cops got here,* I thought.

"Well, all right, Georgie." The voice was deep, sonorous, and a bit scary, like some villain in a dark opera. I could picture him twirling his mustache as he plotted the demise of some fair young maiden. "Is there someplace we can talk privately?"

I glanced over at Dolly, who was fingering the gold crucifix in her bosom and staring at his butt predatorily.

"We can go into my office. I have something I need to talk to you about too." I led him in and sat him down in the armchair. I sat at the desk facing him and waited for him to speak.

"Mrs.— uh, Georgie."

"Yes?"

"I'm looking into the death of Domenic DiTomasso, sometimes known as Big Dom."

"I'm not sure how I can help you." This guy was definitely scary. I guess that's a good thing in law enforcement.

"We understand that you and Mr."—he consulted the notebook again—"Morgan found the body."

"Yes, Keith was giving me a ride to the spa on Valentine Island when we found him."

"You were just motoring on by and saw a floating body?" His tone was skeptical. My hackles rose.

"That's right."

"And you went over to investigate?"

"Yes."

"Why did you disturb the body?"

I took a deep breath and refused to be baited. I'd seen enough winter reruns of cop shows to know that he was trying to throw me off balance and get me to admit to something.

"If you see someone floating in the water, you roll over

the body and see if the person can be saved. That's what we did."

"It was too late, though, wasn't it?"

"It was."

"How well did you know the victim?"

"Not that well. I mean, I would see him around town, and we both own restaurants on the same street, so I knew him in a business sense."

"What type of food do you serve at this restaurant?"

"I can show you a menu if you like. We serve Greek food, burgers, salads, steaks, and lobsters, with various specials throughout the week."

"What type of food did the victim serve at his restaurant?"

"Basically the same, but Italian, at about the same prices. I don't think he emphasized the seafood, though."

"How many other restaurants are there nearby?" he said without looking up. He made some notes.

Was he not from around here? "The Sailor's Rest and the Bonaparte House are the largest of the restaurants in the Bay. The rest are the diner, the pizza shop, the sub shop, and the hot dog stand at the docks."

He pulled a stick of gum out of its paper wrapper and leisurely put it into his mouth. He made a few deliberate chews and swallowed. The prominent knob of his Adam's apple bobbed up and down. "So, would you say that the Sailor's Rest was your business competitor?"

"There's enough business in this town for both of us," I said defensively.

He locked eyes with me. My heart rate ticked up. I'd

intended to tell the police about the threatening notes and about the search of our upstairs rooms. But this conversation was going in a direction I didn't like and I couldn't see a way to turn it around. Detective Hawthorne was treating me like a suspect rather than a victim.

"Where's your husband?"

Crap. How much could I tell him without putting Spiro and Sophie in more danger? I could get Spiro killed. I needed time to think.

"He's out of town," I said.

"Really? Where is he?" The Trooper snapped his gum. "I'd like to talk to him."

I thought fast. "He's gone to Montreal for the week."

"What's he doing up there?"

"He's on vacation."

"In the middle of your busy season?"

I wanted to say that he didn't do much around here anyway, but refrained. "His doctor said he should get away for a few days."

"Does he have a medical condition?"

He would have a fatal medical condition if I couldn't find the thing hidden in this house. "Just nerves. The stress of working seven days a week sometimes takes its toll on him."

"How long have you been married?"

"Twenty years. We have a daughter who's studying in Greece right now."

"Are you aware that bigamy is illegal in this or any other state of the United States?"

Huh? He must have interviewed Inky and found out about his hopes for a future with Spiro.

"Uh, yes. I'd say virtually everyone knows that."

"So how were you planning to legally marry Big Dom? Did you kill your husband so you could?"

"What?" I didn't think I'd heard him right.

"The day before he died, Big Dom drove to Watertown and purchased a diamond ring."

I shook my head in confusion. "Sorry—I don't understand this."

"He told the clerk at the jewelry store that he was planning to ask 'the lovely Mrs. N' to forget her husband and marry him, and that he was going to come into a lot of money very soon. The ring has not been found." He leaned toward me. "So I'm asking you, how long had your affair been going on, what were you planning to do, and where's the ring?"

I was floored. I barely knew Big Dom, and he had been going to ask me to marry him? Everyone in town knew I was already married to Spiro. Then it hit me. There was another Mrs. N in this house. And she was available. The Trooper must have known that—maybe he was just fishing for information. But maybe not. I had to get rid of this guy, and now. If the cops didn't think I killed Dom, they might think Sophie had.

"I'm sorry, but I think your information is incorrect," I said as evenly as I could. "I did not have any sort of relationship at all with Mr. DiTomasso. I must get back to work now. I have a restaurant to run." I stood up.

"I'm not finished with my questions, ma'am."

"But I am. If you want to speak to me again, you'll need to arrange it through my lawyer." I scribbled down the name of the local attorney who handled our business legal work. Whether he was qualified to represent a criminal client, I had no idea. "Good-bye."

He took the paper and fastened it into his notebook with a paper clip that had been attached to the cover. "We'll talk again, Georgie. I'm going to need to talk to your mother-in-law too. Maybe you'd both prefer to do it at the state police barracks."

He stood up with maddening slowness and opened my office door, moving quite gracefully for a man of his size out through the kitchen and into the parking lot. Dolly stared after him, goggle-eyed. I considered handing her a napkin to mop up any drool that might have escaped her parted, frosty pink lips.

"Damn!" she said. "I wish Harold looked like that. He could interrogate me anytime."

I headed up the stairs and banged on Sophie's door. "Come in," she said weakly.

I went inside and found her propped up on a mound of pillows, her bony legs stretched out in front of her on the yellow bedspread. I bet anything that if I had reached under those pillows I would have found that smut novel hidden away. She didn't look tired at all anymore.

"Sophie, I've just had a visit from a State Trooper."

She sat up and put her hand to her throat. "It isn't . . . Spiro?" She seemed to shrink back again and I saw real fear in her eyes.

"He hasn't turned up anywhere, if that's what you mean."

She relaxed. "What did he want?"

"He wanted to ask me some questions about Big Dom's death."

"Oh." She began to fidget. I let her squirm.

"All right, Sophie, I know all about it," I bluffed. "You might as well tell me before that Trooper comes back."

She hesitated, then sat up straighter and began to fiddle with the fringe on one of her floral throw pillows.

"Sophie, I don't have all day."

She sighed, continuing to twist the fringe. "Domenic is—was—very handsome."

Not in my book, but to each her own. "And?"

"He was in love with me, but I resist him." Her eyes took on a dreamy quality that gave me the distinct impression she would not have resisted him forever.

"I don't remember seeing the two of you together recently except that day he was in trying to buy the restaurant again."

"We talk on the phone."

"When?"

"Well, we don't talk out loud so much."

Curiouser and curiouser. "How did you communicate, then?"

"We use that message text. On the cell phone."

Sophie had been texting Big Dom? She had a cell phone, but I had never seen her use it to make or receive a call, let alone text anyone.

"How did you learn how to send text messages?"

"Callista showed me before she left. I talk to her this way all the time," she said proudly.

I wasn't much of a texter, so I was mildly impressed.

"So you and Big Dom were writing back and forth."

"Yes, many times a day. And night," she added.

Please, I thought, *don't let her have been sexting with Big Dom. Or at least don't let her tell me about it.* "He tell me he's in love with me ever since Basil died." She looked very, very sad. "I think Domenic killed himself because I no accept him."

"What do you mean, 'accept him'?"

"He say he want to marry me. I no believe him, though. But then he bring me a ring, and I tell him I will think about it."

I was floored, although I shouldn't have been, given the information the Trooper had just told me. "When did this happen?"

"The day before he died."

"Where is the ring?"

"I keep it here." She patted her heart.

She was not generally a sentimental woman. "No, I mean where is the actual ring?"

"Right here." She reached into the neckline of her blouse and pulled out a rose gold chain on which hung a platinum ring. A dazzling white central diamond of at least two carats was flanked by two smaller sparkling yellow stones—canary diamonds? Her metals didn't match, but who cared? I was skeptical that that ring could have been bought in Watertown, which was a very small city. A ring of that quality and size would have to come from Syracuse or Manhattan, I would think.

I had been standing over her this whole time but now I sat down on the edge of the bed. I reached over and held up the

Susannah Hardy

platinum ring to the sunlight. I was rewarded with a stunning prismatic display that literally took my breath away. I did love jewelry, but I bought all my own now that my husband no longer felt the need to show me how much he loved me.

"Sophie, you must keep this ring hidden for now."

"Why?" She bristled, though I felt sure that was what she had planned anyway, since she was wearing it inside her top and had not seen fit to mention that she had been proposed to.

A thought struck me. "You didn't tell Marina or Dolly about this, did you?" That was all we needed. The place would be swarming with police and gossips and lookie-loos and I would not be able to protect her, or find the thing hidden in the house. *Damn, the treasure.*

"No-oh." She drew the syllable out and I knew there was more.

"Did you tell, or not?"

She played with the pillow fringe some more before she answered. "I tell them I have a secret, but I no tell what it is." She loved to torture people, so she was most likely telling the truth.

I had to ask. "Did you love him?"

"No. But I was thinking about loving him." So she was not completely repulsed by Big Dom, and would have considered the marriage. She had taken the ring. "A woman my age has needs, you know." She looked up at me defiantly.

Please, don't tell me about your unfulfilled needs, I begged silently. I had plenty of my own, and I was decades younger than she.

"I'm still a young woman. Basil died too soon and left me alone."

I was still married yet I was alone too. I could certainly understand how she might want some male companionship. I was surprised that she wanted to have it with Big Dom, though.

"I think he kill himself over me," she reminded me.

"Sophie, I've heard that the police suspect murder."

"Oh." Her face fell. I guess it would theoretically be rather romantic, in a Shakespearean sort of way, to have someone commit suicide over you. "Who offed him?"

I suppressed a snort. "I don't think anyone knows yet. Can you think of a reason someone would want to kill him?" I figured it was worth a try—she'd been secretly texting him for who knew how long now and might know something.

"He was talking about getting some money soon."

"From where?"

"He no say." Extremely unhelpful.

"How much money?"

"A lot of money. Georgie, I hear something."

Oh, for crying out loud. She was always hearing something. "What is it?"

"Listen." She leaned toward one wall and put her finger to her lips.

"I don't hear anything."

She let out a wail. "It's Spiro. He's dead!"

My heart started beating wildly. "Why do you say that?"

"Because I just hear his ghost! He said, '*Mana*.'"

◆ THIRTEEN ◆

"What do you mean, his ghost?" You heard about these things happening all the time, people knowing the exact moment of a loved one's death, even from many miles away, but somehow you don't expect it to happen with people you actually know.

"I just hear him. He say, '*Mana*.' Oh, he's dead. I can feel it." Her big eyes filled with tears.

I stared at the wall and listened, but heard nothing but Sophie's sobs. My eyes drifted downward and fell on the floor, which had some wear. I'd have to get this floor done too. Could she have some maternal sixth sense connecting her to Spiro? Had the kidnapper done away with him before the deadline? Which was tonight. That wave of panic washed over me again and I took a deep breath to calm myself. *No,* I thought. The kidnapper had nothing to gain by killing him—Spiro was his bargaining chip in exchange for the supposed treasure. Still, Spiro might have angered this guy enough that he didn't care and killed him anyway. I know I'd wanted to, often.

I listened again. And heard something this time. A soft, muffled noise coming from the direction of the wall adjoining Spiro's room. I shushed Sophie and hustled over to the wall. I put my ear up to it but heard nothing more. I raced out the door and into Spiro's room. I checked under the bed and inside the closet and bathroom, screwing up my courage and pulling aside the shower curtain, half expecting to see some crazed monster drooling rabidly in the tub, but it was empty. I ran to the window, which was locked from the inside. I'd intended to open it up this morning but had never gotten to it. It was at least a thirty-foot drop. No one could have left that way. No one human, that was. If someone had been here, he or she would have had to have been extraordinarily fast and quiet to get out the door in the couple of seconds between the moment I'd heard the noise and the time it had taken me to get out into the hallway.

Sophie came to the door. "Georgie, I hear him again! My son is dead! He is afraid and wants me! Say a prayer with me!" She got down on her knees and grabbed my hand.

"Sophie, get up. We need to figure this out. We can pray later."

I pulled her up, not as gently as I could have. "Let's not lose our heads here. We heard a noise in your room, right?"

"Yes, my dead son!" she wailed.

"And it came from this direction, right?"

"Yes, it is coming from this room. The dead come back to the place they know."

"But you heard the voice again while I was here, in Spiro's room."

"He was here," she said with awe. "I no feel him now."

"I don't think there was anybody, living or dead, in here with me, Sophie. There has to be an explanation for this. I don't know what it is, but I am going to find out. Spiro isn't dead. I'm going to find him." I hoped I sounded more confident than I felt.

I waited with her while she put on her shoes, splashed water on her face, and ran a comb through her hair. We headed downstairs. I installed her, shaking, in her chair by the cash register and went down to the bar, where I poured a tall glass of orange juice over ice.

I scanned the bottles behind the bar, each marked with a series of black lines showing the level of liquid inside and the initials "SN" on each line. It was a low-tech system Sophie used for keeping track of our liquor inventory. She knew pretty much to the ounce how much alcohol we sold, and since we made a lot of money on drinks, she didn't like to see any of our booze being stolen by our employees.

I located the brand of vodka Sophie liked and poured some into the glass of juice, giving it a stir with a long plastic straw. As I replaced the bottle, I frowned. Something didn't look right. Hmmm. Where was the bottle of Ouzo? We didn't sell a lot of it to customers, but we sometimes had a shot with the employees on Dolly's birthday, whenever it happened to fall, and Spiro and Sophie had an occasional glass. An uneasy feeling settled into the pit of my stomach. There were a lot of bars in town, but Ouzo probably wasn't a big seller anywhere. My thoughts went back to the bottle

I'd seen floating near Dom's body. Had it had hand-drawn black lines and Sophie's initials on the label? I couldn't remember.

Back in the kitchen I handed Sophie the glass and told her to drink up. The first lunch check of the day had just come in. The waitress gave the check to my mother-in-law with a stack of cash. This, combined with a couple of sips of the screwdriver, seemed to restore her to some semblance of her normal self. She handed the change to the waitress and pocketed the money.

"Sophie, I'm going back upstairs." I looked at her significantly. "Stay here," I ordered in what I hoped was a nonnegotiable tone. She nodded and rearranged her apron over her knobby knees.

I raced back upstairs and looked through Cal's room. I didn't take time to pick up the mess, figuring that if an item was on the floor, it had been searched already. I checked the walls, under the bed, and in the closet for any possible hiding places. I made sure the bedroom door was closed and locked from the inside, as I should have done before so Sophie wouldn't be able to get in and see the mess. I went through the bathroom door. I'd already searched here, since she and I shared this bath, and came out back in my own room.

I scanned the damage. I did not even know where to start. I had so much more stuff than the other members of my family that it was going to take much, much longer to put things back together. I resolved then and there that I would clear out my clutter once this ordeal was over. The chances of the treasure being in this room were pretty remote, I thought, since I'd occupied it for a lot of years and I knew the contents. I closed my eyes and tried to clear my mind. I opened them back up and looked about with what I hoped was a fresh perspective. Walls painted a soft spring green, white sheer curtains, white bed linens. I'd had the walls painted last year and was pretty sure that I would have heard about it if any secret wall safes had been discovered.

I looked down at the floors, which seemed to be in excellent shape, and inspected the areas that weren't covered by the large floral area rug and the mess of my personal belongings. I kicked through the clothes on the floor, feeling simultaneously sad and angry that someone had treated me and my family with such disrespect. I toed my overnight bag, which had been overturned and its contents spilled, clothes and papers everywhere.

I moved the bed away from the wall and lifted up all four corners of the rug, checking for secret compartments. I was pretty sure there weren't any. Besides, Spiro had said the thing was "hidden in plain sight." To me that pretty much ruled out my having to look too far under or into anything. I didn't even bother to examine my drawers or the closet. On a whim I lifted the bottom of the reproduction Monet from the wall and didn't see anything behind that. I almost laughed—that would have to be a flat treasure, now, wouldn't it? Well, I guess it could have been cash or stock certificates taped to the back or something, but somehow I felt that what I was looking for was a valuable object of some kind, not money.

I took one last look around but didn't see anything promising. No need to search the kitchen, I felt—there were so many people in and out of the kitchen, if the object had been hidden in some fairly obvious place, it would have been found by now.

There was only one area of the house I hadn't searched—the cupola.

I closed my bedroom door and locked it, putting the key into my pocket. I moved around to the staircase and began the climb up and around the helix that would lead me to the highest point of the house. I didn't look down. I hadn't had any lunch and it had been what seemed like a lifetime ago since my breakfast with Keith. If I looked over the railing I would have gotten dizzy, perhaps sick.

My upward trudge ended at a small landing. The cupola was quite large, almost like an observatory, about ten feet in any direction from the central opening of the stairway. It was filled with stunningly bright light entering from the four windows facing the sun, illuminating a shower of dust motes suspended in the air. It was stiflingly hot up there—only the first-floor restaurant was air-conditioned—and I fanned the bottom of my T-shirt to try to get some air circulating on the exposed skin. I began to sweat nonetheless. It would have been much more comfortable to have come up here after the sun went down, but I didn't have that luxury.

I took a deep breath. That damned treasure, whatever it was, had to be here. Now that I thought about it, this was the most likely place and I would have saved myself a lot of time and worry if I had just come up here to begin with. Sophie and Spiro had told me many times that Basil had loved this spot. If he was going to hide something, this would almost certainly be where he'd do it. Cal and I had spent many happy hours playing up here when she was small, and I smiled even as my eyes teared up. I missed those magical days with my little girl. I shook it off. No time for sentimentality now.

I started at the wall to my left, looking up toward the Pancake Heaven. Aunt Jennie was lit up and smiling. There were no curtains on these windows. I ran my hands along the entire surface of the window frame, hoping to find a hidden catch or spring that might open a secret compartment like in a Nancy Drew story. I moved counterclockwise around the octagon and checked each window in turn, including the wall space in between, coming up empty except for some sticky cobwebs that I wiped on my shorts. I got down on my hands and knees, wincing as I kneeled on the grit on the floor. Dolly's daughter Brandy came in to clean for us once a week, but I sent her up here only at the change of seasons since we used this room so infrequently now. I wished I'd brought a towel to kneel on.

I examined the ancient wood paneling underneath each window, feeling for loose moldings, wobbly panels, metal pieces, but came up empty again. I went to Cal's old toy box and poked around. She had saved a few of her stuffed animals, including that dinosaur the *Ghost Squad* had been messing around with. I squeezed each toy—limbs, head, and tummy—but didn't feel anything unusual inside.

Next I moved to the small wooden table adjacent to Basil's old chair. No drawers, just a central wooden spindle supporting a smooth top on which someone, probably one of the TV guys, had written "clean me" in the dust. Hysterical. There was a basket next to the table on the floor containing some old paperbacks and a cylindrical metal object, which I picked up. Now I remembered what this was. It was the other thing those ghost hunters had been playing with that night. It looked like a telescope but was in fact an old Victorian-era kaleidoscope. Cal and I had played with this many times on sunny days up here. I pawed through the basket but didn't find anything else. I returned the kaleidoscope to the basket and turned my attention back to the chair.

The chair was upholstered in a faded 1950s floral pattern, not slipcovered, and I didn't feel any loose spots that might hide something. I armed some sweat off my face, tipped up the chair, and examined the bottom cambric. It was old and dusty but intact and didn't look as though it had been recently disturbed or replaced. I sneezed at the dust I had released and set the chair upright.

I turned toward the table. I tipped it upside down and felt under the legs. They seemed to be solidly attached and could not be removed without tools. I checked the connection between the top and the turned wood spindle connecting it to its three legs, and found that it was similarly tight.

I froze. Could it be this simple? A frisson of excitement ran through me. I'd been thinking in terms of gold bars or bundles of cash. But what if this table was the treasure? I'd seen television shows about pieces of supposedly junk furniture being bought for a few bucks at garage sales and then turning out to be priceless early-American antiques. I looked at the table again. It was definitely very old. There was some wear but the wood glowed, deep and ancient.

The more I thought about it, the more I knew this had to be it. If this was some colonial-era table made by a famous carpenter, it could be worth a fortune. A check under the top revealed no signature that I could discern.

I realized that I had stopped breathing. I filled my lungs and felt a huge weight lift off my shoulders. I'd found the treasure.

◈ FOURTEEN ◈

Whoever had searched the house hadn't known what to look for either, and certainly hadn't been looking for furniture. I could exchange the table for Spiro and we'd sort out whatever money mess he was in, he could tell the police what, if anything, he knew about Big Dom's death, and everything would get back to normal. Sophie would never have to know. I doubted she'd miss this table. Despite her professions of infirmity, she was quite spry for her age; but it required a heck of a lot of steps to get all the way up here and I felt sure she almost never made the trek. In a couple of months, after we got everything fixed and I sent Sophie and Spiro back to Greece where they'd be out of harm's way, I would alert the authorities to be on the lookout for the seller of a valuable antique table, and we'd be able to bring the kidnapper/extortionist and whatever else he was to justice, and get the table back too.

I needed a short-term plan. The table was unwieldy but not too heavy, so it would be easy enough to get downstairs. I'd have to avoid being seen, though, and there was only the one central staircase, which was visible from most angles of all the downstairs dining rooms. My only choice was to send Sophie out to Marina's again, close up early, and get the thing out of the house when everyone was gone. I'd need to get the table down to the water without damaging it and onto a boat—rather a large hurdle since I didn't own one. Nor did I know how to operate one.

But first things first. I wiped the dusty surface with my arm, obliterating the love note the ghost hunters had left me. I carried the table over to the open stairway and maneuvered it down the stairs to the second floor. Since it was now the peak of the lunch hour and Sophie would be managing the dining room and the kitchen without my help, it didn't seem likely she would come upstairs, but I looked around me to be sure. I set the table down in front of my door, fumbled in my pocket for the key, heart racing, and set the table inside.

I grabbed a random sock from the pile on my floor and gave the whole table a quick going-over. I'd definitely seen a table just like this on *Antiques Roadshow* and it had been appraised at several hundred thousand dollars. I extricated a blanket from the tangle of linens at the foot of my bed and wrapped it up. Digging through the mess, I found what I was looking for—an old army green web belt with an adjustable buckle. Ugh. Had I ever really worn this thing? I secured the belt around the central spoke of the table, making sure all the loose edges of the blanket were secured in it and all the surfaces of the table were covered. It wasn't perfect, but it would do.

So how was I going to transport this priceless wooden antique over water and somehow secure it inside the cave on Devil's Oven Island without getting it wet and damaging it? Couldn't this kidnapper have picked an exchange location on terra firma? Why make it so difficult? I undid the belt and went into the bathroom, unclipping the tropical-flowered plastic shower curtain from its rings. I wrapped the blanketed table in a waterproof layer of plastic and secured the belt again. Not the prettiest package I'd ever wrapped, but certainly the most valuable.

I went back into the bathroom, grabbed a washcloth, and saturated it with cold water. I draped it over my face and luxuriated for a moment in the cool sensation of it. I wiped off my dusty, sweaty arms. A cool shower would have been heavenly, but there was no time. And no shower curtain. So I stripped down to my underwear and took a quick, cool sponge bath. The evaporating moisture felt wonderful. I ran a hairbrush through my hair, applied some fresh deodorant, then changed into clean clothes. I headed back downstairs, being sure to lock the door behind me.

I was ravenous and went straight to the kitchen, which was bustling. We must have had a good crowd out in the dining rooms today. It was Thursday and people were starting to come into town for Pirate Days.

Sophie watched me. She had probably noticed my change of clothes, but didn't say anything. Dolly was working feverishly to keep up with the orders, so I made myself a sandwich. Sliced marinated chicken breast on grilled, buttered bread with lots of melted provolone cheese and some roasted red peppers. I sent one of the busboys down to the bar for a

Diet Coke with a slice of lemon. I slammed down the sand-wich and dropped my plate in the dishwater, then took my drink back to my office.

I fired off a return e-mail to the kidnapper telling him I had found what he wanted and would bring it to the drop-off place tonight as instructed. I couldn't help adding, in what I hoped was a nonthreatening way, that I would be expecting Spiro's safe return tonight or tomorrow. Were you allowed to do that with kidnappers? I hoped he would be so happy to have his demands met that he would overlook any eti-quette breach I might have made.

I found my cell phone and dialed Liza's personal number so I wouldn't have to go through her switchboard.

"It's Georgie."

"I know that," she chided good-naturedly, then turned serious. "Georgie, what is going on with you? I haven't heard from you since you spent the night here, and I was beginning to worry."

"Uh, I've just been busy." Not the answer she was looking for, but true enough. "Li, I have to ask you a favor."

"Of course, ask anything; you know that."

"There's just one thing. Please trust me and don't ask me any questions. It's something I can't talk about right now. Maybe later, but not now, okay?"

"Georgie, what is going on? Are you in trouble?" she demanded.

"Please. I wouldn't do this if it weren't important." A matter of life and death definitely classified as important. I picked up a stray pen on the desk and started to tap nervously with it.

She sighed. "What do you need me to do?"

"Lend me a boat." Liza kept a small motorboat at the village docks so that her employees could transport guests to the island. She kept another, more luxurious one docked at the island so her guests could be treated to a private cruise if they wished.

"Anything that's mine is yours; you know that. But what could you need a boat for? And since when do you know how to operate one?"

"I have to ask you again not to question me. I know what I'm doing."

"I doubt that," she said, then sighed again. I wished she would stop doing that. "The cuddy cabin should be unlocked. There's an ignition key inside a coffee can in the cabinet over the galley sink."

"Thanks. I appreciate this. And I wouldn't ask if it weren't important," I repeated.

"If it's that important, then you shouldn't be attempting it alone," she admonished. "If anything happens to you because I lent you this boat, I will never, ever forgive myself."

"I'll be all right. I promise to wear a life jacket."

"You'll find one in the compartment under the deck cushions at the stern."

Right, the stern. I had no idea what the stern was. "Okay."

"Have you heard from Spiro? He hasn't come back yet, has he?"

"No, he hasn't come back. I'm expecting him tomorrow, though." If everything went according to plan tonight, that was. I crossed my fingers. It was silly superstition, but it couldn't hurt. She didn't press any further.

Remembering the other thing I needed to ask her, I said,

"So, did you find out anything about those farmers we were talking about, the ones that Spiro was—" I caught myself. "Is supposedly involved with?"

"The Sons of Demeter."

"Yes, that's it."

"My sources tell me that Big Dom was involved with them too." I didn't even bother to ask who her sources were; she would never tell me.

"Big Dom?" I swallowed. "Involved how?"

"The SODs are in the money-lending business. The Sailor's Rest and Dom's other restaurant in Watertown haven't been doing all that well the last few years due to his mismanagement. He was also keeping a mistress over in LaFargeville, and she's been getting more and more demanding of his time and money. He apparently borrowed some serious bucks from the SODs to keep everything afloat. And didn't pay them back on time."

"And?" I was afraid to ask.

"And it appears that they had something to do with his murder."

I swallowed hard. Organized, murdering, money-lending farmers? In the North Country? This was unbelievable. And I'd had no idea that Big Dom's restaurants were in trouble.

"How much money are we talking about?" I knew Spiro was into them for at least the seventy-nine thousand dollars he'd withdrawn from his accounts and the cash box under Sophie's bed, but he must have paid them that. How much more could he owe?

"I don't know the exact amount, but it may be in the six figures."

Wow. Big Dom had gotten himself into a mess. A fatal mess. I knew where some of that money was—invested in a honkin' big diamond ring currently ensconced in Sophie's scrawny cleavage. Damn him. He'd been romancing Sophie for her money, plain and simple. If he hadn't already been killed I might have had a go at it myself. I didn't think Sophie had been that emotionally entangled, so hopefully she wouldn't be too hurt when all this came out. Knowing her tough and resilient nature, I predicted she would be spitting mad, not humiliated.

"How in the world are these farmers coming up with that kind of money to lend out?" I didn't realize there was that much money in the whole North Country.

"My guess is extortion and some kind of drug dealing, but I don't have any proof of that. Up until now they've flown way under the radar. It might not be so easy for them now."

Even if Spiro returned safely, how were we going to extricate him from whatever his obligations were and protect him in the future? "Who are these people?"

"Here's the part that surprised me."

"What do you mean?"

"The rumor is that they are headquartered in Rossie."

Rossie was an adjacent township that covered a lot of square miles. "Where?"

"The Sunshine Acres commune."

❖ FIFTEEN ❖

A burp of pepper-flavored acid rose up in my throat and I swallowed it back down. I reached for my Diet Coke and took a big sip, but that did nothing to neutralize the nasty burn, only intensified it. I'd been at Sunshine Acres only a few hours ago. That Hank guy could have been the killer. He must be involved somehow. Spiro must be hidden away in any of the numerous buildings of the compound. And I'd bought groceries from them for years. My God, I was supporting them!

"Georgie, are you there?"

"Uh, yeah. I'm just surprised, is all." I fished around in my desk and came up with a lone antacid tablet wrapped up in a curling peel of paper. I chewed it up.

"Well, I was too. Although when you think about it, it makes perfect sense. They've been organized as a farming and living cooperative for forty years. It's not that big a leap

141

to think that they might have branched out into a more lucrative business now that they're all senior citizens and thinking about retiring. Maybe they want to buy an island someplace tropical. I don't think they're getting a lot of new recruits."

"Who's Hank?" I wasn't sure why I wanted to know, but somehow it seemed important.

"Hank? That must be Hank Miller. He's a local guy. In fact, I think Sunshine Acres started out as his family's farm. He seems to be the unofficial leader of Sunshine Acres. I've always thought he was a pretty decent guy."

"Could there be a secret splinter group within the commune, one that Hank doesn't know about?" For some reason, I wanted Hank to be innocent.

"It's certainly possible. Hank is business savvy. He's been running the Acres for decades. But I wouldn't have thought he could run an extortion business and get away with it till now. I certainly wouldn't have thought he was capable of murder, or being involved in a murder."

I glanced down at my watch. "I've gotta go. Thank you so much for lending me the boat. I'll have it back by midnight." I hoped.

"Why don't you ask Keith to go with you, if you won't tell me what this errand of yours is all about?"

"I can't. I just can't."

"You will call me as soon as you get back, at any hour of the night," she ordered. "If I don't hear from you by one a.m., I am calling the police. Your trust and your friendship are important to me, but I'd rather have you alive and not trusting me than dead. I know this is somehow mixed up with Big Dom's death and Spiro being missing, and I am warning you that you are playing with fire."

That was fair enough, and I would have done the same for her. "I promise I will call as soon as I get back."

I returned to the kitchen and asked Sophie to accompany me into the hall. She got up stiffly, wincing for the benefit of the kitchen staff, and followed. "Sophie, you need to go home with Marina this afternoon, and spend the night with her again," I said in a voice I hoped brooked no opposition. She started to protest, but I gave her a look and she stopped midsentence. "This is important. I think I know where Spiro is. I'm hoping he'll be back tomorrow."

Her face lit up. "You mean, he's not dead?" No doubt she had already been on the phone with the Bay's one funeral home and was trying to figure out the cheapest way to get his corpse back to Greece. Her smile morphed into a furious scowl. "Wait until I get my hands on him, that thieving, ungrateful brat!" She started swearing in Greek, but I put my hand on her arm to stop her.

"Sophie, I have to go and get him." And do some other things, but she didn't need to know that. "I don't want you to be here alone. We're going to shut down the Bonaparte House tonight." I waited for the eruption.

"What? It's Thursday night! Our third busiest night of the week! Do you know how much that will cost me? I'll go bankrupt!" she shrieked. "We are not closing tonight!"

"Yes, we are," I said as calmly as I could. "I am going to

get Spiro, and you are going to Marina's when she leaves to go home for the afternoon. We'll be open again tomorrow for Pirate Days, and we'll be very busy and make lots of money. Call her, and tell her to wait for you until you get there. Now."

I stepped back into the kitchen and asked Dolly to oversee the kitchen cleanup and send everyone home early, assuring the staff that I'd pay them their regular wages. A broad smile showcasing her dentures creased her face. She fiddled with the giant gold cross around her neck again.

"Is that new, Dolly? I haven't seen that pendant before."

"Yup. Russ bought it for me. He's such a good son. It's real, too. I had Roger down at the jewelry shop check it out with that little eye microscope thingie he has."

Russ? Our dishwasher gofer whom we paid twelve dollars an hour, plus the occasional steak? "Does he have another job?"

"Nah. He didn't say where he got this. I don't know if he, uh, paid for it," she added. "I didn't see a receipt."

"Have you talked to him today?"

"Yeah, he called me a while ago. He's sore but all right. He's out in his garage right now getting ready for huntin' season." Hunting season wasn't due to start for two months.

"He'll be in tomorrow?" The busboy hadn't stopped complaining about doing the dishes since I came in. He wouldn't be returning next year.

"Yeah, he'll be back."

"Good. Have a nice evening off."

"How come we're closin' up?"

I thought fast. "I want everyone rested up for Pirate Days." Incredibly lame, but she nodded. I don't think she cared anyway—she was getting the day off and that was all that mattered.

"I'll just finish up here then and head out."

Less than an hour later, the last lunch customers had paid their bills, the evening reservations had been rescheduled, and the staff had made it out in record time. I lugged Sophie's giant suitcase over to the Pancake Heaven and deposited my mother-in-law in a booth at the back of the diner to wait for Marina. A waitress hustled over and brought her a cup of coffee and a raspberry Danish, which looked pretty darn good, but there was no time for a treat.

Marina told me that they would be leaving shortly and that she would keep Sophie home tonight. I replied that Sophie hadn't been feeling well but wouldn't admit it. Marina nodded her understanding. "She has troubles now." She thumped her ample chest. "Heart troubles." My guess was that Sophie wasn't suffering much over Big Dom's death, maybe more like celebrating inwardly at the increase in business she was experiencing, but I decided to allow Sophie her fun and let her cousin make a fuss over her supposedly broken heart. Sophie had spilled the beans to Marina about Big Dom's proposal, though in her defense there had been no reason to keep it secret prior to the murder.

I went back to the empty Bonaparte House and up to my room. There was time to kill so I started to pick up some of the mess. All the clothes went into a laundry basket I kept in the bathroom. Not knowing who had touched them made me squeamish to wear them, as though some kind of kidnapper cooties might have been transferred. I owned only a few items that would need to be dry-cleaned and pressed, so those just went on top of the pile. Tomorrow I would pay Dolly extra to run a few loads of laundry for me after I made up some story about how virtually every towel and article of clothing I owned got dirty at the same time.

I went back out to the linen closet in the hall, which for some reason had not been touched, and retrieved fresh, non-cootie sheets and a spare blanket from the shelf. I stripped the bed, then remade it, and replaced the rest of the flotsam and jetsam that had spilled out of the closet, stuffing everything in and slamming the door before an avalanche ensued.

I righted my overturned overnight bag and picked up the jumble of papers spilling out of a file folder. Spiro's research about the Bonapartes and the supposed plot to bring Napoleon here. Frankly, I'd always had my doubts about whether that story was true, but in light of the fact that I'd just been proven wrong about there being a treasure in this house, I wasn't taking anything for granted anymore. Those ghost hunters might be interested in this stuff for their show. After I had Spiro back, I would scan the most interesting documentation and e-mail it them to see whether maybe they'd want to use any of it as background information.

The room looked presentable, no worse than usual, but I decided to lock my door anyway on my way out. I looked at my watch. Marina and Sophie would definitely be gone by now. I opened my door, took a deep breath, and reached for the blanketed and shower-curtained table near the door. A noise caught my attention. I stood up and listened. There it was again, a very soft and muffled sound coming from Sophie's room across the hall. She'd left her door open, most likely to try to keep the air circulating up here. I looked around for something I could use as a weapon. I grabbed the first thing I saw—a big barrel curling iron I had left out on top of the dresser. Too bad the thing wasn't hot, but I'd be able to inflict some damage if I swung it hard enough.

I cautiously peeked out my door, then moved across the hall to Sophie's door. The noise sounded again, a soft grunt definitely coming from inside. "Come out of there now, whoever you are!" I ordered. I sounded more authoritative than I felt. "People are downstairs and as soon as I scream they will be up here." I walked in, brandishing the curling iron and nearly tripping over the cord. "You can't hurt my family anymore!" The noise sounded again, and it seemed to be coming from . . . the wall. That wall adjoined Spiro's room. I ran over to the wall and put my ear up to it and heard a shuffling sound accompanied by soft moaning.

I ran out into the hallway and flung open Spiro's door. "Come out and show yourself, you bastard!" Adrenaline surged through me and my fear left. I looked under the bed, in the closet, in the bathroom, but there was no one there. The noise came again, softer this time, then faded out completely. I ran to the wall adjoining Sophie's room and put my ear to that, but nothing. I was panting by now and stopped to catch my breath. There was nobody in the room with me. Nobody human, that was.

◈ SIXTEEN ◈

I hightailed it back to my room and grabbed the folder, sticking it under one arm. I brought the table out and set it in the hallway, locking my door behind me. My arms ached and the bundle shifted precariously several times as I carried it down the stairs. I almost dropped the folder more than once on the way down and around the spiral to the main floor.

I set everything down for a moment to catch my breath, then continued on to my office where I grabbed my purse and carried everything out to my car. The wrapped bundle, with some careful maneuvering, just barely fit into my trunk. I tossed my purse onto the passenger's seat along with the folder, which I'd meant to drop off at my office but had neglected to do in the excitement of getting the hell out of that house. I got into the driver's seat and willed myself to relax. Had I just heard a ghost? I'd heard something, all right. Once this was all over I'd have to call in a priest or an exorcist or something. It didn't seem likely there'd be one in the Bay. Maybe those ghost hunters had a connection they could set me up with.

What now? I had several hours to kill—I winced at my own choice of words—before I could attempt to transfer the table to Liza's boat and motor out to the Devil's Oven. I didn't want to wait until it was full dark, but needed the cover of twilight to minimize the chances of my being spotted. The docks were only a hundred yards or so from the Bonaparte House, but it was simply inconceivable that I could carry a shower-curtain-wrapped table through downtown without having to stop and answer a thousand questions. I'd drive down to the Lady Liberty Boat Tours parking lot and leave the car there at dusk, then unload the table onto the boat. There was still a chance I'd be recognized, but it was a risk I'd have to take.

I started up the engine and pulled out of the employee parking lot, turning away from the shops and restaurants to head out of town. I drove inland toward Redwood, a couple of villages over, and stopped at a little mom-and-pop convenience store. I bought a Diet Coke and a bag of chips. On a whim I turned down Hubbard Street, where Russ lived next door to Dolly and her common-law husband, Harold. I pulled up on the other side of the street and put the car in park. I twisted off the cap and took a big glug of the icy cold soda. This seemed as safe a place as any to pass some time, and if anybody questioned me I could say that I'd come to check on Russ.

Dolly had decorated her front yard with a menagerie of lawn animals watched over by a pair of garish, amateurishly repainted gnomes. Her porch was hung with twirling and jingling wind ornaments. She had lots of neon-colored zinnias in a rubber tire planter, and a morning glory with brilliant blue flowers twining up the flagpole. A Virgin Mary statue stood serenely, arms outspread, safe inside the protective shrine of an upended, half-buried cast-iron bathtub, claw feet still attached. Maybe she was Catholic after all. Her house was so cheerful, I had to smile. Her car was gone, so she must be out.

I opened the bag of salt and vinegar chips with a crinkly little pop and crunched absentmindedly on one, which turned out to be one of those extra delicious anomalies both folded over and imbued with an extra dose of the vinegar flavoring. I looked past Dolly's place one door down. A strand of colored lights hung loose from Russ's front porch railing, and the desiccated rusty brown remains of a Christmas tree, tarnished tinsel waving in the afternoon breeze, graced the left side of the front door, which was open to the interior and unprotected by a screen door. That didn't necessarily mean anybody was home, though.

Something looked different about the place—I couldn't quite put my finger on it. Then I realized with a mental slap of the head that there was now a garage at the end of Russ's gravel driveway. It was huge, at least two or three times the square footage of his makeshift double-wide mobile home, and could hold at least three cars or trucks in addition to ATVs and other motorized toys. The building was unfinished, with just a skin of Tyvek insulation flapping loose in several places from the chipboard underneath. A big rack of deer antlers, at least ten points though I couldn't count them clearly from this distance, hung over one of the bay doors. He'd never mentioned that he was building a garage.

Knowing Russ, this was as finished as the structure would ever get. It was unknown how many winters it could survive in this condition, but you'd be surprised how long it takes a building to fall down around you, based on some of the farmhouses and barns I've seen in the Northern New York countryside. I'd bet anything if I looked inside, there would be a row of heavy-duty hooks attached to the rafters for hanging deer in the fall, or any other time of the year he happened to have a hankering for venison.

I was munching on another chip and was leaned over feeling around with a rather greasy hand in the glove compartment for a napkin, when a figure filled my driver's side window. I righted myself and looked out the window, right into a shiny belt buckle emblazoned with "USCG." I looked up as the owner of the belt buckle bent down so I could see his face. He rapped on the window and made a roll-down-the-window gesture, though of course the days of crank windows were long gone. My heart leapt into my throat and I couldn't swallow the potato chip, which was now stuck and dissolving back there. Damn! It was that Captain Jack, if that was his real name. How the hell had he found me here? My gut clenched as I realized he must have followed me. I turned down the radio and cracked the window. Thank goodness my doors were locked.

"Yes?" I squeaked out.

"Georgie, I'm Jack, remember? We spoke a couple of days ago? I've been trying to get in touch with you."

"What do you want?" I tried to calm myself and put my hand surreptitiously on the ignition key so I could make a fast getaway if I needed to.

"Georgie, can I talk to you? I'm not an *a* *murderer*." He grinned at me with his movie-star smile. Damn! There were those cute little crinkles around his eyes again.

"No, you absolutely cannot get any closer," I said through the slit between the window and doorframe. For all I knew, this guy was an assassin hired by the SODs to kill Big Dom. Or kidnap people. My eyes narrowed as I grew braver. "And where's my husband's cell phone? I know you took it from my desk that day you were in my office."

He looked genuinely confused, or he was a very good actor. "What do you mean? I didn't take a cell phone or anything else away from your office, other than a good opinion of you. Which I might have to consider revising," he said. There was that grin again.

It was kind of cute, but I didn't bite. "All I know is that I found it missing after you left."

"What would I want with your husband's cell phone? Look, Georgie, if you don't want to talk to me here, why don't we go someplace public? There's a diner up the road where there will be lots of people and you won't have to worry about my abducting you." He was referring to Jo-Jo's, the home-cooking place up the road. I considered. If he had been going to abduct me or kill me, he wouldn't be standing around here talking about it, would he? I'd already be shot dead, bleeding all over the Honda's upholstery, or bound and gagged in the trunk of his car.

"What do you want to talk about?"

"I know Spiro is missing, Georgie."

I was momentarily speechless. "He's gone out of town for a few days," I bluffed. "Lots of people know he's gone."

"I'm pretty sure he didn't leave town voluntarily."

I didn't know what to say to that, so I said nothing.

"Come on, let's go to the diner and talk. I'll follow you." I glanced in my rearview mirror and saw a Jeep Rubicon parked behind me, its green metallic paint sparkling in the afternoon sun. The top was off.

I still had no reason to trust him, but if he was on the level he might have some information I could use to get Spiro back. There would be enough people at Jo-Jo's that he'd be a fool to try anything with me. I nodded, and said, "No, I'll follow you." That way he couldn't run me off the road. I started my ignition.

"Fine," he said. "I'll see you there."

I watched in the side mirror as he swung his long legs up into the Jeep and drove past me into Russ's driveway to turn around. The doors were off as well. It sure looked like a fun ride, though it would be a wet ride if he got caught in a sudden shower. Jack came back past me and waved. I turned around in Dolly's driveway, just so it wouldn't look like I was imitating him, and followed him up to the stop sign and back out onto the main road.

He put on his blinker and I followed suit, turning in to the parking lot. I shouldered my purse and put my hand inside. All I found in the way of potential weapons was a pen with a sharp point. It wouldn't kill him, but it would hurt if I stabbed him hard enough with it and it might buy me some time to get away. I flipped the cap off and kept my hand on the pen. My suspicions were on high alert with this guy. Keith had said that nobody at the Coast Guard station knew why Jack Conway was in town. Conway was asking

Susannah Hardy

a lot of questions about things he shouldn't have had an interest in. He might have taken Spiro's cell phone from my office though I couldn't see how he'd done it. And he was a stranger to Bonaparte Bay. I almost laughed. Bonaparte Bay's entire economy was built on strangers. But this guy was no ordinary tourist. Given everything that was happening around me, it paid to be cautious.

He waited for me at the door of the restaurant, then gallantly held it open for me. I made sure I waved conspicuously at Brianne Bowers behind the counter, and she waved back. There were four or five booths occupied as well as three of the counter stools. This was a seat-yourself place, so I headed to the booth in the back corner. I parked myself on the cracked pleather with my back to the wall, facing the exit and next to the big plate-glass window so I could see if some henchman or accomplice came in to get me. I shifted position so that my bare legs were not directly on top of the sticky duct tape that was holding the upholstery together. Jack sat down opposite me.

Patty came out from behind the counter with two menus, each page encased in maroon-edged plastic folders with gold-colored tips on each of the corners. You could get breakfast anytime of day or night here. She handed one to Jack and looked at him appreciatively, then back at me with a smile and a raise of her penciled-on eyebrows. "What can I get you?" she asked Jack flirtatiously. Her polyester uniform matched the menus.

"Large Coke, extra ice, and another one of your smiles," he flirted back.

I mentally rolled my eyes. "Diet Coke with a slice of lemon," I piped up. She wrote it down without looking at me, continuing to smile at Jack. I scanned the specials and ordered a cheeseburger with pickles and grilled onions and a basket of fries. He ordered a prime rib sandwich and onion rings. He handed his menu back to Patty, who held on to it as though it were some magical link to his hand. Or other parts. She continued to stare into his eyes. "This'll be done in no time." She smiled at him again. I poked her with my menu and she grabbed it, still without looking at me, as she left to put in our orders.

"So." He sat back and took a sip of his ice water.

"So, what?" I could wait him out. For a while anyway.

"Have you heard from Spiro?" Nothing like getting right to the point.

I hesitated. "No, but I'm expecting him back tomorrow."

He leaned toward me interestedly. "Really? If you haven't heard from him, how do you know he's coming back tomorrow?" Damn, he had me there.

"Look, why do you care?" I figured my best escape was to turn his question back on him.

"Georgie, have you heard of the Sunshine Acres commune?"

My heart started to race.

"Yes. My restaurant buys its produce and dairy there."

"Well, I think something fishy is going on out there and I'm trying to find out what it is."

"What does that have to do with me?" At that moment my cell phone rang, saving me from having to go any further with this. I pulled it out of my purse and saw Keith's name flashing on the screen. "Excuse me, I have to take this." Jack nodded and started fiddling with his straw wrapper, twisting it into a rope and then untwisting it again. "Hello?" I said.

"Hi, beautiful." I could feel myself blush, but Jack didn't seem to be looking at me so I guessed it didn't matter.

"Hi," I said.

"What are you doing?" he asked. "Want to come over tonight after the restaurant closes so we can complete our unfinished business from last night?"

The heat in my face intensified and I knew I was tomato red. *I'll be back,* I mouthed to Jack and got up from the table and headed toward the hallway by the restrooms. "Uh, we're closed tonight."

"You're kidding. How did you talk Sophie into that?"

"She's staying with Marina."

"Even better. Shall I come over there?"

"Uh, I'm not home right now."

"Oh, where are you? Want me to come and pick you up somewhere?"

"Uh, no, I have my car. I'm out at Jo-Jo's having dinner."

"I'll join you—tell Patty to hold your order and I'll be there in ten minutes."

"I'm not alone, Keith." I didn't know why I was so reluctant to talk to him. I should have been grateful that somebody would know where I was.

There was a silence. "I see," he said, coldly.

"Keith, I would like to get together again. Maybe next week after Pirate Days is over," I offered.

"But not tonight?"

"Uh, I've got some things going on tonight, so I can't."

"I'll bet you've got things going on," he said icily. "Goodbye, Georgie."

"I'll talk to you soon," I promised.

"Maybe," he said, and rung off.

Well. We weren't even dating—how did he get off being so huffy with me? It wasn't any of his business who I was with. I slapped my phone shut and dropped it into my bag, returned to the booth, and slid in, wincing as I dragged my thigh painfully across the sticky duct tape on the seat. The drinks had arrived and I took a big slurp with the straw, then squeezed the lemon into the glass.

"Everything okay?" Jack asked.

"Yeah, just fine."

Patty came over and set my plate down unceremoniously in front of me. She dropped the basket of fries next to the plate, spilling some on the table but not bothering to apologize or pick them up. She placed Jack's sandwich down gently and made sure she accidentally brushed his hand, giggling as she did so. I wanted to vomit. Why did grown women make such fools of themselves? I could understand a little flirting, but this pretending you were thirteen when you were middle-aged was for the birds. I poured a puddle of ketchup next to my burger and dipped in a French fry.

"Where were we?" I wanted to smack that self-satisfied smile off his face. Where did he get those teeth anyway? He must have spent a fortune on cosmetic dental work. And what kind of a guy would do that? Well, my husband might, I had to admit.

"You were telling me that you think something is going on at"—I lowered my voice and looked around, but there was nobody at this end of the counter and nobody in the adjacent booth—"the farm."

He lowered his voice too. "Georgie, you must have

figured out by now that there's a money operation going on out there." I wasn't sure how he knew that I knew that, but I nodded and let him go on.

"Well, I think there's more. I think there's a drug operation too." That wouldn't surprise me. The people who lived there were aging hippies with a lot of acreage in a remote area. The chances were good that they were growing some recreational (or, at this stage of their lives, it could be medicinal) marijuana.

"Is that why you're involved?" *If you're really with the Coast Guard,* I wanted to add, but didn't.

"My interest is personal, not professional. The Coast Guard wouldn't have the authority to investigate that far inland, any more than the army over at Fort Drum would."

"Looking to make a purchase?" I couldn't help asking.

He ignored my little jibe. "I'm going to level with you, Georgie. My best friend was in the Reserves and was killed in Iraq. His son, who's been like a nephew to me, has moved out to the commune with his girlfriend. I think he's in over his head out there."

My heart broke for this poor boy who'd lost his father that way. "I'm sorry about your friend and his son, but I don't see what this has to do with me."

"I think we can help each other."

"Again, I don't see how."

"Spiro was involved with the SODs."

I guess if Liza could find that out, other people could too. "I just learned that. I don't know anything about it other than that there's a connection."

"My sources tell me that he invested quite a bit of capital with them."

"Our finances are kept separately. I don't know what, if anything, he does with his money." Small fib there. I knew that at least seventy-nine thousand dollars was missing.

"Look, I'll cut to the chase. You want to find your husband. At least, I assume you do." He looked at me pointedly. "I want to find Brian and get him out of the trouble he's either in or going to get himself in. Drugs and teenagers don't mix. The chances are very good that Spiro is being held somewhere out on that farm if he hasn't skipped town. So I'm saying, let's take a ride out to the farm and see if we can find out anything."

The cheeseburger was at my lips and rested there, unbitten. I set it back down. "Are you suggesting that I get in a car with you, a man I know nothing about, and go out to a farm in the middle of nowhere that is run by a bunch of drug-dealing loan sharks? You've got to be kidding."

He looked at me levelly. "I will tell you anything you want to know about me, anytime. In fact, I'd love to."

I squirmed uncomfortably. This wasn't going the way I wanted it to. "Look, you seem like a nice guy." I was surprised to find I almost believed that. "But I'm just not the type to go snooping around a commune full of criminal types with somebody I don't know. And I have somewhere I have to be tonight, if that's what you're suggesting."

"Was that your boyfriend on the phone earlier?"

My face grew hot. "I don't have a boyfriend. I'm married, remember?"

"You should have a boyfriend."

He could be right. In fact, he was right. I resolved to call Keith tomorrow after he'd cooled off and tell him I wanted to give it a try. So there. My God. I was acting like I was . . . thirteen.

"Where are you going tonight?" He was maddeningly cool.

"None of your business," I snapped. If I'd had some gum I would have pulled a long string of it out of my mouth and twirled it around my finger.

"No, it isn't, but I'd like to help, if I could." Why did he have to be so nice? I thought of Ted Bundy again, so handsome and smooth—and also a serial killer.

I took a big bite of the cheeseburger and felt a glob of ketchup ooze out onto my chin. Jack grabbed a napkin and reached over, dabbing it away. His fingers brushed my jaw as he cleaned me up, and I understood what had driven Patty to want to touch him. It was all I could do not to jump over the table and beg him to put his arms around me. This was nothing like my wanting Keith to kiss me the other day—the attraction was strong and deep on some animal level and my breath caught. He wadded up the napkin and placed it under the rim of his plate, then leaned back and smiled, tucking in to his sandwich. There was that smile again that made me want to slap him, although I was afraid if I did, I'd never take my hand away from his face.

"I could go with you."

"No!" I gulped.

"Does anybody know where you're going?"

"Look, it's my business, okay? I have something I have to do, that's all. In fact, I should be going."

"Give me your cell phone."

"What?"

"Give me your phone. I want to program my number into it so if you need me, you can reach me."

I considered, then gave it to him. It wasn't a bad idea. He punched in some numbers and handed the phone back to me. "I put myself as number one on your speed dial," he said. "All you have to do is press and hold the one key, and it will call me."

That was presumptuous. Not that I had anybody in my speed dial, since I didn't know how to program it myself. "Fine," I said huffily.

I replaced the phone in my purse and pulled out my wallet. "No, no, this is on me," he said.

"I'd like to pay for my own dinner."

"I insist. It's been a long time since I've taken a woman out to dinner. Next time I'll take you someplace nicer."

"I own someplace nicer," I said, and got up.

He stood up too and took my hand, looking into my eyes. "Call me if you need anything. Anything," he emphasized. "And if Spiro doesn't come back tomorrow, please consider going out to the farm with me and having a look around."

I forced myself to let go of his hand. "I'll think about it. I hope you can help Brian."

"Me too. Be careful."

I was certainly planning to do that. I walked down the aisle and turned my head back as I reached the door. Patty was sliding onto the seat next to Jack. Well, he was a big boy and looked like he could take care of himself.

◈ SEVENTEEN ◈

The sun was low on the horizon as I drove back into town. I parked at the docks at the farthest edge of the lot with my front end facing the water. The *Lady Liberty II* was loading for its daily sunset booze cruise on the river, and I intended to wait a decent interval after it left to make sure the docks were clear before I loaded the table onto Liza's boat. My little blue car was as nondescript as they came. I closed my eyes and leaned back. It had been a long, long day, and there was no end in sight. I was dog tired.

Forty-five minutes later I awoke with a start. Damn! I had not intended to fall asleep. The sun had not quite set but was close to, and the big tour boat was gone. I exited the car and popped the trunk with the remote key. I maneuvered the wrapped table out with care, set it down, and closed the trunk lid. A quick scan of the parking lot and docks showed just a person here and there, no one I recognized. Hefting the table, I began the trek to Liza's boat, which was moored down near the end of the main dock. I set my bundle down on the boards, stepped onto the *Heartsong*, and reached over the edge of the boat to clumsily lift the table onto the back deck. A deep pain stabbed my side, causing me to suck in a breath. A pulled muscle, no doubt, caused by my unaccustomed feat of strength. I massaged my side and turned toward the cabin doors.

"Hi, Georgie," a thick voice said from my left.

I'd been spotted. I turned toward the speaker. It was Brenda Jones, her hands resting on a shopping cart I recognized as coming from inside the front door of the Big B Supermarket out on Route 12. It was filled with cans and bottles. She had apparently just emptied the trash can on the land side of the dock and was headed to the receptacle at the water end. Her hair, wild and frizzy, was a peculiar shade of Raggedy Ann red today. Her eyes were bloodshot, the crimson veins making the blue of each iris stand out in almost three-dimensional contrast.

"Uh, hi, Brenda. How's it going?"

"Not too bad. I'll have a pretty good weekend, what with all the pirates coming into town," she said.

"Well, good luck with that." I had to get rid of her. It was getting late. "I don't want to keep you. It looks like you need to go empty your cart."

"Yeah, I probably should."

"Okay, bye, now." I started back toward the cabin doors.

"Where you going?" she asked. "I've never seen you driving a boat before. Course, you were riding in a boat with Keith Morgan the other night. You know, the night you found Big Dom?" She gave me a watery wink and waited expectantly for some more information, but I didn't give her any. "What's that thing you've got all wrapped up there?"

"Brenda, did you check out in back of the Bonaparte House? I left you the returnables in the usual spot."

A lame attempt at distraction, but it seemed to work. Or she allowed it to work. I was pretty sure there was a lot more to Bonaparte Bay's Dumpster Diva than met the eye.

"I guess I should go before it gets too dark here. See ya, Georgie." She pushed the cart back to shore, the wheels rattling across the boards of the dock.

I breathed a sigh of relief and grabbed the table. I took it belowdecks and stowed it inside one of the beds—what do you call those things? Berths, that was it. I fumbled around for the latch on the cabinet over the sink in the tiny kitchen and located the coffee can, which contained the set of keys Liza had promised. I fisted the keys and went back up the few stairs to the captain's chair.

Now what? I sat down and put the key into the ignition. The engine caught on the first try. Success made me cocky. This was going to be easy—just like driving a car. I pushed the throttle forward and bumped the boat in front of me. Panicked, I pushed the throttle back, and bumped the boat in back of me. The front end of the boat (the stern? the bow? Oh, what did it matter anyway?) swung out away from the dock and pointed toward the open water. This was good! I pushed the throttle forward again and the boat refused to go anywhere, despite the engines making a lot of revving noise. Something was holding me back, so I gave it some more gas. The boat ripped free. My body jerked forward but

I somehow managed to keep myself upright. Over my shoulder I saw the ropes—which I had neglected to untie—drifting on the water, tethered to a big chunk of floating wood that had been ripped away from the dock. Oops.

The boat was racing right toward a pair of big sailboats moored out in the harbor. I tried to pull back on the throttle but that didn't stop the forward momentum and I had to steer like an Indy 500 driver between them. I congratulated myself on making it through unscathed until I realized I was headed right for a big green buoy. My eyes closed involuntarily, then opened to see that my maneuver had been successful. I'd missed it, though I'd steered too hard to the left. The boat listed, then righted itself

My pulse increased. This was crazy. I should have just told Detective Hawthorne everything and let people who knew what they were doing handle it, even if it meant I was under suspicion for a while. But what choice was there? Spiro and Sophie could be hurt. If all it took to ensure their safety was an old wooden table, I had to try. Of course there was no guarantee the perpetrator would honor the deal, but I had to think this was about money, plain and simple. Once I had Spiro back safely, we'd all lawyer up and present ourselves to the police.

And to add to the Top Ten List of Crazy Things Georgie Has Done, I was not wearing a life vest. I clearly needed one. I was far enough out into the main channel by now that I thought I could safely drift for a while, so I cut the engine. Where had Liza said the life jackets were? In a compartment somewhere up on the deck. I searched around in the fading light and finally lifted up a cushion just in front of the outboard engine to find a vest, which I quickly donned.

Feeling safer, I turned the engines back on and guided the boat downriver. I didn't know how far it was to my destination, but I knew it was in this direction. There was still some dim light from what had been a spectacular sunset, and I should have just enough time to get to the small island and unload my cargo before it got totally dark. What I would do after that, I did not know, but I would worry about that later. *Do boats have headlights?* I wondered.

I gave the boat some gas and it accelerated. This was kind of fun. The breeze was cool and I wished I'd brought my light fleece jacket. My hair whipped back and I reached up with one hand to brush the stray strands from my eyes, which turned out to be a mistake because I narrowly missed a chunk of wood floating on the water. I didn't know what kind of damage I'd already done to Liza's boat, but I didn't want to do any more. I decelerated and decided to keep both hands on the wheel.

The island shouldn't be far downriver and should be coming up any moment now. I scanned the shore for familiar cottages to use as a guide, but the number of times I'd been out for a ride on this stunningly beautiful piece of the earth was shameful, and nothing was recognizable. I'd spent the last twenty-three summers working seven days a week, sometimes sixteen or seventeen hours a day, and I'd never made the time to get out and do anything. See anything. That was going to have to change.

I decelerated more and kept watch to my right. I was pretty sure I would not be able to miss the gaping maw that was the entrance to the cave, and it was only five or so more minutes before I saw it. I was about to cut the throttle but realized that I was coming toward the rocky shore of the island too fast, and so I decided to motor around it and make another attempt. This time I slowed the engine as low as it would go and steered the pointy front end of the boat toward the cave opening. There were some rocks on the shore but they didn't look too big, so I cut the engine and just let the boat go forward with its own momentum until it hit land with a thud that made me jerk backward, then forward in the captain's chair, hitting my head on the steering wheel. Damn!

The blow to my head hadn't been that hard, and I shook it off. All in all, that had gone pretty well and a small feeling of accomplishment washed over me. Until it occurred to me to wonder how much money I was going to owe Liza in repairs.

Well, I knew a pretty good boat restorer. Once this was all over I planned to make up with Keith and see whether our friendship could go any further. He was handsome and kind and funny, and I thought maybe I could love him someday. It would be nice to be in love again. Why should my husband be the only one in love? I realized with a pang that if I didn't get this package delivered, Spiro might not live to be in love. Panic rose again as I wondered whether whoever had him could reach across the ocean and get to Callista. I willed myself to relax. *All I have to do is stick to my plan.* I would deliver the table as instructed, and hope that the kidnapper would honor his end of the bargain and deliver Spiro to me.

I looked over the side of the boat. Now what? There was no dock. The bow of the boat was up on the shore, and the back end was in the water. Options included jumping over the side onto dry land, an unappealing eight-foot drop, or I could go over the back wall by the engines and get awfully wet—less appealing, but the safer alternative. I went belowdecks and brought up the wrapped table, depositing it near the engines. The water must be at least three or four feet deep based on how low the engines were riding and the sharp angle at which the boat was pitched. This was a problem, just one of many on this little adventure. How was I going to get a half-million-dollar table onto the island without soaking it? I did not have enough confidence in my wrapping job to think that it would keep out all moisture.

I looked around the boat, hoping for inspiration. A tool or implement of some kind—that was what I needed. If some Neolithic humans could figure out how to make fire, bring down mastodons, and survive the Ice Age, I could figure out how to get a table onto an island.

My first scan yielded nothing. The second time I hit the jackpot. A long pole with a hook on the end was secured to the outer wall of the boat. I undid the Velcro with a satisfying rip and awkwardly removed the pole from its bed. The pole was the telescoping kind, and it extended to about seven feet, more than adequate for my needs. I hooked the end under the ugly belt securing the shower curtain to the table, and gave a test lift. The pole bowed in the middle, but it looked like it would hold. I lifted the pole awkwardly and lowered my bundle, which had started to swing rather wildly, over the side. There didn't seem to be any way to slow it down, since any movement I made intensified the swinging. I said a quick prayer and decided to go for it, hoping that the blanket and the shower curtain would provide enough padding if my fish decided to drop. I lowered the swinging bundle, leaning over the side of the boat. My weight caused the boat to list and I wondered whether it would tip it over, but it stopped at about a thirty-degree angle. The table now rested safely on the shore. The soft metal of the boat hook had bent into a gentle arc, and it didn't look fixable. One more thing to replace for Liza.

Now for me. I went to the back of the boat and peered over. The water was black and weedy. I had a sudden vision of the live tank downtown that contained specimens of some of the marine life residing in the river. A sudden onset of the willies caused me to shiver. I steeled myself, opened the short door that led out onto a platform next to the engines, and jumped down into the water.

Cold and wet doesn't begin to describe the experience. I found myself standing in water almost to my crotch. Something brushed against my leg and I choked back a scream. Snapping turtle? Muskellunge? Giant river sturgeon? The display down at the docks said those prehistoric beasties could grow to twelve feet or more and I felt a deep knot form in the pit of my stomach. *You can do this, Georgie. You have to do this.* I held on to the boat as much as I could to prevent being dragged down into the depths of the river by some nasty monster and made my way around to the shore, grateful beyond words when my soggy left Teva sandal reached the island. I stood for a moment to calm my breathing, difficult since I was also shivering, and made my way to the mouth of the cave.

I expected some kind of instructions, but either there weren't any or perhaps in the fading light they just weren't visible. I leaned around to the inside, trying to keep out of the water, although I was already wet so it didn't matter. Still, the water might get deeper inside, and I did not want to know what might be living inside that underwater cavern. It would have been smart to bring a flashlight from the boat, but I was not going back through that cold water any more times than I had to.

A quick survey of the island revealed that it was only about twenty by thirty feet, containing a half dozen trees and no buildings. *This kidnapper must be some kind of amateur,* I thought, not for the first time. The table could not be left inside the cave where it would certainly be ruined by the watery floor.

A glance at the sky told me there were only a few minutes of daylight left. I unwrapped the belt and repositioned it, lashing the table to a tree. It was pretty conspicuous, and unless the kidnapper was a complete moron, it would be hard to miss it. It was hidden by some other trees, though, so it didn't seem to be visible from the water. I felt a momentary pang of guilt at leaving this valuable antique out to the elements, despite its being protected as well as it could be on short notice, but there was no help for it. Was rain forecast for the weekend? Sophie and Spiro were inveterate weather watchers, the weather being a pretty good predictor of what kind of business the Bonaparte House would do. The table should be all right as long as the guy showed up soon. I'd e-mail him when I got back home and tell him where to find it.

I surveyed my handiwork and double-checked the plastic to make sure it was as tight and weatherproof as possible. Time to get back home and wait. I headed back toward the boat, stepping over the rocks and fallen branches. A squirrel ran in front of me. These islands were full of wildlife, which made its way across the ice during the winter from the mainland. This island was quite small, though, and wouldn't support anything much larger than my little friend, so at least I didn't have to worry about being eaten by a bear or crushed by a moose. I reached the shore where I had disembarked.

No *Heartsong*.

My eyes strained in the darkness. No boat. I did not have the best sense of direction, but I had not gotten turned around and gone to the wrong side of the island. There was the entrance to the cave, and I was certain that that was where I'd left it. A brilliant white moon had risen and begun to cast its light over the river. There, about twenty yards offshore and drifting peacefully along like a ghost ship in a pirate movie, was my boat. Liza's boat. Which I had neglected to tie off.

◈ EIGHTEEN ◈

Damn. The boat was gone. I could swim to save my life but was no athlete, and only a complete idiot would try to catch up to it. Of course, only a complete idiot would not tie the thing up in the first place, but that went without saying. I patted my pockets with the vain hope of finding my cell phone, but I knew that was making its way toward Montreal right about now. Tears welled up.

Now what? I sat down on the rocks and wrapped my arms around myself to try to stop the shivering. I reached up and wiped the tears from my face. *Buck up, Georgie. This could be worse. Pretend you're on* Survivor. A few boats might go by, but the chances of them seeing me were slim. I could yell, but a boat engine makes quite a bit of noise and it was unlikely I'd be heard. It looked like I was here till morning, when one of the tour boats would pass. I could attract enough attention then by yelling and waving my arms at the blue-haired ladies on the first boat of the morning. It was going to be a long, cold night. I could only hope the killer/kidnapper didn't plan to retrieve the table tonight.

What I needed was a fire. What I did not have was any means of starting one—no matches or lighter, which would have been soaked anyway. It looked like it was me and my furry friend the squirrel for the evening, and he or she wasn't going to be much company.

I headed farther back into the interior of the island, where I hoped it would be a bit warmer within the shelter of the trees. It was still cold, and I wasn't drying. I looked around for materials to construct some type of windbreak. Some branches that had probably come down in the last big rainstorm lay nearby. I dragged some over by the tree to which I'd lashed the table and piled them up into a makeshift lean-to. I crawled inside to test it out for size and felt a bit warmer. Wait! The table was wrapped in both a blanket and a shower curtain. I had the belt. If I used the shower curtain to wrap the lean-to, and wrapped myself in the blanket, I'd be damp but pretty snug till morning.

The small rocks and twigs of the island's surface cut painfully into my knees and palms as I crawled out, stood stiffly, and stretched. My left arm tapped the wall of the shelter. It collapsed.

The waves lapped against the shore. In the bright sunshine it would have been a happy sound. Here in the moonlight it would be soothing and romantic if somebody special had been with me. Alone, wet, and cold, it was ominous like the slobbery tongue of a river monster licking the shore and getting closer to me all the time. The sound was mesmerizing and I shook my head to break the spell, willing myself to return to the task at hand. As I began to unhook the belt, another sound reached my ears. Not a natural sound like the waves, but a low thrum that was increasing in intensity. It was coming from the water and moving toward me.

I held my breath. It had to be a boat. It could be some kids coming out here to party. There were enough beer cans and graffiti littering the island that this was a very good possibility.

It could also be the kidnapper, who certainly hadn't left me much time if he was here already. Still, if he'd been watching me, he would have seen the boat float away and would probably have figured that I just couldn't get the thing started. He—or she—was dead wrong about that. I'd had no trouble getting the thing started. Driving it and securing it were other matters, though.

My hopes soared at the thought that it might be kids. If they hadn't started their evening imbibing, I could make up some story and get them to take me back to the mainland. The promise of a couple of twenties upon my safe delivery would secure that deal, no problem. Still, I should be cautious. If it was the kidnapper, he was not going to want to find me still here.

I moved back toward the interior of the island, cringing as each step made a crunching sound. I hid behind a tree on the channel side and held my breath. The motor grew closer and the engine abruptly cut out, leaving a sound void that was then filled up again by the increased lapping of the waves from the boat's wake. Any thoughts of rescue by a pack of rowdy teenagers were dashed. There were no sounds of boisterous merriment coming from the craft.

I ventured a peek around the tree trunk as my heart raced. A boat on its own momentum was coming toward the shore. The operator was evidently an experienced sailor, because the boat stopped well short of the shore. I heard the metal-on-metal rasping of a chain being lowered by a crank—an anchor. That had been my mistake with Liza's boat, not that I would have known how to work it anyway. A soft splash sounded as the driver exited the boat. I was perversely gratified to think that the perp would be as cold and wet as I was. A stout stick lay on the ground just out of arm's reach. It wasn't much as a weapon, and it wasn't yet in hand, but I knew where it was if I needed it.

A dark figure emerged from the water. I had a sudden image of the Creature from the Black Lagoon and stifled a very inappropriate, semi-hysterical laugh. The figure moved purposefully and didn't seem to care how much noise he made. I could see around the tree trunk that it was a tall man, but the moon was to his back and the facial features were indistinguishable. He looked left, then apparently decided to head to the right. He switched on a flashlight and shined it into the cave. The angle was wrong for me to get even a glimpse of him. While he was inspecting the interior of the cave, I decided to chance reaching for the stick. I held on with one hand to the trunk of the tree, and leaned over precariously toward the stick. As I reached to pick it up, my grip on the dew-wet bark slipped and I fell over into the debris. A shot of pain ran through my arm as I landed on it.

The crash caused the kidnapper to look up. He shined the flashlight in a slow, broad arc. I lay still, damp, and cold as a dead fish. Fortunately or unfortunately, I had landed on my cudgel. The tingling in my arm made me wonder whether either the stick or my arm would be any use to me. There was virtually no chance that I would not be discovered. Should I go on the offensive? I might be able to use the element of surprise. I ventured a look up. My pursuer was nowhere to be seen and must be searching the woods nearer the cave.

The flashlight beam was not visible, so I gingerly sat up. My arm was sore and the probing fingers of my other hand traced the tender, raised ridge of a nasty scratch. I didn't feel any blood, which was good because I wasn't about to go ripping off pieces of my clothing for bandages like in some Wild West movie. I got up, brushed off the pine needles that had stuck to me, and looked around, my weapon in hand.

A cold wet hand caressed my shoulder. I screamed. I heard a dull thwack and the hand let go. I spun around, a hard lump of fear twisting through my innards, and looked into the upturned face of my mother-in-law.

❖ NINETEEN ❖

"Sophie!" I was so shocked to see her I croaked out the name. "Marina?" I looked from one to the other in disbelief. Sophie was holding an oar in both hands and using it to poke at a crumpled figure on the ground. The figure began to moan softly as she prodded.

"Serves you right," she spat out. "Come on, Georgie, let's leave this place. It's starting to give me the spookies." Marina nodded in agreement, her plastic rain bonnet sliding back and forth over her pin curls.

A wave of relief washed over me at being rescued, but was quickly replaced by anger. And curiosity. I grabbed the flashlight from Marina's hand and shined it down onto the face of Captain Jack Conway.

I knew it! I knew he had to be involved in this somehow. That cockamamie story about his dead friend's son was all fabricated to make me feel sorry for him. He must have managed to escape the clutches of Patty at the diner and followed me to the docks. I hadn't been exactly inconspicuous as I got the boat under way. He would have seen the *Heartsong* float off and figured that I was on it, so he could come and pick up his booty. He hadn't expected that I would be here stranded.

"Let's go, girls, before he wakes up." They hooked elbows with each other in the Greek way and moved toward the channel side of the island, where it turned out there was a quite serviceable rocky natural dock on which they'd tied up a small motorboat. I'd apparently missed that on my circuits of the island in the bigger boat.

"Life jacket, please." Marina handed me the flotation device, which glowed eerily orange in the bright moonlight.

Marina fired up the engine and deftly maneuvered us out into the main channel. We sped full throttle back toward Bonaparte Bay. My jaw clenched at the speed she was coaxing out of this little craft, but she seemed to know what she was doing. Sophie held on to her rain bonnet, which looked to be an exact match for Marina's, probably both purchased from the impulse-buy rack at the cash registers at Kinney's Drugstore. We didn't speak, as we would not have been able to hear one another over the high-pitched buzz of the motor. In no time we had pulled up at the Bonaparte Bay docks.

Marina opened up the diner and we sat in the back booth while she fired up the coffeepot. I went to the ladies' room in the back and washed up as well as I could. When I returned, Marina had produced a plate of this morning's cinnamon rolls, which she had sliced into round halves and grilled with butter. I ate hungrily and took a long sip of the hot liquid before I spoke.

"How in the world did you find me?" I forked in another delicious buttery bite and waited for an answer.

"You been acting funny, Georgie." Sophie stared at me, her face unreadable. "I want to see where you go."

The old biddy had been spying on me! But if she hadn't been so nosy, I'd still be on that island, injured. Or dead.

"Where I go is none of your business!" I was saying that a lot lately. Damn, but that woman could irk me.

She continued to stare at me. I stared back.

"You seeing that Keith guy."

"I've told you before, and I'll tell you again. I am not seeing anybody." *Yet.*

"What you doing in a boat? You don't know how to drive a boat." She couldn't accuse me of that anymore, thank you very much. I'd done an okay job. Except for the property damage and the fact that said boat was currently missing in action.

"Sophie, how did you two find me?"

Marina let out a little giggle. "We don't go right back to my house. We decide to have dinner downtown. Your little blue car was down at the docks and along came Brenda."

Brenda! I should have known.

"How much did you pay her?"

Sophie looked smug. "Very cheap. Only five dollars."

Was I so uninteresting that information about me only cost five dollars? I was kind of offended.

"So what you doing out there at night?" Marina asked. "What happened to your boat?"

"It sort of floated away. I'll have to call Rick at the police station to let the towns upriver know to be on the lookout for it."

"Hmm." They both continued to stare at me.

"How come that guy was after you?" Sophie demanded. "I give him a good whack, didn't I?" she added. She sure had. I could hardly believe she had been able to generate enough force to knock out a man of Jack Conway's size. I wondered, not for the first time, whether she had something to do with Big Dom's death, then shook it off. This was my mother-in-law, whom I'd known for two decades. She was many things, but she wasn't a killer no matter how much she wanted a bigger piece of the Bonaparte Bay restaurant business. I hoped.

If I didn't give them something, they'd never leave this alone. "I was supposed to meet someone there. Someone who might"—I bit into the pastry—"have a message from Spiro."

Four penetrating eyes, two chocolate brown and two olive green, glared back at me. "Why he no call himself?" Sophie asked, suspicion undisguised in her voice. "Why he no call his mother? Why he no call you? You're his wife." Marina cut her eyes significantly to Sophie, and they exchanged glances. Good Lord! Could they possibly think I did not know that my husband preferred men?

"He forgot his cell phone."

"He is dead!" Sophie shrieked. "He don't go nowhere without his phone!"

Marina patted her arm and cooed sympathetically.

I sighed. "Sophie, I think he's okay." Not that I had any

proof of that at all, just a gut feeling. "He should be back tonight. Maybe tomorrow."

She looked up, hopeful. Her eyes narrowed again. "How you know this?"

"You'll just have to trust me."

"Hmmmm." She gave me another long look and then turned her attention to the tiny cup of thick, bitter liquid in front of her. I'd never developed a taste for Greek coffee myself.

"Sophie, you and Marina need to go back to Marina's house. I'll stay here and wait for Spiro."

Her eyes narrowed. "You not gonna meet that Keith guy, are you?"

I sighed. "Sophie, I do not have any plans to meet anybody. I am going home to take a hot bath, get into my pajamas, and turn on a Lifetime channel movie while I wait for Spiro. Period."

"I have spies, you know." How well I knew the truth of that statement. "You call me as soon as you hear from him," she demanded.

"It's very late. Let's all go now. I promise you I will call as soon as I know where he is." *Let's just hope that's not floating belly-up like a dead muskellunge in the St. Lawrence.*

Sophie and Marina glanced at each other, and Sophie nodded. "Here. You take this." Marina offered me a tiny gun with a pretty pearly grip. I'd never handled a firearm in my life, and I was afraid to touch it. "Take it," she insisted. "You just take off the safety, point at the bad guy, and pull the trigger." She sounded as though she were teaching a five-year-old.

"Is this thing legal?"

"Legal, shmegal. Who cares? You gotta take it."

I looked from one senior citizen to the other and sighed, taking the gun and stowing it inside a paper bag Marina handed me since my purse was out on the river somewhere. Did I have it in me to use a gun? Hopefully I wouldn't have to find out.

The cousins got into Marina's car and drove away. I waited impatiently for a few minutes to make sure they didn't circle back, then headed for the Bonaparte House. My key clicked in the lock and the door swung open. Ghost be damned. I was going in.

No noises greeted me other than the hum of the coolers and the ice machine. I switched on all the lights, feeling only a bit guilty at the waste of electricity, and left them on behind me.

I reached the door to my office and pocketed my spare set of keys. I booted up my laptop and fired off a return message to the kidnapper, that criminal Jack Conway. "The package has been delivered. Return Spiro to me now." I didn't care if the bossy tone of the e-mail angered him. Though maybe I should. Sophie had hit him pretty hard and he might take revenge on Spiro. Too late to think about that now. The e-mail was sent. As soon as I had my family safe, I was going to call every authority I could think of and get Conway's cute but sorry ass court-martialed.

Then I would get my table back, convince Sophie to sell it, and send her back to Greece more or less permanently. That should more than make up for the money Spiro took, if it couldn't be recovered. And as long as I paid her a percentage of the restaurant's profits and some rent while the place was closed for the winter, she could live in style and lord it over her Greek cousins for the rest of her days. I'd have to buy out Spiro, but I had some money saved and was pretty sure he might be receptive.

This whole ordeal had made it crystal clear to me that my life wasn't headed anywhere, and wasn't going anywhere unless I took some action. I loved this restaurant. I loved what I did and the people I worked with. But I deserved a life of my own. Keith had been right about that.

I dialed Cal's cell phone. She'd be working today, but I didn't care. "Mom! Hi! Is everything okay?" Her voice was tinny but I could detect a note of worry in it. How was I going to answer that question? Everything was definitely not okay, but it would be soon.

"Sure, sweetie," I lied. "I haven't talked to you in so long, and I missed you, that's all."

"I miss you too, Mom."

"Everything's okay with you?"

"Oh sure, I'm busy, but that's good. Sakis is taking me out tonight."

"That's great. Have fun."

"Is Daddy there? Can I say hi?"

"Err, Daddy's gone out, but I'll tell him you said hello." I paused. "Be careful, Cal."

"Mom, I'm always careful." Uh-huh. At nineteen, everyone is untouchable and immortal. Perhaps it was for the best that she didn't yet understand that life is precious and too short.

"You're at work. I'll let you go now. I love you." I would never live long enough to say that enough times to my darling girl.

"I love you too, Mom. I'll see you when you get here for Christmas, unless I can swing a long weekend sometime between now and then."

"Bye-bye, Cal." I hated to let her go.

"Bye, Mom."

I headed upstairs, stripped out of my still-damp-and-starting-to-smell clothes, and ran a hot shower. I looked longingly at my bed, unmade though it was. The prospect of snuggling in and watching a movie, as I had told Marina and Sophie I would, was infinitely tempting, but there was too much to do. I left my bedroom door open as well as the bathroom door to let the steam escape.

Jack Conway was out on Devil's Oven Island, and if he wasn't still conked out, he was no threat for a while. He'd wake up from his Sophie-induced nap with a nice headache and the horrifying realization (I felt a twinge of unwarranted sympathy) that he was stuck there. Before we left the island, we had taken the liberty of untying his lines. His boat was now headed toward a rendezvous with Liza's boat some-where around Morristown by now. Of course, that meant that he would be unable to return Spiro until morning, but that wasn't a problem. I was about to take matters into my own hands.

◈ TWENTY ◈

With the last of the St. Lawrence rinsed away, I toweled off and left a trail of wet footprints on the wooden floorboards as I crossed the room. I ran a comb through my hair, then tied it back with a scrunchie. It would dry funny and look wonky tomorrow, but it was good enough for my purposes tonight.

I hurriedly dressed in some of the clothes that had been thrown around by whoever had searched my room, doing my best to overcome my squeamishness about them because I had no choice. Picking up my spare keys from the dresser where I had left them, I headed back downstairs to the kitchen door, grabbing a fleece jacket somebody had left on the hooks near the walk-in. My body heat activated the odor of stale cigarette smoke trapped in the synthetic fibers, eliciting a grimace from me, but there was no time to look for a fresher coat. I locked the door behind me and made my way back to the docks, where my Honda sat as I had left it in the parking lot.

"Somebody was looking for you," a voice said.

I started and turned to face Brenda.

"Uh, yeah. I could maybe tell you who it was . . ."

"That's all right. They found me." Her face fell as the anticipated baksheesh wasn't forthcoming. "I'll see you, Brenda. Come by the restaurant on Saturday and I'll give you breakfast on the house." Even though she'd ratted me out to Sophie and Marina, she'd also been the one who'd saved me from a long night of exposure to the elements and quite a bit of embarrassment the next morning. I guessed I could spare a couple of eggs and some toast.

She smiled. "Okay, thanks!" I doubted she'd remember, but she might just show up.

I keyed the lock and got into my beloved little car. I fished around in the glove compartment and came up with a can of windshield deicer. I shook it to see whether I would need to buy a new can come November and felt some liquid sloshing around. I tossed it back in and then found the tiny LED flashlight I knew had to be in there somewhere. It switched on and emitted a bright beam of light, so the batteries were good. My cell phone was gone, but I did have the little pistol Marina had given me shoved into my jeans pocket. I removed it gingerly, before I shot myself. Now that I was about to embark on a torrid love affair, I had a sudden interest in the well-being of my nether regions. I placed the gun in the center console and covered it up with a wad of Donut Dee Light napkins I'd picked up on my last trip to Watertown.

The drive north on Route 12 was silent on this trip to

Sunshine Acres, no eighties music to distract me from my mission. About a mile out of town a soft metallic clink sounded from somewhere in the car. I stopped breathing to minimize the interior noise. There it was again. I focused my gaze to the dark road in front of me, wondering whether the car was about to break down. I nearly ran off the road when a face appeared in the mirror. I yanked the wheel to the right, slammed the car into park, grabbed the pistol, and spun in my seat.

"Don't shoot, Georgie! Jeezum, it's just me."

My breath released in a whoosh. "Inky? What are you doing in my car? You scared the hell out of me!" I lowered the gun, but kept it in my lap.

"I've been trying to reach you for hours, but you didn't answer your phone, and you weren't at the restaurant. I saw you at the Pancake Heaven, but I didn't want to come in to meet the rest of the family without Spiro. Your car was in the parking lot so I knew you'd be back. It was getting chilly"—he did a little fake shiver—"so I decided to wait for you inside." His voice was singsong-y and melodious and put me at ease. I was pretty sure Inky wouldn't hurt anybody, but it paid to be cautious.

"How did you get in?"

"Oh, I grew up in Bassport. They taught us how to break into cars as part of the kindergarten curriculum."

"Why did you want to see me?" His lovesick expression told me what he would say even before the words came out.

"I miss Spiro. And I know he must be missing me. I can feel it right here." He made a fist and tapped the left side of his chest. "Just like Jane Eyre and Mr. Rochester, but hopefully without the blindness and the horrible burn scars. I feel like he's calling me psychically. And I just wanted to know if you'd heard from him, not that I think he would call you before me, no offense."

"None taken."

"So, any news?"

I considered. He was going to throw a monkey wrench into my plans for tonight, no question. "Inky, I think I should take you home. I have somewhere to go tonight. If everything goes according to plan, Spiro will be home by morning." I regretted my words.

"Plan? What plan? Why do we need a plan?"

"Not *we*, Inky. I need to do this alone."

"Is this like a commando raid? Do you know where he is, and we're going to take him home by force? Is that why he hasn't called me? Is that why you have a gun? Ooh, that is so sexy! Count me in, baby!"

I was running out of time. I had to get this show on the road. A thought occurred to me. "Inky, do you have a phone?"

"Does a Kardashian know how to work a room? Are you kidding? Of course I have a phone."

If I'd been smart I would have borrowed Sophie's phone, just to have it. I considered taking Inky's by force, then dumping him on the side of the road to find his own way home, but I couldn't help liking him. I sighed. "Okay, you can come with me. But you have to do as I say."

"You're the boss. I can't wait to see Spiro again. Where are we going?" He climbed nimbly over the seat and deposited himself next to me.

"We are going to find Spiro." I pulled out and drove north. "Next time, use the door, okay?"

"Like I said, you're the boss."

Twenty minutes later we had pulled off on the side road leading to the farm. "We're on foot from here, Inky."

"You have your gun, right? Did you bring one for me? I should have brought a weapon, shouldn't I? Damn! A stun gun, or a shiv—that's what I need. Do you see a shiv anywhere?"

"No. You don't need one. We're just going to go and look around. We're not going to hurt anybody." *If we can help it*.

I calculated it was about a quarter mile to get to the Sunshine Acres compound. I breathed deeply of the cool air. A gentle breeze blew the stink of the smoky jacket behind me, making me feel cleaner. I looked up. The stars were an incredible sight. Here in the North Country where there is virtually no light pollution, the sheer number of twinkly orbs in the night sky is fascinating. Overwhelming, sometimes, if you're a city type.

Inky kept up a constant stream of chatter. "I was reading those papers in that folder in your car while I was waiting for you. It was über interesting! Like, did you know that your house was built for Napoleon, but he croaked"—he made a slashing motion across his heavily patterned throat—"before he could escape and come live in it?"

"Yes," I answered absentmindedly. I considered switching on the little flashlight I'd brought, but decided against it. The stars reflected enough light to see by now that my eyes had adjusted.

"His friends put all these expensive furniture and paintings and things in the house for him, but he never got to use them. It's kind of sad. I bet that's where that painting of Napoleon came from in your front room."

"Hmmm." I don't recall Inky ever being in the Bonaparte House, so how would he know about that painting unless Spiro brought him in? On second thought, I did not want to know any more. The guy could talk; that was for sure. I was searching my memory for the layout of the farm. There were about a half dozen buildings, some of which—the dormitory-like residence for example—I would not be able to search because there would be people sleeping in there. These were farmers and it was the height of their work season. They would not be staying up late. I judged it unlikely that Spiro would be hidden there anyway. I doubted that the whole commune was in on the business that was going on here. More likely he would be hidden somewhere in one of the little-used outbuildings.

"Did you know he had a brother? Well, lots of brothers. And sisters too?"

"I think I knew that." We'd start with the big barn to rule that out. There couldn't be that many hiding places in a big open space.

"And as he conquered countries, he made his brothers kings. His oldest brother was the king of Spain. His name was Joseph, but his real name was Giuseppe, which he should have kept, in my opinion. It's so much more romantic, don't you think?"

"Uh, sure." The smaller buildings might be more problematic. I had no idea what they were used for, so I couldn't predict how extensive the search was going to have to be.

"Joseph owned lots of land in this area. Well, farther north, up by Harrisville and Natural Bridge. Lake Bonaparte is named after him. There's supposed to be a cave there named after him too. Ooh, just last week I was reading about a cute little bed-and-breakfast on Lake Bonaparte. They'll lend you a boat so you can go explore the lake. Do you think you can spare Spiro for a night or two when we get him back? I could call in somebody from my shop in Watertown to cover for me here."

"Yeah, sure," I repeated. Spare Spiro from the restaurant? I thought that could be arranged, seeing as how we hadn't needed him at all during the days he'd been gone.

Inky prattled on. "Guess how he bought all the land up here? The Spanish kicked him out as their king, and he escaped with the Spanish crown jewels! They say he sold them so he had wads of cash to buy whatever he wanted. He built a hunting lodge on Lake Bonaparte—well, it was called Lake Diana then—and he had a gondola that he had himself rowed around in, and he used to wear a green velvet hunting suit. How tacky! Can you imagine? And he and his mistress and their daughter would go on picnics and he'd wear that awful suit and eat off gold plates out in the woods. Did you know he had an American daughter? Well, he had two daughters, but one got killed as a little girl when a flowerpot fell on her head. The one that lived married some loser guy that spent all her money and they lived in Oxbow. A Bonaparte in Oxbow? Have you ever been to Oxbow? That's hard to believe."

By now we had reached the driveway to Sunshine Acres. I lowered my voice. "Inky, we can't talk anymore, okay? We are going to search these buildings for Spiro, but we have to be quiet. That means no talking. Or we could put him in danger." Or ourselves.

"Got it, sweetie. My lips are like totally zipped." I waited. There it was, the zipping motion across his lips. The muscles of his inked arms exploded into an impressive display of biceps, triceps, and deltoids. I could see why Spiro was attracted to him. He was certainly fit.

"Let's go."

We walked up the grass along the side of the driveway, sticking as close to the line of trees as possible to avoid being seen. We passed the large rocky enclosure where the goats were kept. The animals must be in for the night. The large front doors of the big barn were closed, of course, and I just knew they would make a big squeaky noise when they were opened. We slipped around the corner looking for a side door, which I knew had to be here somewhere. Locating it, I put my ear up to the wood, heard nothing, and lifted the latch. The door swung open a crack. I peeked inside, being careful to keep most of my body hidden by the door. The coast seemed clear, so I motioned for Inky to follow me.

The building was large and cavernous, the air black and thick and unlit by the stars outside. The soft fluttering of wings sounded overhead. Ugh! *Please, not bats.* I had to risk turning on my little flashlight or we'd never be able to find our way around in here. I switched it on and its bluish beam cut through the darkness. I swung it around in a semicircle.

We were in an equipment storage building. In the center

of the space were tractors in many shapes and sizes, giant scary machines with big toothy appendages out front, which I imagined were used for harvesting crops or tilling the soil. Surely Spiro wouldn't be hidden inside those machines, so I turned the beam on the walls. We walked around the perimeter of the building, searching for any nooks or crannies or interior doors. About halfway around we found a door. I opened it, then jumped back as an avalanche of wooden poles fell out with a deafening clatter that reverberated around the barn. Another flutter of wings heading in the direction of the driveway end of the barn made me look up. I shined the flashlight up toward the peak of the roof and, sure enough, about a million bats were now exiting the building through a ventilation window. I shuddered, steeled my nerves, then directed the beam down on the tangled pile of rakes and hoes and other wooden-handled farm implements that was now resting at my feet.

"Whoa," Inky whispered. "That was a little scary."

I shushed him and shined the light into the interior of the shallow closet. I stepped over the pile and scanned the walls for evidence of another door or latch or false wall, but it looked ordinary enough. Should I try to restore the cubby to some kind of order? No, we'd be better off getting out of there before someone came down from the house to investigate. I did not know whether the noise would have reached that far or whether anyone would be awake to hear it, but we couldn't take the chance. We completed our circuit of the exterior walls without finding anything more and exited by the same door we had come in, switching off the light.

We paused for a moment to allow our heart rates to return

to something approaching normal. I ventured a look toward the house, but didn't see anyone coming in response to the noise we'd made, so we ran toward the next building, the one containing the store I'd been to—could it be possible?—the day before yesterday. I was surprised to find the door to the shop unlocked, and we entered. The big cooler containing the dairy products hummed, and its permanently on light gave a soft blue glow by which we could see easily.

I heard Inky draw in a breath and I turned, panicked. "Oh, my God!" he whispered.

"What!" My heart pounded in my chest and a drip of sweat made its way down the center of my back.

"Look at this Amish quilt!" he gushed. "It's extraordinary! I love the bright colors. Give me the light so I can get a better look at the stitching."

I relaxed a bit. "Inky, we *do not* have time to look at the quilts." I could see the pout forming on his face, the snake tattoo glowing weirdly in the blue light from the cooler.

"I just wanted to look," he said peevishly.

"Maybe I'll get you one for a wedding present." Now, *that* was weird, planning to get a wedding present for my husband and his fiancé. I didn't even know whether they were officially engaged. Could you be engaged to one person while you were still married to someone else? But this was not the time to think about that.

Inky's face brightened. He did not grasp the subtleties of our relationship. "Oh, that would be so swell! I like this one right here." He winked at me and pointed to the quilt done in bold shades of red, purple, and black in, if I wasn't mistaken, the Tumbling Blocks pattern. Good, he hadn't chosen the one I wanted for myself.

I checked behind the counter, just out of nosiness. Nothing. A scan of the walls revealed a doorway that presumably led out into the larger part of the building. I opened it. The lights were on and my eyes blinked rapidly in response. The windowless room appeared to be empty. I entered, Inky right behind me. I had been expecting a storage room of some kind since this was where Hank had gone to retrieve the restaurant's order the other day. I was therefore surprised to find that the room was some sort of office, containing a table with a half dozen or so chairs arranged around it. A computer sat on the table, attached to a long extension cord and a cable that was presumably an Internet connection that reached to the far wall. A pile of papers flanked the computer. I began to rifle through them. "Inky, walk around the edge of the room and look for doors, will you?"

Aha! About halfway down I found a list of names. At the top of the list—Domenic DiTomasso. Crossed off. I gulped, screwed up my courage, and read on. Number two—Spiro Nikolopatos. Both names were misspelled. I felt encouraged that Spiro's name had not been struck through, though that was of course no guarantee at all that he was still alive. Inky came bounding over to me before I got further. I replaced the papers and followed him toward the far wall. A door painted the same color as the surrounding walls opened into another small room, this one filled with boxes. It looked promising, but Spiro was not hidden here.

We gave up and headed back toward the door. I held up

a hand for Inky to stop. Someone was in the other room. A chair scraped across the rough wooden floor accompanied by the unmistakable jingle and whir of a computer being booted up. I held my breath and looked back to warn Inky, but the look on his face told me that he had heard it too.

We had left the door to our little room ajar, but the person apparently hadn't noticed it yet. I looked around for another way out but saw none. Now I understood why the doors had been unlocked and the lights had been on and I wanted to kick myself for being so dumb. If this person was going to be Web surfing or playing solitaire on the computer, he (or she) could be here for hours. Much as I'd grown to like Inky, the prospect of being trapped in here with him for that long, unable to move or make any noise at all, was unbearable.

"Good boy!" A male voice cooed. "Who's Daddy's good boy?" Inky and I looked at each other and he shrugged. A bark rang out in the other room. A deep, throaty bark, the kind that can only be made by a big and deadly dog. Inky's face froze and melted into a cold pool of panic. He pointed at his chest, then pantomimed a sneeze. He was allergic to dogs.

❖ TWENTY-ONE ❖

It was only a minute or two before the inevitable happened. A longish snout poked into the open doorway, fangs bared and growling. The rest of the head and the shoulders appeared. It was a large German shepherd, dark and muscular, although it could have been part wolf, it was that menacing. It kept up the growl and we backed away slowly. Inky fell backward over one of the boxes and banged his head on the wall. He lay there, momentarily stunned as the dog prepared to pounce. I grabbed one of the boxes. It was heavy and I had no idea what was in it, but I heaved it at the dog and managed to hit the beast with one corner. A sharp pain raced through my side from the muscle I'd pulled, and I gasped. The box broke open and some plastic bags of dry brownish shreds fell out. The dog yelped and ran back out into the main room, passing his master who now appeared in the doorway.

Hank. Somehow I knew it would be Hank. Maybe because he was the only person I'd ever met here at Sunshine Acres. His red plaid flannel shirt was untucked over a white T-shirt, ratty at the neck where it could be seen under his ridiculously long beard. A packet of cigarettes bulged from the shirt pocket, a Native American logo showing through a hole in the threadbare fabric. Must be he bought his cigarettes at a discount from the Akwesasne Mohawk reservation to the northeast. A greasy John Deere ball cap, grubby faded blue jeans hanging loose in the butt, and scuffed work boots completed the ensemble.

"What the . . . ?" He didn't complete the sentence. Inky got up, rubbing his head, then launched himself over the boxes at Hank, catching him square in the chest with his shoulder. Hank went down, cursing. The dog came running, but Inky had enough momentum going to propel him out the door and past the dog. I snapped out of my stupor and jumped over Hank. He was lying on the floor moaning, but as I flew over him he managed to reach up and grab my leg. I went sprawling on top of him and heard the breath go out of his bony chest in a whoosh. I recovered and sprang up, none too gracefully, and slammed the door. Inky flew over to me with a chair, jamming it under the doorknob. There was a lock on the door but we didn't have a key. I felt a little twinge of guilt and hoped Hank hadn't broken a hip or anything even though he was involved in criminal activity and was probably holding Spiro here somewhere. His breath came in ragged wheezes, muffled by the door. His footsteps approached and the knob rattled as he tried it. He pounded on the heavy old wood, and I hoped it would hold. The dog barked like crazy and scratched at the door.

Inky and I ran past the table. I grabbed the sheaf of papers. Too bad the computer wasn't a laptop, or I would have taken that as well. We ran for the door. This one had a lock on the inside, which I set before we exited. Inside the store, I tested the lock; then Inky and I dragged over a crate full of maple syrup jugs and stuffed that under the doorknob for good measure.

I peeked out the exterior door. The coast seemed to be clear, so we ventured out into the cool night air. I took a moment to align the edges of the stack of papers I had lifted and stuffed them into the front of my fleece jacket. I tucked the bottom of the fleece into the front of my jeans and zipped it all the way up to secure the papers. Not too stylish, but it should keep this evidence contained until I could deliver it to the police.

We hightailed it back down the driveway, again keeping close to the trees. We jogged the quarter mile back to the side road where we'd left my car, then climbed in. My breath came hard and fast, and my side continued to ache. I vowed again to start exercising once my life returned to normal. Inky had not even broken a sweat. He was clearly in much better shape than I. He set something down with a dull thud between his feet.

"What the heck is that?"

"Pancakes for breakfast! Wanna come over in the morning?"

It was already morning. I looked down and could just make out the outline of a gallon jug of maple syrup.

"I couldn't resist," he said with a grin.

Whatever. I'd always hated it when Cal said that to me, and here I was thinking it. Whatever.

"We'd better get out of here." I turned the key in the ignition and the engine started up. I did a U-turn and went as fast as I dared on the gravel road back out to the two-lane highway.

"Have you got any cigarette papers?"

"Huh?"

"Have you got any cigarette papers?" he repeated.

"Uh, no, Inky. Fresh out."

"That's a shame. 'Cause look what else I picked up while we were there!" He held up one of the plastic bags that had fallen out of the broken box. "This looks like some decent stuff."

"Crap! Inky, is that drugs? In my car?"

"Well, yeah. I was going to test it out tonight, then offer you some with the pancakes tomorrow," he said defensively.

Like I didn't have enough trouble already. "Just keep the bag out of sight, okay?"

"Duh! I am aware that this stuff is illegal, you know."

I was glad to hear that, at least. We had almost reached the village limits when a blue flashing light appeared in my rearview mirror. *Damn!* I was moving along, but I didn't think I had been going more than a few miles an hour over the speed limit. I pulled over and took a deep breath to compose myself. "Inky, put that bag somewhere out of sight. Now." He shoved it into the glove compartment. I was about to tell him to move it, but the cop was already striding toward the car. I certainly didn't want the cop to see Inky fumbling around in there. "Let me do the talking," I hissed.

"Chill out, babe. It's just a cop."

But it wasn't just a cop. A face appeared in my window. A large, clean-shaven face under the brim of a big gray State Trooper's hat. The same State Trooper who had visited me in my office not long ago. What were the odds?

I rolled down the window. "Well, hello! Detective Hawthorne, isn't it?" I tried to sound cheerful and innocent but probably failed miserably.

"Well, well, well. Mrs. Nik," he said.

"Just Georgie, remember?" I put on what I hoped was a winning smile.

"Well, then, Georgie." His voice was sonorous and sexy here in the night air and Inky leaned over to get a better look at him. "Do you know why I stopped you?"

I hated that question, especially when it was delivered in that cop tone of voice. It made me want to slap him but that didn't seem wise. "No, I'm afraid I don't."

"You've got a taillight out."

This was news to me. I'd have to send Russ out for a bulb tomorrow. "I didn't realize it was out, but I'll get that fixed right away." I hoped that would be enough to satisfy him. It wasn't.

"What are you doing out this time of night?"

Inky leaned over even farther, invading my personal space to a slightly annoying degree. "Hello, Officer," he purred. "I'm Inky. From the tattoo shop in town?" I groaned inwardly. This was going to be a disaster. "My friend Georgie and I went to dinner at this fabulous Chinese restaurant up in Prescott."

The Trooper shined his light into the car and square into Inky's face. He didn't even flinch. "Where did you cross the Canadian border?"

"The Burg, of course."

"And this was at what time?"

My smile tightened.

"Oh, about, oh, what time was it, Georgie?"

I shrugged, unable to speak.

"Oh, right, it was about nine o'clock or so, wasn't it? Just after I closed up the shop."

I nodded stupidly, too dumbfounded to contribute any weft to the warp in the coverlet of lies being woven here.

"Let me get this straight. You drove all the way to Ogdensburg at nine o'clock at night, then went over the bridge, cleared Customs, and went to Prescott for some Chinese food?" His skepticism was frightening. Couldn't two friends go get some Kung Pao chicken without being suspected of something? My nervousness was replaced by something approaching affront.

"You've obviously never had the food at Lucky Ling's Buffet. When the craving for that General Tso's chicken hits, you just gotta go!" Inky smiled broadly.

"You know, Georgie," Trooper Hawthorne turned the light back onto me, but was kind enough to point it down at my boobs rather than into my eyes, a bit longer than necessary, "I'd still like to talk to you about that little matter we were discussing the other day."

"She's available! For anything," Inky said, and I just

knew he was winking. If there hadn't been a State Trooper bulking up my driver's side window, I would have elbowed him to shut up. Hard.

"Stay here. I'll be right back." I watched him in the side mirror without turning my head as he strode back to his unmarked cruiser.

Great, just great! "Couldn't you have come up with a better story than that?" I asked. Actually, the story about going out to dinner wasn't bad. We could have been at any restaurant and said we'd paid cash, and Detective Hawthorne might not have bothered to check it out. Crossing into Canada was another matter, though. One simple inquiry to the Border Patrol and that story was sunk.

"It was the best I could do on short notice," he fired back at me. "And I could see you were starting to go catatonic. Somebody had to step in. And besides"—he poked at me with one of his long slender fingers—"I was hungry and thinking about Chinese food! I was at the shop all day and only had a protein bar for dinner in between tats. It's been a stressful night, you know!"

That was an understatement. It had been a stressful several days, and the lack of sleep was starting to affect me. Come to think of it, I was ready to gnaw off my own arm if I thought it would taste good. I'd have to eat something when I got back to the restaurant. If I got back to the restaurant.

I glanced in the mirror again. The detective was out of his car and moving toward us. He was illuminated from behind by the flashing of his Kojak light, and his jaw had a set to it that did not seem, um, happy.

"Inky, hold on." I'd made a sudden, stupid decision, but

I was committed now. There was no way I could allow that Trooper to search this car and find that bag of dope. No. Way. In. Hell. I jammed the accelerator to the floor and peeled out. Inky flew to one side, then righted himself. In the rearview mirror I could see the Trooper pulling out his radio and running back to his cruiser. *Good luck trying to call for backup,* I thought. Detective Hawthorne was almost certainly the only Trooper around for miles. And the Bay's police department would all be sleeping, whether an officer was on duty or not.

I hung a quick right under the arch emblazoned "Welcome to Bonaparte Bay, Gateway to the 1000 Islands" in glowing pink neon. Inky squealed with delight. The Trooper's siren wailed in the distance, getting closer. I turned down a side street, then down another, and pulled over. "Get out, and put that bag inside your jacket," I ordered.

"Get out?"

"Just do it!" The sheaf of papers from Sunshine Acres was still in the front of my fleece and I resecured the load. "Follow me, and move!" Like he couldn't run circles around me.

We hightailed it through the night and didn't stop until we arrived, panting, at the door to Keith's boat shop. This would be the test of whether Keith was appropriate boyfriend material. I was going to have to trust him. And he was going to have to trust me.

"Keep an eye out for that cop," I ordered again.

"You betcha!" How could he be so darn cheerful? I was now in as much trouble as I'd ever been in my life, and Inky sounded as though he'd just won a trip to Dollywood. My knuckles rapped softly on the door. I didn't hold out much hope for Keith hearing me, since the door was at the bottom of a stairwell and it was three o'clock in the morning. He'd almost certainly be asleep. I tried the knob. The door was locked, as expected.

We circled around to the dock and went inside the open boathouse. A half dozen boats in various states of repair were tied up to the cleats on the dock. If worse came to worst, we could hide out belowdecks in one of these. There was an empty slip at one end of the dock. I walked to the interior door, which I knew also opened into Keith's apartment. Locked. Damn! I knocked again, not wanting to make any superfluous noise in case the Trooper had tracked us down, but there was no answer. The intercom next to the door made a god-awful buzz as I pressed the button, reverberating around the building and no doubt out over the water. Inky was examining the racks of hand tools on the wall. He did not seem the type to enjoy woodworking, but I didn't know anything about him.

"Inky, can I borrow your phone? I need to check my phone messages at the Bonaparte House."

He handed me the device, an expensive iPhone that I was unfamiliar with. "Er, you'll have to show me how to use it too," I admitted.

"Here, the Bonaparte House is on speed dial." He deftly pressed some buttons and I connected to the restaurant's voice mail system. There was a call from Sophie, demanding to know why I hadn't called her.

Beep. "Georgie, I'm sorry I was so nasty to you earlier tonight," Keith's voice said. "What you do is your business.

When can I see you again? I'm willing to challenge whoever you were with to a duel if necessary. I'm off to Syracuse to pick up some specialty wood, but I'll be back tomorrow. Call me, okay? I miss you." My heart gave a little tug.

Beep. "Georgie!" It was Liza. "Would you like to explain, dearest friend, why you haven't called me tonight to let me know you're all right? Also why the Morristown Police Department, all one of them, called about a certain boat registered to me that was found drifting up the St. Lawrence? They have your purse and cell phone, by the way. I don't care about the boat. I own a castle and have scads of money and I can buy a new boat if necessary. I cannot buy a new friend. Well, I suppose it would be easy to buy some new friends, but I cannot buy a new you. If you don't call me by morning, I am going to have to have Chief Moriarty start dragging the river. Call me!"

Aw, that was so sweet. She was worried about me. I could not ask for a better bestie.

No message from the kidnapper, but I hadn't expected one. Jack Conway was most likely still on the island, unless he had come to and called an accomplice to rescue him. Now, that was a scary thought, one that hadn't occurred to me. If he had somebody working with him, I had absolutely no idea who that might be. Hank from Sunshine Acres seemed to be the most logical choice. We'd slowed Hank down, but he could certainly be out by now. He wouldn't have had time to escape from his makeshift prison, put a boat in the water, and retrieve Jack. But he might be on his way.

And now I knew why Keith wasn't answering our knocks.

He wasn't even here. So much for that idea. Still, this wasn't a bad place to hide out if necessary.

"You can check your e-mail too, you know. I can't go for more than a few hours without checking my e-mail." Inky brought me out of my thoughts. "Here, let me connect to the Internet."

Inky pulled up the touch screen and told me to punch in my username and password. This was so much nicer than my own cell phone. The little machine was not only adorable but useful too. Someday, when I was not so tangled up with kidnappers, extortionists, drug-dealing aged hippies, and men trying to steal my husband, I could shop for a new phone.

Okay, that last was a little excessive. There would be no stealing necessary. I was ready to set Spiro free, and myself in the process. What I would do with my newfound freedom remained to be seen.

I scrolled through the spam until I got to a message from Cal. "I'm fine, Aunt Athena is watching me like a hawk! Heading out to work now. Tell Daddy and Yiayia I love them (U2, of course!). Say hi to Russ and Dolly for me too. Bye bye! (Heart, xxxxxoooooooxxxxx) Cal." She used the Greek word for "grandmother" to refer to Sophie. Fluent in both her parents' languages, Callista could also speak quite good French. I did a quick calculation of the time differential and figured that she had sent it just an hour or so ago. That was a relief.

I stared at the most recent e-mail, the one I had been avoiding by looking at the older stuff first. I took a deep breath. My apprehension must have showed on my face or else Inky was quite perceptive, because he took my arm and asked with concern, "What is it?"

"I don't know yet."

WHAT THE HELL ARE YOU UP TO? YOU ARE NOT FOL-LOWING INSTRUCTOINS. YOU WERE NOT SUPOSED TO BRING ME A TABLE. I'M FEELING GENERUS SO I'M GIVING YOU A REPREEVE. BUT HE IS GOING TO START LOSING BODY PARTS IF YOU DON'T DELIVER THE GOODS BY NOON TOMOROW.

Best not to tell Inky about the missing body parts. Panic welled up in me. If there'd been anything in my stomach, it would have come up too.

If this nebulous treasure was not a priceless antique table, what the hell was it? Even if I did manage to figure it out, the bonehead had not told me where to bring the thing. My panic was replaced with anger. I was done. Exhausted, hungry, and done. The e-mail had been sent more than an hour ago. Jack Conway wouldn't have been able to send this message—unless he hadn't been unconscious for long and had a smartphone like the one I was now using. He hadn't said anything about having been clocked by Sophie. Maybe he had big clumsy fingers and wasn't good with the little keyboard, so he had to keep his messages short.

I had to get back to the Bonaparte House and try to figure this out. Walking through the streets of the Bay to get there was out of the question. There were only about a dozen streets in the whole village and I couldn't anticipate where Detective Hawthorne might be. Even worse, he might have been able to rouse another Trooper or one of the Bay's tiny police force to come and join in the search. He would almost certainly have found my car by now. I'd purposely left it unlocked so that he could search the inside, thinking that would buy us some time to get to Keith's. It was probably illegal for him to do so, but I was counting on the idea that he wouldn't be able to resist. Not that he'd find anything other than an empty doughnut shop bag and some spare change in the center console.

Once I got inside the Bonaparte House, I should be okay. I just wouldn't answer the door. Which I hoped he wouldn't break down. Without getting a judge out of bed he probably couldn't get a search warrant before morning, but it was possible. A lump that seemed to be the size of a small eggplant formed in my throat. I was piling one bad decision on top of another and it was only a matter of time before they all came crashing down around me.

"Inky, we have to get back to the restaurant. We can't go on foot. Do you know how to drive a boat?"

He looked at me as though I had two heads. "Are you kidding? Of course I know how to drive a boat. I've lived my entire life on the river."

I had lived my entire life on the river, and I had never driven a boat until a few hours ago. "I think we should take one of these boats, preferably one that isn't broken, and go around to the docks by the boat tour office. But we won't get out there. We'll go a little bit farther up the shore and go ashore over by the Taj Mahal Motel. Then we can sneak through the back alley and go in the side door. If the cops are watching anywhere, they'll be watching the front and back entrances." I only hoped that was true.

"What about Spiro?" he demanded. "You said we were going to get him back tonight."

"I'm working on it." I had no idea what I would do once I got back to the restaurant, but I knew I couldn't stay here.

Inky took the little flashlight I offered and examined the boats tied up at the docks. "This one looks like our best bet. It's small and won't make a lot of engine noise, and we won't need the deep water at the docks to land it."

"Is there a key?" I could not imagine that Keith would leave the keys in the ignition when the front of this boathouse was open to the water and anyone could walk in. Like me.

"Honey, I don't need a key. I'm a Bassport boy, remember?" Oh right, his childhood training had apparently included petty crime, or at least he had learned the skills for it. "Let's see here." He opened the engine hatch and shined the flashlight inside. "Oh, this will be easy. A piece of baklava, as my Greek god would say." I felt a little twinge of nostalgia. I'd called Spiro that a long, long time ago. I didn't miss the man, but I missed the feeling.

"What are you doing? Don't you have to crack open the steering column or something?" I'd seen that on TV and in movies.

"No! That's why this is so easy. See, in a car, the key also unlocks the steering column. On a boat the key just activates an electrical switch. So all I have to do is disconnect these wires back here and splice into them. Any Bassport kid can do this by the time he's ten."

I was intrigued by this mechanical skill Inky possessed. He was going to be a valuable addition to the family. Now I wouldn't have to rely on Russ all the time when stuff broke around the house. "See if you can find me a pair of wire strippers, will you?"

Wire strippers? I did not have the foggiest idea what wire strippers were. "Uh," I faltered. "What do they look like?"

"They're like a pair of flat pliers—oh, never mind," he said. He reached into his pocket and pulled out a shiny red Swiss Army Knife and fiddled with something in the engine compartment. In less than a minute the engine turned over. "Okay, grab a couple of life jackets and let's get this show on the road."

We found vests and put them on. I climbed into the boat and took a seat. Inky sat in the captain's chair and put the engine into reverse, backing us expertly out of the boat-house. He turned us around and we headed out to the main channel. Despite my newfound skill with watercraft, I was happy to leave this particular trip to someone with more experience. It was one thing for me to wreck Liza's boat, but it would be quite another to damage one belonging to one of Keith's clients. I felt incredibly guilty at having borrowed this one, but I saw no alternative.

We ran at a slow speed so as to keep the noise down, with just the smallest possible light illuminating the black water ahead of us. It was close to dawn.

We passed the docks, scaring a seagull from its roost atop the giant paddle wheel affixed to the back of the *Lady Liberty II* tour boat. Inky cut the engine. We drifted into the shore near the Taj Mahal Motel and Inky stepped out into the cold water, rope in hand. He found a small upright post to serve as a cleat and tied off the boat. Then he came back and offered me a hand. Mechanically inclined and a gentleman too. I moved to the front of the boat and stepped over, a bit awkwardly, onto dry land.

Seeing no observers, we made our way the short distance to the motel. We cut under the motel's carport and past the pink-painted office, keeping close to the unlit back of the building. From the end unit it was only a few yards to the Bonaparte House. I glanced involuntarily up at the windows, looking for any signs of activity, human or supernatural, but everything looked normal. We arrived at the emergency exit, which fronted on a strip of lawn facing the adjacent ice cream shop. If we ever had an evacuation-worthy emergency, there would be quite a traffic jam in this narrow alley.

My hand reached for the window in an attempt to raise the sash from outside so we could crawl in. Inky waved his hand at me and pointed to a rock to the left of the flat, irregular-sided slab of reddish sandstone that served as a stoop. He bent down and turned over the rock, producing a key, with which he swiftly and silently opened the door. Once inside, he turned to me and whispered, "Spiro put this there for me." Didn't take a genius to realize he'd used it more than once.

I decided not to comment. "Come with me," I said, my voice low.

"Can I get something to eat?" he whined. "I'm starving!"

I was hungry too. "Sorry, but that would mean turning on a light in the kitchen. If that cop is watching the parking lot waiting for us to try to come in that way, we'll be seen through the door."

I could feel his pout in the dark. "What are we going to do, then?"

"Come on." I led him past the restrooms and through the

front dining room. The sun had not yet breached the horizon, but the sky was lightening in preparation, and the room was dimly lit. Napoleon gazed down at us, incarcerated in his heavy gilt frame.

"That picture gives me the creeps," Inky said.

Funny, it had never bothered me, but I took another look and could see the faint menace in the hard thin line of that mouth. A frisson went through me and I shuddered.

We passed my office and headed toward the kitchen. I felt bad to be leading Inky toward the makings of a nice sandwich and a cup of tea without delivering, but it couldn't be helped. I opened a door and switched on the light.

"What are you doing?" he cried.

The sudden illumination after so long in the dark made me squint. "Don't worry," I said as we descended the unpainted wooden stairs down into the damp cool of the basement. "There are no outside windows or doors down here, so we're safe to turn on the light. The walls are solid rock, eighteen inches thick, so sound is not going to carry outside. Remember, this house was built for Napoleon to hide out from the monarchists and the revolutionaries, and as far as I know it's solid as a fortress."

"Well, okay, then. Anything to eat down here?" He looked around at the boxes of canned goods and pasta and extra china and glassware we stored in a rough semicircle around the outer walls. His gaze landed on a door. "What's in there?"

"Oh, that's where we store the expensive wine." He made a beeline for the door and flung it open.

"Ooh, I wondered where Spiro was coming up with this

stuff. This is a good one!" He held up a bottle of expensive French champagne. "Let's have a glass!"

The idea was tempting, even at five o'clock in the morning, but I needed to keep a clear head, and so did Inky. "Let's wait until we find Spiro, okay?"

His face fell, but then brightened. "A welcome-home party! That is such a good idea! We can make some horse doovers to go with it." I thought he was making a joke, but he did grow up in Bassport and I couldn't be sure. "How are we going to find him?"

No clue. He handed me the bottle and I replaced it on the shelves in the large closet. I felt a little draft of air as I did so. Air? How could there be a draft of air when there were no openings to the outside? We'd never had problems with water seeping in. As far as I knew every stone in the rough-cut foundation was sealed with mortar. I had made sure the cellar door was closed behind Inky.

The air seemed to be moving inside the wine closet. "Inky, come here, will you?"

He had been foraging among the boxes looking for something edible, but returned to the closet. "Yikes, it's cold. Do you have some kind of cooling system to maintain the temperature for the vino?"

Nope. Even on the hottest day of summer it was fifty-three degrees down here.

"Look around in here and see if you can find the source of that draft."

There was a gap of about two feet between the freestanding shelving and the cold stone walls. I examined them without success. After a minute or two, Inky said from his side of the closet, "Well, here's where it's coming from. There's a door back here behind these boxes of French wine."

A door? I had lived in this house for twenty years and been down here countless times, and I had never known there was a door in the wine closet.

"Where does it go?" Inky asked.

"Beats me."

"I'm going to open it. I can't resist!"

I was curious myself. There wasn't room for two of us to stand abreast behind the shelves, so I stood behind him on my tiptoes as he opened the door, which was built into an interior wall, not the stone foundation. A blast of air hit us, momentarily stopping my breath. "Check it out!" Inky exclaimed. "It's a staircase."

He turned ninety degrees so I could see around him and up the dark passage. I shook my head. Had I been plucked out of my life and set down in a Nancy Drew novel? I thought I knew everything about this house, and here was a secret staircase leading to . . . I had no damn clue.

"You don't know where this goes, do you? We're gonna see, right? I don't think I could stand not knowing."

Me either. "Do you see a light switch anywhere?"

He ran his hands up and down on both sides of the stairway walls, finding nothing. I pulled the LED flashlight out of my pocket and shined it on the walls. I moved the beam up and illuminated an old-fashioned beaded metal chain with a little bell-like cap affixed to the end. He pulled the chain and the passageway lit up with a click.

Cobwebs lined the juncture of the narrow walls and the

low ceiling. The stairway itself was dusty in the corners of the risers, but the treads were bare. Somebody had been up here recently.

"Did you hear that?" Inky whispered.

"What?" I aligned my right ear with the stairwell and listened.

"There it is again!" This time there was no mistake. A muffled moan floated down from the top of the stairs.

"The ghost," I whispered.

"Ghost? Are you telling me those ghost hunters found something? I was meaning to ask you about that."

My flight of fancy crash-landed back on terra firma. "They found something, but I'm pretty sure it wasn't a ghost. Come on."

I pushed past him and led the way up the stairs, each tread sounding a distinctive creak. At the top of the stairs I took a deep breath and opened the door.

My little light preceded me as I entered a long, narrow, triangular room, facing a very acute angle where two walls met. I fumbled unsuccessfully on the wall for a light switch, then shined the beam up again to find another pull chain. I gave it a yank and a dim light filled the room.

Motionless, on the bare floor, was the prone form of a man.

◈ TWENTY-TWO ◈

"Oh, my God!" Inky rushed past me and knelt over the body. Spiro. His olive skin had taken on the bloodless, greenish pallor of a mushroom and his classically beautiful face was as still as an ancient Greek statue. My heart sank. Inky put his ear to Spiro's chest and breathed a sigh of relief. "He's alive!"

His arms were bound behind him, and his ankles were also tied together. Inky pulled out his pocketknife and set to work on the ropes. Spiro made some soft, incoherent noises, but seemed unaware of our presence. Inky gingerly pulled back one of his eyelids. "Drugged," he pronounced.

"Where are we?" I tried to orient myself in the house. We were on the second floor, but there was no stairway opening into any of the bedrooms corresponding to this room. I thought about the weird triangular shape of this space and I understood. The bedrooms were all regular rectangles. The house, though, was octagonal. That meant that each of the bedrooms had a space just like this on the other side of the wall. I doubted I would find three more secret stairways, but the configuration offered some interesting possibilities as far as additional closet space.

This explained why I was hearing ghostly noises from Spiro's room and from Sophie's room, but hadn't been able to locate the source. Poor Spiro had been up here for days. No way of telling whether he'd been fed, but several empty water bottles and some bent straws littered the floor, so it looked as though he'd at least had some water. I did not know, and didn't want to know, how he had relieved himself. My missing bottle of Ouzo, now empty, lay on its side in one corner. Looked like somebody had been having a few shots while he kept Spiro sedated.

"Who did this to you?" Inky spoke softly to him, but Spiro didn't answer. Inky looked at me. "We have to get him out of here."

"Let's get him to his room and then call the EMTs." Inky nodded and hoisted him up in a fireman's carry. Inky was made of some strong stuff. He turned and faced the top of the stairs, then sucked in a breath.

I whipped around to see what had startled him and felt my heart jump into my throat. A figure stood in the doorway, brandishing a gun.

Russ Riley pointed the gun at Inky's chest. "Put him down. Now."

"Russ, what the hell are you doing?" I was too shocked to be frightened. Russ? I'd known him since he was a kindergartner, gave him a job every year, and looked the other way when he stole from me. Now he had turned on me and my family?

"Shut up, Georgie." He grinned his crooked jack-o'-lantern grin, which I'd always thought was cute in a redneck sort of way. Now it just looked evil. His smile looked different for another reason as well. Was he missing a couple more teeth? "I always wanted to say that! Now put him down, or I'll shoot all three of you." He gestured with the deer rifle and Inky obeyed, laying the still-unconscious Spiro gently on the floor. "Now put your hands up. Both of you." A hideously mottled green-and-purple bruise covered the left side of his face, and he had quite a shiner.

We complied. "You, Snakeman." He pointed a finger at Inky. "You are going to stay here, and you are going to keep your mouth shut." Inky pursed his lips and didn't say a word, but cut his eyes to me.

"You, *boss*, are going to get them valuables for me. Now."

"Russ, I am telling you the absolute truth when I say I don't know where the valuables are. Or what they are."

"There's money in this house. I've heard it all my life and I've looked for it all my life. You got it hid somewhere, and you are going to take me to it. Now."

So he was the one who'd been snooping around and had ransacked the bedrooms. Ewww. His sausage-like fingers, the ones with the homemade tattoos spelling out "H-E-L-L" and "Y-E-S," had been through my underwear drawer. I was going to throw out everything and buy new stuff posthaste.

He poked me with the barrel of the gun. "Watch it," I said, my temper flaring. Shooting a deer was very different from shooting a human, and I didn't think he had it in him.

A sudden vision of Big Dom's corpse floating on the river came to mind. Had Russ killed Big Dom? It was possible. But he couldn't be working alone. Unless I'd grossly underestimated him all these years, he was simply too . . . simple to be a criminal mastermind. He was working for Jack Conway. I'd bet on it.

I moved toward the top of the stairs, Russ prodding me along with the gun. I looked back at Inky, who nodded at me. Russ locked the door behind us when we reached the bottom.

"Go on upstairs to the kitchen," he ordered. "Unless it's down here somewhere."

"Uh, no, it's not down here. So," I said conversationally, trying to buy some time, for what I wasn't yet sure, "how come you have Spiro tied up?"

"I don't. Well, I do. But it wasn't my idea. Wish it was. I'm getting paid, a helluva lot more than I get paid for being a dishwasher." I should hope so, if he was taking this kind of risk. Kidnapping was a felony and he was facing serious prison time when this was over.

"Who's paying you?"

"Nice try. But guess what? I ain't telling. Now, where is it?"

"Uh, okay. I do know where it is."

"I thought so. Now, get it, so I can give it to the guy paying me and I can get my cut. Then I'm blowing this town. I'm going to Florida. And I'm stayin' there. Girls in bikinis on the beach. And no more damned snow to shovel."

"Do you even know who is paying you?"

"Well," he hesitated. "No, I don't. But as soon as I get this thing I'm gonna take it to him. Then I'll find out."

"How much have you gotten paid already?"

"None of your damn business. But a lot," he said. Now I knew where the money had come from to build that gargantuan garage and to buy that giant gold necklace Dolly had been sporting.

"Look, Russ," I said. "I've been up all night, and I'm hungry and thirsty. How about I make us an egg sandwich and then I'll go get it? It's outside," I added, "and it's going to take some work to dig it up."

He considered. "You got bacon to go on that? And American cheese? Extra American cheese. And make sure I got ketchup on the side. And a Coke to go with it." He sat down in Sophie's armchair by the cash register, still pointing the gun at me as I gathered ingredients from the cooler. "Start cookin'. And don't try nothin' funny."

Me? I wouldn't dream of it. I turned on the range and heated up a heavy, copper-bottomed sauté pan. I dropped a big glob of butter in the pan and it sizzled happily. I had a vague plan that I could somehow use this hot frying pan as a weapon. How I would get it close enough to him without arousing his suspicion and getting myself shot in the process, I had not yet worked out. Plan B was to get a shovel from the gardening shed under the pretense of digging up the treasure, then smack him over the head with it. "You want this on toast or English muffin?" I called out.

"Toast. None of that fancy wheat stuff either. White."

"Sure thing." I dropped four eggs, one by one, into the pan, and put yesterday's cooked bacon on a layer of paper towels into our high-powered microwave to warm up. Four slices of bread went into the toaster, two white and two homemade wheat. I had just begun to flip the eggs when a knock sounded at the kitchen door. We both looked up.

"Who is it?" Russ demanded.

"I don't know. I'm not expecting anybody here this early."

"Go see who it is and get rid of them."

"The eggs are going to get overcooked if I leave them."

He paused. "Come in!" he bellowed as he got up and stood behind the armchair, holding the gun low so it was not visible.

The door swung open and Brenda Jones walked in. Her hair was combed down and back into a frizzy ponytail, and she had inexpertly applied some makeup. She looked as nice as I'd ever seen her, and she was sober to boot. "I'm here for breakfast," she announced.

I forgot I'd invited her. "The restaurant isn't open yet, Brenda, but I'm just making some bacon, egg, and cheese sandwiches. You can either come in and have one with me and Russ, or you can come back in a couple hours." The invitation might get me shot, but I was betting on the fact that Russ wanted the treasure more than he wanted me dead, and he thought I knew where it was. He wouldn't want to take the chance of shooting either Brenda or me and giving the other the chance to escape. Russ glared at me, and I went back to flipping eggs.

"Russ, you handsome dog, you," she cooed at him, fingering the neckline of her turquoise tank top. She turned to me. "I think I'll take one of those egg sandwiches too. Russ, where've you been? I haven't seen you around lately."

While she flirted I made a few more pieces of toast and assembled the sandwiches, giving Russ two eggs, and one each to Brenda and me. I set the plates down on the counter. "Should we eat in the dining room?" He wouldn't take the gun with him and tip off Brenda.

"No! We'll eat right here." He patted the back of the armchair. "Just set it right here. And where's my Coke?" That demanding tone was annoying me. I was definitely going to fire his sorry ass when this was all over. In fact, he could consider himself fired, effective immediately. I handed him the plate and a can of Coke from the fridge, which he set on the narrow shelf next to the chair.

"Brenda, would you mind going out into the hallway and getting us a couple of those folding chairs?"

After she had left, he whispered, "Don't try nothing. I still got my gun back here."

"Yeah, I know."

Brenda came back in and set down the chairs, which she arranged next to the armchair.

"Come on out from behind there and sit with us," Brenda suggested, her voice hopeful.

"Naw, I'm fine right where I am."

"So whatcha doing here so early?" she asked, cutting her darkly mascaraed blue eyes at him.

Russ didn't answer, just took a big bite of the sandwich. Brenda looked at me and shrugged.

At that moment the back door flew open. Russ dropped his sandwich and shouldered the gun, faster than I would have thought possible for someone at his level of physical conditioning. "Who the hell is it now?" We all froze, Brenda in midbite, and turned to stare.

"Ma?"

"Russell Riley, what the hell are you doing? Put that gun down. Now!" Dolly strode toward him unafraid. He attempted to maneuver out from behind the chair, but it wasn't as easy as it looked while still holding the gun, and he bumped one hip against the chair. It moved and blocked his way, slowing him down long enough for me to grab the waist-length tail of his mullet and yank him off balance. I hooked my ankle behind his leg and pushed. Brenda grabbed the gun away from him as he sat down hard in the chair. She trained the weapon on him.

"You can put that gun down, Brenda," Dolly said. "He ain't going nowhere till he tells me what he's been doing. Now, mister." The morning light sparkled on the jewel pasted onto her long hot pink gel nail as she poked it into his chest. "You want to explain to me how come I just got a phone call from the tattoo man telling me to get over here because you were doing something stupid? Huh?" She jabbed him again and he winced. It looked like it hurt.

Brenda sat rapt as the harangue continued.

"I had to go over to your house this morning and take care of that damn barking dog of yours, since you apparently decided not to come home last night. I thought you were in that car wreck out on Route 12 a couple hours ago, you dumb son of a bitch."

Inky, bless him, had phoned Dolly rather than the police. It was a genius move, really, since the police had to be looking for us. What had Dolly said, though? There was a car wreck? That would explain why Detective Hawthorne and the rest of the local police force weren't knocking at my door like everybody else this morning. Yet.

I ran out into the hallway and downstairs. I tried the door to the secret stairs but remembered when the handle wouldn't turn that Russ had the key. I ran back up, breathing more heavily than I would have liked. "Russ, give me the key."

"You know something," he spat back out at me. "I quit." Fine by me. I wouldn't have to sign off on his unemployment in November.

"Give her what she wants. Now. And watch your mouth." Dolly put out her hand, palm up, and Russ reluctantly offered up the key. She handed it to me. "Sorry, Georgie, about this dumbass boy of mine." She gave him a slap on the side of the head.

"Thanks, Dolly." I raced back to the wine cellar and up the narrow stairs to the triangle room.

"Inky, that was brilliant! How did you think to call Dolly?"

"I had her in my phone book because she came in for a tat a few months ago—you know, the butterfly on her ass?" Well, I didn't know, and didn't want to know any more about that. "And I always keep the numbers for my local customers handy so I can make follow-up calls later, you know, see if they're healing all right, or if they're ready for another one."

"Has Spiro come to yet?"

"No," he said sadly. "He must have had a pretty good dose of whatever he's on; plus he's weak from lack of food."

"Let's get him to his room and lay him down where he'll be comfortable." Inky nodded. I steeled myself for the physical exertion ahead. We were going to have to carry his limp body down these back stairs, then up to the main floor through the cellar, then through the hallway and up and around the circular staircase. It would have to be done, though. There was nowhere downstairs to put him. "I'm ready."

Inky picked Spiro up under the arms. His unconscious head lolled to one side. I went for his feet, bracing myself against the wall. It moved. Huh? I pushed back again and the wall moved again. "Inky, did you see that?" I looked toward the sharp corner opposite the door. A gap had appeared. Inky set Spiro down again and we both walked toward the corner. Inky pushed on the wall and the corner separated farther.

"Check this out! We only have to move him a few feet. There's his bedroom right there." I peered through the opening at the pale blue walls and antiseptic cleanliness of Spiro's room.

"The walls must have some kind of pivot points back here." He pointed behind us. "In this position, they can only be moved from this space. If you push on the walls from the bedroom side, nothing will happen because they have a common point, here in the corner."

I sort of understood. As long as the bedroom was a perfect rectangle, the walls wouldn't move from that side. They could open out from the triangle room, but not in from the bedroom.

We both gave the wall another shove and made an opening large enough to bring Spiro through. Inky picked him up in the fireman's carry again, and I went ahead and pulled down the comforter. Inky laid him down and we covered him up. "I'll stay with him till he wakes up. If it looks like he needs an ambulance sooner, I'll call."

"That might not be too long. Russ was no doubt here to give him another dose as well as to bother me, so he must be close to coming around."

"What are we going to do about Russ?"

I'd been wondering the same thing. "Somebody's been paying him to kidnap Spiro and to look around this house for whatever's hidden here. Or whatever somebody thinks is hidden here. He doesn't know who it is. I'm tempted to lock him up in that room after I ask him a few more questions."

"Not a bad plan. We definitely need to find out if he knows anything else, and I'm just itching to give him a piece of my mind too. But if we lock him up over there, he's gonna make a hell of a noise, and that's going to disturb Spiro. Plus, he's healthy. He could push the walls open after we close them, unless there's some sort of locking mechanism." He stroked his chin, where a light stubble had appeared since I'd first seen him hours ago. "We could leave him to Dolly."

"She's tough and smart, no question, but he's bigger than she is. I'm going to have to think about this." It was just a matter of time before the police got involved, and rightly so. But there was one piece of this puzzle missing, and for the sake of my family, I was going to find out for sure who that piece was.

Back downstairs in the kitchen I found Brenda helping herself to coffee. Had she made a pot on her own? She stirred in several spoonfuls of sugar as she listened to Dolly going to work on Russ, who had started to squirm.

"Dolly." She didn't even notice me, just kept on him.

"Dolly," I repeated, a bit louder this time. I tapped her shoulder and she turned to me.

"What?!" she snapped, then apologized.

"No problem. I just need to talk to Russ for a minute."

She moved aside and I took her place in front of him. I could see the gun leaning up against the prep counter within arm's reach, so I moved to block it from his easy access.

"Who's been paying you?"

"I said I don't know."

"How are you communicating with him?"

"He sends me e-mails."

"What have you been drugging Spiro with?" I might need this information if he didn't come out of it soon.

"Beats me. The guy left a bunch of pills in my mailbox and I been crushing them up and putting them in the water I give him."

"Where's Spiro's Mercedes?"

"In my garage." He looked up at me spitefully. "It might have a few scratches on it. I been driving it after-hours." It probably reeked of cigarettes too. I could see a pack of Chiefs in his shirt pocket, so he'd gone back to smoking. Spiro would be trading in that car sooner than he'd planned.

"Where's his cell phone?" Jack Conway had said he didn't have it, not that I believed him.

"In the car." His tone implied that the rest of that sentence was, "stupid." I restrained myself from slapping him. "Hope he had unlimited minutes."

I turned. "Dolly, is Harold working today?"

"Naw, it's his day off."

"Russ has been storing Spiro's car in his garage. Do you

think Harold could drive it over here; then you could give him a ride back home? I'll pay you," I added.

"Sure. He was coming into town today anyway."

"Brenda, what have you got planned?"

"Well, today's the day the pirates come in on the tall ships, remember?" No, I had forgotten that. "So it's one of my biggest days for collecting returnables. But I don't start until late afternoon."

"How'd you like a job?"

Fifteen minutes later, with Dolly's blessing ("It'll teach him a lesson, the goofy bastard"), we had herded Russ at gunpoint up into the cupola. We tied him up to Basil's old flowered armchair and told him to keep it quiet. I locked him in and installed Brenda outside the door with the rifle. I didn't want him running off and e-mailing the mastermind, putting us all in more danger.

"Don't shoot unless you absolutely have to." She nodded, serious. "I'll bring you up something to drink in a few minutes."

Back in the kitchen, Dolly was prepping for the day as if nothing had happened. We opened for breakfast on the weekends, and Dolly cooked the breakfast orders. She was cracking eggs and mixing them up in a pitcher so they'd be ready to pour onto the griddle when a scrambled egg order came in. I was not doing any more business with Sunshine Acres, not that Hank would probably want my business anyway after Inky's and my little nighttime escapade. So we were going to have to make do with what we had until I could get another supply of perishables in from Watertown. I thought if I begged and pleaded and paid a premium, I could get them delivered before eleven.

Sophie came in looking fresh as a daisy. "You look very bad," she scolded me.

"Spiro is home." Her face lit up and she headed for the hallway. I put out a hand to stop her.

"He's not feeling too well. And he's sleeping right now."

"I will leave him to rest, then," she declared. "I'll go see him later."

"Yes, that would be best."

"And then I'm going to wring his neck until he tells me where my money is!"

I went into my office and checked my e-mail. There was the one I'd been expecting, the one from the unknown sender. The instructions were to bring it (still no clue what "it" was) to Riverfront Park at eleven this morning. I was to wait at the picnic table closest to the soda machines, and someone would contact me for the handoff. I was done with this business. Spiro was back, a bit worse for the wear, and as soon as he woke up I planned to pry the whole story out of him. The kidnapper, however, probably didn't know that I had both his leverage and his henchman, so I had no intention of wasting any more time trying to figure out what the treasure was. I'd go down to the police station and turn myself in, and make a complaint against Jack Conway this afternoon. First I would try to keep my restaurant running for the next couple of hours.

I considered trying to grab a quick nap, but decided against it. I was already up and oddly alert, so I decided to leave well enough alone. My backup supplier in Watertown agreed to get me enough vegetables and dairy for the weekend. I sent off an e-mail to Cal and told her that her father was a little under the weather but that he would call her soon. I reiterated my admonition about being careful. The reservations for the evening meal were processed in record time. Upstairs, Brenda seemed to be enjoying herself. I handed her a trashy celebrity gossip magazine and a bottle of water and reminded her to stay alert in case Russ tried to make a break for it. He was being relatively quiet, but that might have had something to do with the gag we'd tied around his mouth.

I descended to the second floor and gave two other bottles to Inky, who had set up camp in the side chair and was watching *Jerry Springer* on the flat-screen TV with the volume turned low. "It's research," he informed me. A lot of tattoos were showcased on that program, and he was always looking for new ideas. He'd called in one of his artists from the shop near Fort Drum to watch his store downtown so as not to miss out on any of the drunk pirate business that would be coming in this afternoon and evening. Spiro had still not awakened, but was breathing deeply and evenly and seemed healthy enough.

I went to my room and ran a comb through my hair, then splashed some water on my face. I applied a light sunscreen, then put on some lip balm with a hint of color and a swipe of eye shadow and mascara. Looking decent—or as decent as possible after my all-nighter—would give me courage for my upcoming encounter. I dug out a spare purse and dropped in a few essentials. Still no wallet or cell, though. Those would have to be retrieved from the police station later on.

Back in the kitchen, Sophie stared at my shoulder bag. "Where you going?" she demanded. "Today going to be very, very busy." A look of rapture crossed her face as she contemplated the day's potential take. "I need you here."

"Sophie, I'm going out to"—I paused—"run some errands. I'll be back as soon as I can. In the meantime, you and Dolly can handle things back here, and you can have Lizzie manage the dining room. I think we ought to make her dining room manager anyway."

She snorted. "Lizzie! What about Spiro? You said he was back?" she asked suspiciously.

"He is back, and he's sleeping. I want you to stay downstairs and leave him alone."

She snorted again and turned back to her breakfast.

I exited through the kitchen door and made my way through the short maze of streets to where I'd left my car on Vincent Street. No one seemed to be watching, so I darted over to my little blue baby and slipped inside. I drove it over to the Bonaparte House lot and left it there. If the police did show up, Sophie could truthfully say that she didn't know where I was.

On foot, I made my way up Theresa Street and up past the tattoo shop and the Windlass Guest House to Riverfront Park. There were already crowds of people milling around, waiting for the ships to arrive. I found an empty seat at one of the picnic tables at the covered pavilion and fished around in the bottom of the large purse I'd brought, coming up with enough change to buy a Diet Coke. I fed my coins into the machine and pressed the button for the lime variety. The machine vended out a cold bottle, the condensation which formed confirming that it was already a hot day, and it was going to get hotter and muggier. I sat back down and waited.

A pair of young children dressed in their adorable beads and pirate hats, curly mustaches drawn on their little faces with their mom's eyebrow pencils, ran around excitedly, fencing with their plastic swords. I felt a twinge of nostalgia as I remembered bringing Cal here when she was little. I think I still had the black skull-and-crossbones bandannas we had tied pirate-wise around our heads. The atmosphere was palpable with fun and excitement, the unmistakable air of a tourist town where people come to get away from their normal lives, where cares and troubles are left behind for a few days. It felt good to be a part of that in some small way, providing meals that tasted great and didn't have to be cooked or cleaned up after by the consumer. *A vacation,* I mused. *A vacation would be so nice.* Of course, most people would consider spending a few months on a Greek island every winter a pretty nice vacation. But I was thinking about doing some real traveling after we closed up this season. With e-mail and the Internet and cell phones, I could leave all the after-season paperwork and closing up to the accountant.

Where would I like to go, I wondered. Maybe California. Well, maybe not. I might run into my mother. Not that I'd recognize her after so many years. How about Hawaii? Or Peru? Or Copenhagen? Cal would be in school, so she wouldn't be able to come with me, but maybe I could convince Liza to take a month off for a girlfriends' tour. Or, I allowed myself to fantasize a bit, maybe Keith could come with me. I blushed and sipped the cold soda, bringing myself back to the present.

My watch read a quarter to eleven. No one around me seemed to be my contact. Captain Jack would not show up to do this job himself. He'd send somebody else. The entire park was filling up with pirates of varying ages, sizes, and degrees of costuming. Nearly everyone had a bandanna tied around his or her head, and lots of brightly colored plastic beads around their necks. Two of my evening waitresses were hanging out over in the far corner of the pavilion, but I didn't think they noticed me. *They'd better be sober when they get to work tonight,* I thought.

A man with a pair of binoculars pointed across the river to the Canadian side. "They're leaving port! I can see them!" The crowd pushed toward the river side of the pavilion and spilled out into the park. I couldn't help myself and stood up, craning my neck. The energy level all around me was building and I was feeling it too. The distinct boom of gun-fire blanks sounded over the buzz of the throng. I went up on my tiptoes to try to get a better look, and I could just see the masts, each flying the Jolly Roger, coming into view. It wasn't a long trip across the river and they'd be here soon. The noise of the crowd intensified as the ships approached. Children waved their flags and danced excitedly. By now only a few stragglers like me were left behind at the pavilion. I screwed the cap onto my soda and stowed the bottle in my big bag.

The tall ships glided up and dropped anchor about a dozen feet from shore, where the water was deep enough to hold them. A voice, amplified by a decidedly non-period bullhorn, advised: "Citizens of Bonaparte Bay—surrender or be taken with no mercy!" Squeals and shouts went up from the crowd as two dozen pirates descended rope ladders into prams that had been unlashed from the sides of the ships. They continued to whoop as they rowed into shore and began to mingle with the tourists, pausing long enough for photos snapped with digital cameras and cell phones. They dropped more beads over the heads of the children as they passed.

I spotted my waitresses over by one of the barbecue grills. One of them had her fingers tangled up in the strand of beads around the neck of one of the pirates and was boldly planting a kiss on him. He pulled back, then gave her a look that pretty clearly said that the kiss might be repeated and extended later on. I hoped she was having fun.

I was so engrossed in watching the spectacle that it came as a surprise to me when someone came up behind me and put a string of beads around my neck. I whirled around and was greeted by a black eye pencil coming toward me. Before I could protest, two lines had been drawn under my nose into what I assumed was a mustache. I looked into a face I did not recognize, brown eyes rimmed with black liner, a long ratty wig held in place by a red bandanna. The face was young, sprinkled with a few reddish blond hairs that tried to pass for a beard. "Come on now, and come quietly." The voice was soft and urgent with just the hint of a crack. I punched out to push him away, but he grabbed my wrists and held on. He was surprisingly strong for someone as young and skinny as he was.

"Now, smile and get moving. Look natural."

"Where are we going?" He didn't answer, but transferred both my wrists into one of his very large hands and deftly wound a piece of clothesline around my wrists with the other. My shoulder bag was now dangling from the crook of my elbow.

"I have a gun, and I will use it on you if I have to." He marched me down the steps of the pavilion, waving and smiling at the tourists and other pirates as he did so. A couple of thumbs went up, accompanied by catcalls. *These pigs think I am enjoying being carried off.* Well, maybe if I'd been the age of my waitresses and the pirate was cute, I would have. The forced march halted when we got to the beach and stepped over the side into a small rowboat, where another pirate was waiting. We shoved off and he started rowing out toward the ships. I considered going over the side. It was daylight and the swim to shore would be short and doable even for me, but I did not want to take the chance of being shot. And of course my hands were tied, which would make swimming next to impossible. There were also those lurking muskellunge and sturgeons to consider too. I shuddered.

Add one more bad decision to the mountain I'd already amassed in the last few days. Why had I thought I could do this? I should have brought somebody, anybody, with me. I could even have gotten one of the rent-a-cops in the crowd to sit with me. But I'd thought I'd be safe with all these people around, that by pretending I had the treasure in my oversized bag and telling the go-between I'd only deal with Captain Jack directly, I could draw him out. Stupid, stupid, stupid.

"Now get moving. And don't try anything, or I'll shoot you." His voice cracked again and I thought furiously for a means of escape, but the cold metal cylinder of a gun pressed into the small of my back convinced me not to try anything. He prodded me and I began to ascend the rope ladder, not an easy feat with my hands tied together. "Hurry up!"

"I'm going as fast as I can," I shot back. "It would help if you untied me." He might have a gun, but there was a limit to what I could take from this brat who was young enough to be my son.

"Shut up and go."

I reached the top edge of the boat and swung my legs over. I'd never been on one of these ships before and if circumstances had been different, it would have been pretty cool. The wood all around me was polished and beautiful. The masts rose up to magnificent heights, covered in yards and yards of billowing snowy sails. I could picture myself sailing up the river in one of these. It would be so nice at sunset, maybe with a cocktail and some handsome sailor to snuggle up to. Instead I had Junior here poking me again with a pistol.

"Down here." He opened a hatch in the deck and forced me down the narrow dark stairs. He switched on a light— electric? The romance dimmed a bit. I'd expected the flickering chiaroscuro of an oil lamp. We were in some kind of holding area. Wooden barrels encircled with shiny bands lined the walls of the ship. The kid pushed me forward and opened a short door toward the front of the boat. "Get inside," he ordered.

I complied because there didn't seem to be any other choice. I found myself in a cramped little room with a low ceiling. "Now, stay here. Oh yeah." He laughed. "I'm gonna lock the door behind me, so you can't go anywhere."

"Does your mother know what you're doing?" If he shot me, he shot me. My limit had been reached today.

A look of sadness crossed his face, replaced by anger. "You shut up about my mother," he snapped. "Just shut up!"

He stormed out and slammed the door behind him. The metallic grating of the key in the lock proved he'd kept his promise to lock me in. *Now what, Georgie?* I began to twist and turn my wrists in an attempt to loosen the knots binding my hands, but the rope stayed tight. The kid would never pass for a Boy Scout, but he could apparently tie a square knot. The room around me was empty, the walls bare.

My shoulder bag was still looped over my arm, though. The boy genius had neglected to take that away from me. I was more convinced than ever that I was dealing with a bunch of amateurs. Of course, I'd been abducted and was stuck here, so they knew something. I reviewed what I'd put in the bag. No pocketknife, not even a nail file.

I examined the ropes again. Definitely cotton clothesline, the kind sold in any grocery or hardware store and the same thing that was still strung between two trees out back of the Bonaparte House, though it hadn't been used in a long time. I pictured Cal's little purple bathing suit, the one with the polka dots she had loved so much as a little girl, hanging next to her big flowery beach towel. The line in my memory sagged from the weight of the wet fabric. *Cotton clothesline stretches when it's wet.* I maneuvered the purse down my arm so that its handle lay across both wrists. The zipper was partly open and it was just possible to get my fingers inside to grasp the cap end of the bottle of Diet Coke.

Holding the container between my feet and extending my bound wrists, I managed to twist off the cap. My intent was to pour the liquid onto the ropes, but I succeeded only in spilling it on my hands. The bottle fell onto the floor of the ship and formed a large brown puddle. So I simply dipped the ropes directly into the puddle. The smell of the soda wafted up to me, and in this small room it was intensified to a sickly sweetness. I let the ropes absorb as much of the liquid as they would take, then tried to pull my hands apart.

The clothesline stretched. Not enough. Only the undersides of my wrists were wet, while the tops remained dry. I needed these ropes fully soaked if this was going to work. It proved impossible to turn my wrists over so my palms were facing up. Perhaps for a double-jointed contortionist, but not for me. *Think, Georgie, think.* Yes! I lay down on my back on the floor, and stretched my arms out above my head into the pool. No telling what, other than soda, was on this floor. I'd be showering until I was pruney when I got out of here. I laid my hands in the liquid, which was by now breeding all sorts of bacteria, I just knew, until the ropes wouldn't wick up any more. My arms were stiff from being in that unaccustomed position so long, and soda dripped onto my face as I brought them back to the front of my body. I spat and sat up, arming the sticky yuck off my face. I was going to call Dr. Phelps and get myself on some antibiotics right after the shower.

With my legs tucked up under me, I began to work at the ropes. This time they expanded, and by twisting and maneuvering I made progress. A deep vibration began to rumble all around the walls of my prison. My jaws rattled, like a pair of chattering teeth in a joke shop window. It was loud as hell in there. A metallic grating noise—a chain scraping in its housing?—sent shivers up my arms. The anchor. Unless I was mistaken, we were under way.

❖ TWENTY-THREE ❖

I swallowed down the lump of panic that had risen to my throat. Where were we headed? These tall ships were supposed to be anchored in the Bay overnight and not leave until midafternoon Sunday, so as to allow the maximum number of tourists to see them. My plan, such as it was, was to escape Houdini-like from this locked room, then make my way out a porthole or over the side into the water, where I would swim for shore. This was still possible even if we were moving, but it was a lot more dangerous if the engines were running. The farther downriver we got, the deeper the water would get and the wider the river, making the swim much more difficult for me. It would take a crew of at least four or five to run this tub, I figured, so there would be that many more pairs of eyes watching me too.

I worked frantically at the ropes and finally managed to extricate one hand by squeezing my hands together and then pulling them apart parallel to each other. My wrists stung, rubbed red and raw from the ropes, but I was free.

Not exactly free, I reminded myself. The engine was so loud there was no way to tell whether someone was stationed on the other side of the door. I gingerly twisted the knob and found it locked, just as I had suspected. Lock picking was not part of my skill set. If Dolly had been here, she could have lent me a bobby pin from the depths of her coiffure. Not that I would wish this situation on anyone.

My usual purse contained a metal nail file, but that was sitting in the Morristown police station waiting for me to retrieve it. Dismantling the pen in the bag I had with me might work, but would be messy. Ah, this was better. A small wirebound notebook, which read, "MacKenzie Motor Lodge, Bonaparte Bay, NY," in gold foil letters on the cover. I began to uncoil the thin metal. Beads of blood appeared on my hand where I scraped the sharp end against my skin, and I winced. When the last coil pulled free, the papers fluttered loose to the floor in a shower of white, lined rectangles.

The wire was thin and floppy, and it surely wouldn't work in its current state. I bent it in half and twisted it around itself, creating a two-ply rod that was much more rigid. I gave it a little wave like a movie swashbuckler. A giddy laugh escaped my lips. Who was I kidding? I was in way, way over my head. But the need to put an end to this giant fiasco, the need to keep my family safe, overrode my insecurities and forced me to press on.

Poking the wire into the keyhole, I felt resistance and tried again in another spot. Again and again, different angles produced no results and I bit my lip in frustration. This was not turning out to be as easy as I had hoped. Where was Inky with his early-life-of-petty-crime skills when you needed him? Something clicked. My heart leapt and I wanted to give myself a high five. But not only had the lock released, the doorknob was turning as well.

I yanked out my ersatz pick and leapt backward, into the puddle of soda. My feet went out from under me on the slick surface and I fell hard on my behind. Yelping in pain, I whipped the tool behind me just as my young pirate friend opened the door. He snickered as he saw me sitting there and I wanted to slap that snarky little smile off his adolescent face. "I see you've been busy untying yourself," he commented. "Well, it doesn't matter. The captain wants to see you."

The captain? I knew it. That damned Captain Jack was behind this. If he really was Coast Guard (not for long, if I had anything to say about it), he could handle a ship like this. What his motive was, and how he thought he was going to get away with it, I did not know. We weren't inconspicuous in this replica sailing ship, and there must be faster boats than this out there that could catch us. I was ready to rip into him, and I didn't care what he did to me. Although, letting me live would be ideal.

"Follow me," he said in a sonorous monotone, then cracked up. "Get it? I'm Lurch!" He was so young, he must have been watching that old show on the classic TV channel late at night.

"Funny." I picked up my shoulder bag and exited behind him, my bottom uncomfortably wet. I'd be a sticky mess when I started to dry. We threaded our way through the maze of barrels. He put his black-booted foot on the bottom rung of the stairs to the hatch on the upper deck.

Here was my opportunity. He took a few more steps up. I slipped my wire around his ankles and pulled back as hard as I could, jumping to the side as he fell. He hit his head on one of the barrels, and tipped it over. He lay there stunned as I dragged him across the floor by his feet. He was awkward because of his gangly height, but he was skinny and didn't weigh much. Should I try to immobilize him? No time for that, and he was out cold. And he wasn't in charge. Maternal guilt squeezed my heart as I considered whether he needed medical attention. The kid was young, and he was somebody's son. What if he had a concussion? I was sorry, but there were bigger fish to fry.

I maneuvered around the barrel the boy had tipped over. The top had come loose. Out of curiosity I looked inside. It was filled to the top with plastic bags. Each plastic bag was filled with a dry, grassy substance. I'd bet anything it was the same stuff I'd discovered out at Sunshine Acres. There must be hundreds of packages in a barrel this size. A quick look around showed at least fifty barrels in here. If all of them were filled with these little bags, the amount of marijuana this ship was carrying was staggering. And we could be headed anywhere. Anywhere. With enough supplies and a competent crew, this ship could sail all the way down the St. Lawrence and out across the Atlantic, I thought. Or, if we were sailing in the other direction, we could be on Lake Ontario in less than an hour and making our way through the rest of the chain of the Great Lakes to some Midwestern port.

I shouldered my bag and took a deep breath as I ascended the ladder. The kid had left the hatch open and I poked my head up cautiously. Seeing no one, I came up onto the deck, squinting into the bright sunshine, and considered. Where would I find the captain? He could be driving the ship, or he could be anywhere on board while he left the driving to some underling—what were they called? Right, mates. The wheel of the ship must be up front. I hadn't seen any kind of raised bridge from which to navigate. The shores were whizzing past me at a pretty good clip, too fast for me to get a good look at any of the houses or other landmarks on either side. We hadn't come about, so I figured my first guess was right: we were headed out to the open sea, not inland.

I moved toward the bow of the boat, doing my best to keep my balance as the boat rocked and swayed. A little wave of nausea rose up and I closed my eyes and took a deep breath to quell the queasy feeling in the pit of my stomach. *What a time to get seasick.* I kept my eyes straight ahead and not on the passing shorelines to either side, and made my way to the bow. There was, in fact, a ship's wheel there, but the helm was empty. Huh? What was this, some kind of ghost ship? Who was driving us? Another glance around showed a little glass-windowed cabin I had missed before. A figure stared out at me, but the facial features were indistinguishable. I squared my shoulders, adjusted the bra strap that had fallen onto one upper arm, and headed for the structure.

Someone grabbed me. It wasn't my young friend who'd abducted me from the mainland, but another guy, dressed in a black-and-white horizontally striped shirt, a long wig with a tricornered hat, and a luxuriant dark mustache he'd waxed to stiff, curly points on either side of his lips. His eyes were rimmed with a heavy application of black eyeliner, which intensified their chocolatey depths. They would have been beautiful if they hadn't been bloodshot and watery. Based on the stale-sweet quality of his breath, he'd been drinking rum, and a lot of it. He didn't have a good grip on me. Almost without thinking I reached for one of the gold hoop earrings he was wearing and yanked as hard as I could, wincing as the flesh tore. He let go with a curse and put his hand to his bleeding ear. I gave him a sharp elbow to the gut. The breath whooshed out of him as I kicked his kneecap for good measure and ran to the side of the boat.

We were at least twenty feet above the surface of the water. This boat had a big engine and I could easily be sucked into it. My diving experience? Nil. I climbed up onto the edge and prepared to jump out as far away from the boat as possible. But I was grabbed. Again. This was getting tiresome. He pulled me back down onto the deck. This assailant had me locked in his arms and began to drag me toward the cabin despite my struggles. I heard a staticky noise. I owled my head around as far as it would go to see that the guy was wearing a headset, a wig, gold earrings, and a scarf tied around his head. His puffy white shirt with ruffles edged in scratchy lace irritated the rope burns on my wrists. He tightened his grip and I cried out in pain. Dragging my feet in an attempt to impede our progress or, even better, to trip him up, proved impossible since he was at least a foot taller and sixty pounds heavier than I, and almost certainly in much better shape. He manhandled me to the cabin door.

The door was ajar and he brought me in, depositing me on a small couch. "Don't move," he warned, pulling out a gun and training it on me. I glared at him, but complied.

"Who's paying you?" I spat out at him.

He didn't answer, but looked toward the front of the cabin.

A chair spun around with agonizing slowness. A knife twisted in my gut and my throat went dry. I looked into a face I knew well, and had hoped to know much better.

"Keith," I whispered.

"Now, now, Georgie, don't look so sad." His voice was patronizing. "This will all work out very well for all of us, if you're smart."

"What's going on here? What do you want with me?"

He chuckled. "Now, that's a loaded question." He gave me a leer, his eyes lingering on my chest. He waved his hand to his henchman. "Go find something to do," he told him. "I can handle this from here. Now, Georgie," he began.

"Yes?" I hoped the hurt and betrayal and disappointment I was feeling did not come through in my voice. I wouldn't give him the satisfaction, if I could help it. "How long have you been dealing drugs?"

He laughed again. "Honey, dealing is for amateurs. I run more of a wholesale operation. That's where the money is."

"But you have lucrative legitimate businesses going with the boats and the furniture. Surely you're making a comfortable living at that?"

"Chump change," he snorted. "I've got my eye on a villa in the South Pacific. With this score"—he waved his arm around—"and the treasure from the Bonaparte House, which I'm still waiting for, by the way, I'll be set for life."

I fought back my disgust. "I haven't found that, you know. If it's not the table, I don't have the foggiest idea what it is."

"Now, you see, Georgie, this is what is so hard for me to believe." He tapped his fingers together in the classic steeple formation of villains everywhere. "You've lived in that house for a number of years." He lowered his voice and said confidentially, "We won't say how many." My hackles rose and my hurt was elbowed out of the way by anger. "How is it possible that you don't know that Joseph Bonaparte left a stash of jewels in that house for the use of his brother Napoleon when he escaped?"

I thought back. What had Inky told me about Joseph Bonaparte? That he had stolen the Spanish crown jewels before he was deposed and used them to finance his lavish lifestyle in the Americas. Was it possible there was a cache of priceless jewels hidden somewhere in my home?

"I'm telling you I've looked everywhere in that house and I have not found anything," I said.

"You are beautiful, even when you're lying." The color rushed up into my face. This guy had some nerve.

"Where are we going?"

"We have a meeting with an outbound laker in a few hours up toward Gaspé."

"Gaspé?" That was a peninsula at the far tip of Quebec out on the Atlantic seaboard.

"Yes, Gaspé." He spoke as if to a child. "We'll be off-loading our cargo and on our way by evening."

"What do you mean, 'our way'?" I had a bad feeling about this, even worse than having been kidnapped.

"You're coming with me."

I gulped. "Where?"

He smiled and a dreamy look came over him. "Tahiti."

I stalled. "What about my restaurant? I can't just leave."

"You already did."

I tried another tack. "Did you kidnap Spiro?"

"No." There was that patronizing tone again that I was beginning to hate. "I did not kidnap Spiro. I paid someone else to do it."

"But why?"

"He is a damned nuisance." I couldn't argue with that. "He finally paid me the money he owed me, but he refused to deliver up the real prize, the jewels. I had planned to kill him—that would solve so many problems for everybody—but I needed him alive in case you couldn't find the jewels. Which you say you can't." He gave me a penetrating gaze. "And, since I want to get our relationship off on the right foot, I've decided to believe you."

What was that expression Cal always used? *As if.* But I played along. "What about Big Dom? Did you take care of him too?" I gave him what I hoped was an encouraging smile.

"Oh, yes. He was another nuisance. He owed me money too, and he took too long to get it back to me. And then he threatened to go to the Feds about me and my enterprises."

I gulped again. Drug running, extortion, and kidnapping were one thing. Murder was quite another.

"Those people at Sunshine Acres, are they part of your business too?"

"They're just my growers. Or, I should say they were my growers. We've already harvested, and I'm getting out of the business. I've instructed them to burn off any residual crop, not that there better be much left, and plow under all the fields."

"The rumor around town is that the Sunshine Acres people are running the money operation."

He snorted. "Hah! That bunch of gray-bearded burnouts? You've got to be kidding me! Still." He paused. "It did suit my purposes to have everyone believe that it was them, rather than me."

"What are you going to do about your businesses? Your house? Your shop?"

"That's the beauty of this plan. I've mortgaged everything to the hilt. I've maxed out all my credit cards with cash advances. I've taken all that cash, along with the money I've made from my other endeavors, and invested it all in offshore accounts. It's completely safe from the Feds. I'm just going to walk away. Or I should say sail away. And never come back. Never live through another six months of winter again. And you, my love"—he picked up my hand and brushed his murderous lips against my damaged wrist—"get to come with me."

I fought back a wave of revulsion and smiled at him. "What about this ship?"

He chuckled. "I had only intended to borrow it and pick up something else to get me to the islands, but I've rather come to like it, you know?" He caressed the varnished wood steering wheel. "It has style. So I've decided to keep it. The price was certainly right." His lips twisted into a grin. "I'll make a few alterations when we get there, and no one will ever be the wiser. Now, come over here."

With only a moment's hesitation, I complied. He pulled me down onto his lap, knocking my rib cage on the steering wheel. I sat down rather harder than I had intended and he let out a breath. His face darkened, but then he smiled. "We'll get you a chef and a personal trainer when we get to the villa."

Jerk. I batted my eyes at him flirtatiously. Well, I hoped it was flirtatiously. He reached around me with both arms and put them on the wheel, pinning me in. It would have been sexy if he hadn't been a criminal. I thought of Cal being motherless, and it called up the pain of my own mother abandoning me when I was younger than she. Something in me changed. I smiled at him and put my left hand up to his ear, which I lightly traced with one finger. He made a little coo of pleasure. "Plenty of time for that later, honey," he said, but he was enjoying it.

I raised my right hand, and he took his eyes away from the water for a moment to see what I'd do next. I touched my throat with my fingers, and trailed them slowly down into my cleavage. He sucked in a breath, and I could feel him shift under me. "This is so tempting, honey, but I have to get this cargo delivered." I fingered the V-neck of my T-shirt and he started to breathe heavily. I reached down inside my bra and I thought he was going to pass out.

"I always fantasized that you were like this, you know."

I did the thing with my other hand and his ear. I reached farther down into my bra.

"Just give me a few hours and I'll be able to help you

with that." His eyes were almost popping out of his head and I wished he'd keep them on the water so we didn't crash into anything, like the Ogdensburg Bridge to Canada, which I could see coming up far ahead of us. Could the masts of this ship fit under the bridge? No time to worry about that now. I arched my back so he could get a better view of my chest and neck, reached down beneath my cleavage, and pulled out Marina's tiny gun.

◆ TWENTY-FOUR ◆

"Now, Keith." I jammed the gun up against his side. "You are going to pull into the port at Ogdensburg and let me off this ship. Do it, and I won't turn you in," I lied. I planned to sic as many authorities as I could find on him just as soon as I got back to land.

"I don't know if I like this side of you. You never seemed to have this much spice." He considered. "Yes, I do think I like it. Where'd you get that gun? The toy aisle at Kinney's?"

"Are you going to do as I say?"

"Mmm, no, I don't think so. You won't shoot me."

I poked him harder with the gun. I hoped he couldn't feel that my hand was shaking. "Try me," I said.

He still had both hands around me and on the wheel. He was much stronger than me and there was no way I'd be able to break through the circle of his arms. We stared at each other like greasy gunfighters in a spaghetti western, at a temporary impasse. "We're going to be so good together," he mused.

"We're not going to be anything together." I punched at his crotch but wasn't able to get much force behind it because of my angle and having to use my nondominant hand, but it was enough. He cried out and dropped one hand to his privates. I used the opportunity to swing my legs over him and stand up. I trained the gun on him.

"Damn it! That wasn't very nice, honey," he gasped.

"Stop calling me 'honey.'" I took a few steps back. I didn't think he'd try to come after me, because somebody had to drive the ship.

I was wrong. He lunged. I scrambled to one side and his momentum carried him past me. I ran for the door. Locked or jammed, it wouldn't open. I fiddled with the handle, desperate. He came up behind me and pawed at me. I twisted out of his grip and tried the handle again. I whirled around and smacked him on the head with the butt end of the gun. It was too small to do much damage. He put a hand up to his head, then caught me by the shirt, grabbing a handful of boob in the process. He looked pleased, and continued to hold on. I brought the gun up again, but he smacked it away with his free arm. The gun skittered away across the polished wood floor and ended up against the back wall, out of reach.

Keith dragged me over to the bridge and gave the wheel a turn, away from the American shoreline where we had started to drift. He reached into a drawer near the wheel and pulled out a gun, quite a bit larger than mine. He stuck it into my ribs. "See, I just want you to understand that this doesn't feel good. If our relationship is going to work at all, we can't be trying to shoot each other all the time. It's kind of a turn-on, though." My God, he was delusional.

I gulped and nodded. "Now I'm going to call up Wally on the radio and have him come up here and babysit you while I finish this business deal. Somebody in this family has to make a living, you know." He picked up a microphone and pushed a button. "Wally, come on up here. Over." No response. He tried again, yelling this time. "Damn it, get up here now." He pressed the button again. "Over." He turned to me. "I am going to fire him."

He tried calling up two more of his crew, but still got no response. "You generously pay these people a year's salary to help you out with one day's work, and this is the kind of response you get. I'm telling you, there is no work ethic anymore." He poked the gun into my ribs for emphasis.

He kept buzzing and buzzing, getting more frustrated with each press of the button. I glanced around the cabin for something close by that I could use as a weapon. I'd dropped my twisted notebook wire belowdecks, so that was useless to me.

The door burst open. "It's about goddamned time you got here. I'm cutting your pay." Keith whipped around. His jaw dropped. I turned to look. Jack Conway stood in the doorway, with a gun pointed in our direction.

❖ TWENTY-FIVE ❖

.

"Put the gun down, Morgan. Georgie, come over here behind me."

"Conway, with all due respect for your rank and all"—he snickered—"I've got a gun too. And I've got our Georgie here keeping it warm for me. If she moves, I'll shoot her. You have to agree, that would be a shame."

"You might as well give it up. I've secured your entire crew, and you can consider yourself boarded. The U.S. Coast Guard is now commanding this vessel."

Keith's face purpled with anger. "This is my ship, and I'm going to finish my job and spend the rest of my life on a tropical island."

"I've got a dozen trained men outside who say you're not going anywhere except on an Adirondack vacation at Dannemora or Ray Brook penitentiary. Now drop the gun, and let her go."

"Make me." Had he regressed to grade school? I half expected him to stick out his tongue.

"Morgan, look out your front glass."

We turned simultaneously, the gun still pressed against my torso. The Ogdensburg Bridge to Canada loomed in front of us. We were drifting toward the Canadian side, where the clearance above the water was lower. If we didn't move under the highest span of the bridge, and soon, we were going to hit.

"Crap!" He took the wheel with both hands, holding the gun up against the wooden circle. Jack motioned and I ran over to the far wall and retrieved the little pearl-handled pistol. "I'm not letting this boat break up! I'm not!"

Jack moved quicker than I would have thought possible for a man of his size and came up behind Keith, who was still frantically trying to correct our course. He jabbed out with his right arm, but Keith swiveled around in the chair and ducked the blow. He sprang up and the two grabbed onto each other, landing on the deck. Neither was letting go and they began to writhe around like a pair of Greco-Roman wrestlers at the summer Olympics. I stared, fascinated.

"Georgie," Jack gasped through the chokehold Keith was trying to put on him. I shook my head to bring myself back to reality. "Steer the boat!"

"I can't!"

"Yes, you can!" I don't know which of them said it, but I sat down in the captain's chair and took the wheel. My breath was coming in ragged puffs as I saw what I had to do. Panic surfaced. A thought flashed absurdly back to the books I used to read Cal when she was little. Madeline. The little French orphan girl. What was it she used to say? "I'm

Madeline, and I can do anything!" I took a deep breath and said out loud, "I'm Georgie. And I can do anything!"

"Huh?" I heard from the floor.

I gripped the wheel with a smidgen more confidence and aimed for the highest span of the bridge. I had to think that if those giant lakers could make it, so could we, but I didn't know for sure. Our masts were very tall. I steered, too hard, and the boat listed to one side.

"Ease up, or we're going to capsize!" I heard from the flailing tangle of bodies beneath me. They were both panting and I wasn't sure how much longer they could keep this up. These guys weren't kids, but they were both in good shape. The boat righted itself. I vaguely wondered why the rest of Jack's Coast Guard contingent hadn't come in to help, but I had to turn my attention back to the water ahead of me. I kept my hands on the wheel and steered, more smoothly this time, aiming us toward one of the arches of the Can-Am bridge. A smallish motorboat was right in front of us. There was no way I could maneuver this ship around it. The driver looked up at us in a panic. *I'm sorry,* I mouthed, not that he could have read my lips from his position. Our momentum continued to carry us forward. The small craft's engine gunned and passed from my sight, right in front of us. I lost sight of it and closed my eyes. My heart sank as I waited for the sickening crunch. It didn't come. I opened my eyes and the boat darted out to my left, intact, leaving a plume of white foam in its wake. I said a silent thank-you. Grunts and groans were coming up from the deck, but I didn't dare turn around to see what was happening.

"Georgie," one of them rasped. "Cut the engine!"

The engine. Of course! I scanned the console. *Okay, if I were a throttle on a tall ship, where would I be?*

"I can't find it!"

"Keep looking! And keep steering!" I still didn't know which of them was talking to me, but it didn't matter.

I glanced back and forth between the console and the rapidly approaching bridge. Was that it? It had to be it. I said a little prayer, then jammed down the lever as fast as I could. I heard a thud; then we were all whiplashed forward and back. The two men on the floor rolled right up against the console at my feet. I glanced down and saw that Jack had ended up on top. He landed a barrage of heavy blows to Keith's gut, and I heard the wind rush out of him. "Georgie, hand me that line!"

I tossed him the coil of rope that was within my reach and he deftly trussed up Keith while he was still gagging and coughing. Jack got up, panting, and dragged Keith, still struggling but unable to get a purchase, over to a chair. I turned back to the water ahead of me. The boat had slowed but our momentum was carrying us forward.

"Untie me, Conway, now! You don't know what's at stake!"

We were right at the bridge. I closed my eyes involuntarily. A muffled wooden crack like the sound of a baseball bat being broken sounded high above us. I opened my eyes and we were on the other side of the bridge, passing the Port of Ogdensburg at a slower and slower pace. I couldn't see behind us but I hoped that no drivers going over the bridge were injured.

"You've ruined my boat! You've ruined everything!" Keith yelled.

"Shut up," Jack said calmly, and hauled off and smacked him in the jaw. Keith's head lolled to one side as he lost consciousness.

"What did I do?" I was starting to panic again.

"You did fine," Jack reassured me. "I'll go out onto the deck and take a look at the damage."

"Can I come with you? I don't want to stay in here alone with him."

"He's not going anywhere. And somebody's got to drive the ship, Georgie."

Oh, yeah. "Well, hurry up, okay?"

He grinned at me, his lower lip already swollen on one side. His smile was devastating, despite the injury, and I felt a little flutter in the pit of my stomach. *Get a grip, Georgie,* I told myself. *You almost took out the Can-Am bridge driving a ship full of illegal drugs and nearly killed yourself and who knows how many other people. Now is not the time.* The boat was now drifting along with the river current and all I had to do was keep a steady course down the middle. Jack brushed back a lock of my hair that had fallen in my face and I could see that his knuckles were raw and already bruising. I looked up into his blue-green eyes, and he looked into mine. He leaned in and brushed his lips against mine. My breath caught and it was a second or two before I could draw in air again. He massaged his thumb across my upper lip and pulled it away, rubbing his thumb and forefinger together. A dark oily smudge covered both digits.

"I've never kissed a woman with a mustache before," he commented. "Well, except my great-aunt Tillie. Hers was more prickly."

Damn! I must look ridiculous, I thought, as the heat rushed toward my hairline. I put my own finger to my lip and rubbed, probably making it even worse, as if that were possible. I was too mortified to speak.

"Don't worry about it," he assured me. "You're beautiful even with fake facial hair."

I blushed again.

"I'm going above to check the masts. Just keep a steady course and keep the red nuns to your port side."

"Huh, what's a nun?" I looked for some kind of black-and-white object, but didn't see anything.

"Those nuns, the red bullet-shaped buoys—see over there? Just keep them to your left, and keep the green can buoys to your right, and you'll be fine."

I located the channel markers and nodded. Jack went upstairs. I steered us on, although we were just drifting along at this point, so it wasn't too hard. Keith groaned but didn't regain consciousness. I had to hope Jack's knots would hold—well, he was a sailor, right?

Jack reappeared in the doorway. "You didn't do too badly, all things considered. You clipped the bridge with the main mast. The mast is cracked, but I think it'll hold until we get to port if we keep the sail furled."

"What about the bridge?"

"It's still standing, if that's what you mean."

I guessed that would have to be good enough. "Where are all your men? The ones who are waiting to take him away?" I nodded in Keith's direction.

"Err, there's something I should tell you about that," he said.

"Like what?" I'd still not gotten rid of my suspicion that he knew more than he was telling me. The muscles of my shoulders tensed into tight knots.

"I'm sort of here by myself."

"You were bluffing?" I was incredulous. "What about the rest of the crew of this ship?"

"As I said, I secured them."

"What do you mean, 'secured'?" That ever-present lump of panic resurfaced.

"Relax, Georgie. I didn't kill anybody, if that's what you mean. I just tied them all up. Somebody already started the job for me belowdecks," he added. "I found one of them facedown on the boards, out cold."

The guilt struck me again. "He's just a kid. We should get him to the ER when we land this thing. By the way, when are we landing?"

"We've already left the Burg behind, and to be honest"—he grinned—"I've always wanted to sail one of these things. I think we'll head farther downriver and put in at Massena. I'd love to try to get this through the Eisenhower Locks, but I guess we'll have to forgo that bit of fun," he said regretfully.

"You do know that we're carrying a full cargo of drugs?"

"I do. Here, do you mind if I take over?"

Did I mind? I moved aside and he took my place in the captain's chair. He restarted the engine and leaned back, resting his hand on the wheel.

"This would be a lot more fun if we could use the sails instead of the engines," he mused, "but I'd need a competent crew to work the rigging. Still, you don't get to do this every day, now, do you?" He smiled and drove us along.

"You didn't happen to notice a bathroom on this thing?" At this point all sense of personal dignity had drained away from me, but I wanted to see whether I could freshen up a little before we docked and I rejoined humanity on dry land.

"It's called the head, Georgie, and I think I saw one toward the stern." He paused, registering my blank stare. "The back of the boat," he said. "I'll make a sailor of you yet." He gave me that devastating, temporarily damaged smile again and I nearly melted into a puddle right there on the deck.

I passed the still-unconscious Keith, resisting the urge to give him a kick in the shins, and exited the cabin door, toward the back of the boat. I located the head and entered. I closed my eyes and raised my face to the mirror, opened my eyes, then closed them up tight again. It was as bad, no, worse, than I had feared. My hair was an Einstein mess, frizzed out into an unflattering and unnatural shape. I made my fingers into combs and tried to smooth out the tangled mess. This was going to require a lot of conditioner when I got home. I found some soap and made a lather in my hands, then scrubbed at the greasy black smudge across my lip. The lather turned gray and oily and I looked back in the mirror to see that the smudge was now less intense but had expanded onto both cheeks. I rinsed off my hands and started again. This time, with some scrubbing, the makeup came off, leaving fresh pink skin underneath.

I put the toilet seat down and sat on the closed lid, trying to collect myself. I should have felt relieved, but I was still keyed up. After a few deep breaths, my heart rate slowed to an acceptable level. I went out onto the deck into the fresh air and headed up toward the cabin. The hairs stood up on

the back of my neck. *Not again!* I thought. *What now?* I
returned to the cabin. Jack was practically humming at the
wheel.

"Hey, Georgie, you're back! Did you find it?" He spun
around in the chair and his face froze. "Brian!?"

"Uncle Jack?"

◆ TWENTY-SIX ◆

I looked behind me. There was the tall gangly kid who had kidnapped me. He was rubbing his head.

"Get in here right now!" Jack ordered. The boy lifted his chin in defiance. "Brian, move it!" He gave in, probably from force of habit being raised in a military family, and stepped into the interior of the cabin. "Take off that stupid wig and get over here." He stood up. Brian moved closer. Jack took a step toward him and wrapped him in a bear hug. "You dope! What the hell are you doing? I've been worried sick about you!"

Brian hung his head. "I'm sorry, Uncle Jack."

"Sorry doesn't cut it. Why haven't you called me? What are you doing mixed up in this mess?"

"I heard about the Acres and I thought it sounded like a nice place to go, you know, to get my head together after Dad died." His voice faltered and when it returned, it was just above a whisper. "Then they offered me this extra job, you know, loading the barrels."

"Do you know what's in the barrels?" Jack's voice was wary.

"I know they're damn heavy!" He turned to me. "Sorry, ma'am." He tapped his foot nervously. "But the barrels were all sealed up, so no, I don't know what's in 'em. They just asked me to move them from the veggie truck onto this ship last night."

Last night? The ship just sailed over from Canada a few hours ago; I'd seen it from the park.

As if he'd read my mind, he continued. "I guess they brought it over in the middle of the night, and then I came down and helped load it up. Then they sailed it back across, and came back again this morning."

I believed, or wanted to believe, that he hadn't known what he was doing. But Jack could deal with him and decide whether to turn him in to the police.

Up ahead white smoke billowed from the smokestacks at the aluminum plants at Massena. Jack pushed a button on the console and spoke up. "Harbormaster, this is Captain Jack Conway from the Coast Guard."

"Roger that." The voice was staticky but understandable. "Captain Jack? Are you kidding?" I thought I heard a snicker.

Jack ignored the remark. "Harbormaster, I've recovered the tall ship stolen from Bonaparte Bay. I've called the Coast Guard station and they are sending a team to secure the ship and its cargo. I'll need a deep water mooring, so I'll be anchoring offshore, not at the docks. Please clear the area so the team can do their work."

"Roger, will do."

"And call the state police and have them send a couple of cars. I've got some people on board they'll be interested in."

I glanced over at Brian. His head jerked up and he cut his eyes to Jack.

Jack shut down the engine and the heavy anchor scraped the bottom of the St. Lawrence. The ship glided to a gradual stop about a hundred yards offshore.

"Georgie, this is where you get off."

"Huh?"

"I'm going to need to stay here and get things cleared up."

"What am I supposed to do?" I hadn't thought this far ahead. How was I going to get home? It wasn't like there was any kind of regularly running public transportation in the North Country, and we were at least fifty miles from the Bay.

"Do you have somebody you can call to come and get you?" Jack asked.

I considered. Keith, still tied up and unconscious in the corner of the cabin, was certainly out of the question. Sophie wouldn't drive this far and Dolly would be busy at the restaurant. It would take Liza too long to get here, and I wouldn't want to take her away from the island in the middle of the day. Russ? No, I wouldn't be asking him for any more favors. I wondered what was happening at home and felt an overpowering urge to get there as soon as I could.

"I'll find a ride. You do what you need to do here."

He stood up and came closer to me. "You are an amazing woman—you know that?" He put his arms around me in a protective hug and then pulled back enough to look down at me.

I screwed up my courage and looked up into his face. He pushed my hair back over one shoulder and bent down. His lips were on mine, his kiss soft and warm. I closed my eyes and let him kiss me. And then I kissed him back. *I could get used to this,* I thought. *I'd like to get used to this.*

We launched a small rowboat over the side. I climbed down the rope ladder and into the craft. I clipped on a life jacket and reached for the oars. "Wait, Georgie," Jack called out. "Brian, row her over to shore and wait for me. Find something to do, because I'm going to be a while, but you'd better be there when I come ashore."

"Okay, Uncle Jack." He boarded the little boat and took the oars. Deep fatigue settled into my bones and I fought to keep my eyes open. I had already decided I wouldn't be pressing charges against this boy for kidnapping me, but I had a feeling that Jack was going to hold him accountable for his actions. I hoped he'd be able to avoid a criminal record.

The thought stopped me cold. I hoped *I'd* be able to avoid a criminal record. We had Big Dom's killer, so I would be cleared of that suspicion, but there was still the matter of my having done some breaking and entering. Oh, yeah, and ditching a State Trooper. At least he didn't know about the bag of dope and that jug of maple syrup Inky had.

We pulled up to shore and I climbed up onto the wooden docks. Brian tied off the pram and followed me. I unfastened my life vest and dropped it down into the little boat, where it landed with a soft thud. Brian took his vest with him, laid it down on the end of a park bench in front of the harbormaster's office, and put his head on it, curling his long legs up onto the wooden slats. He closed his eyes and it looked like he intended to sleep until Jack came back to deliver his punishment, whatever that would be. Couldn't say I blamed him. I'd been up for a lot of hours, and I'd love to go to sleep myself.

"Sorry," he said to me. "I'm so sorry."

"Thanks, Brian. I hope your head's all right."

He mumbled something and shifted on the bench before settling into sleep.

I headed toward an official-looking building. The entire wall facing the water was plate glass. Bright blue lights whirled on top of police cruisers beyond in the parking lot. Sirens screamed in the distance. I wondered how long it would take Channel 7 to get a news crew here from Watertown. They'd have to hustle since it was at least a sixty-mile drive. I opened the glass doors of the harbormaster's office, intending to ask to use a telephone to call a cab, which was going to cost me a fortune.

"Hello, Georgie," a sickeningly familiar voice drawled. I would have spun on my heel and walked out if I thought I could have gotten away with it. As I turned around, my nervous face was reflected in the mirrored sunglasses of my favorite State Trooper.

A lump formed in my throat, but I swallowed it down. "Hello," I squeaked. I cleared my throat.

"Nice to see you again." The voice was deep and scary, just like I remembered it. He could have a nice second career doing voice-overs for horror movies.

"Uh, you too." Damn! I was destined to spend the night in the county lockup. I just knew it. No, wait. Liza would come and bail me out. I was cheered by that thought, anyway.

Detective Hawthorne lowered his chin and peered at me over the tops of his glasses. He had big dark eyes that showed no emotion at all, fringed with extra-long eyelashes. Such a waste on a guy. "Need a ride home?" he asked.

"Er, well, yes, I do, as a matter of fact. I don't have my cell phone, so I was just about to borrow one from somebody here."

"Who were you going to call? Your colorful friend? Maybe you could stop for Chinese food on the way home," he suggested drily. "How about I give you a ride, and you and I can have a little chat?" It didn't sound like a request, more like an order.

"Sure, that would be nice." I hoped I sounded sincere. My heart was pounding. I summoned up a smile and followed him to the parking lot, where he opened the back door of his unmarked cruiser. He spared me the indignity of pressing my head down with his hand as I got into the car. Even better, he hadn't cuffed me and the news crew hadn't arrived yet.

Once inside, I had to admit this was sort of interesting. Embarrassing and terrifying, but interesting. I'd always wondered what it was like in the back of a police car, and here I was, staring at the pattern made by the metal mesh screen separating me from the detective. I hoped nobody I knew saw me. Fat chance of that, I thought ruefully. Living in the North Country is like living in a reality television show where anybody can just tune in to your life anytime, then discuss it around the watercooler. Sophie would have heard about this before we even left the Massena town limits.

We drove back along the river toward the Bay, the Trooper

lecturing me all the way. It was all I could do to stay awake, between the drone of his voice, the lull of the asphalt, and the fact that I hadn't slept in more than twenty-four hours. I pressed a fingernail into my palm, then jerked myself awake with the pain. A livid crescent appeared where I'd inflicted the wound, and I shook my hand to dissipate the ache. It hurt, but at least I was awake. Until I dozed off again.

Finally we pulled into the parking lot of the Bonaparte House. Wait. The restaurant? He wasn't taking me to jail? I should have been paying more attention to his monologue on the way home. Maybe I could have saved myself some needless worrying.

". . . so don't leave town. This investigation is going to take a while, and I'm going to want to talk to you. Sorry I had to make you ride in the back, but it's procedure." Relief washed over me as he exited the car and came around to open my door. He offered me a hand and I pulled myself out into the open air. "I'll be in touch soon."

I should tell him about Russ, but decided to keep it to myself for now. "Sure. I'm not going anywhere."

"Keep it that way." He got back in the car and peeled out, kicking up gravel as he left the parking lot.

I stood there for a moment, steeling myself. I breathed deep and long, relaxed my shoulders, and walked into the Bonaparte House.

Sophie wheeled around when she heard the screen door open. "Where you been?!" she demanded. "You don't look so good."

Yeah, I was aware of that.

"How come you didn't tell me you got a prisoner upstairs?" Dolly. She must have spilled the beans. Well, I guessed I couldn't blame her. I'd been away for hours.

"I didn't think I'd be gone so long."

"How much are we gonna have to pay Brenda to be the warden? How come there's a very jingly guy in my son's room?" she continued. "He looks like a junkyard, all that metal."

"That's Inky." God, I did not want to have to be the one to explain this situation to her.

"Is that Spiro's . . . friend?"

Of course she would know already. I sighed. "Yes, that's Inky. He's a very nice guy. You'll like him when you get to know him."

She grabbed my arm and whispered to me, "You're not gonna leave me too, are you?"

I looked into her face, suddenly old, and saw the fear. She understood, either overtly or intuitively, as did I, that something was different about the relationship between Inky and Spiro. Something permanent. Something that might make him want to make a life somewhere else. I made a decision. "No, Sophie. I'm not going to leave you. I love you, and I love the restaurant, and this is my home."

She patted my arm. I gave her a spontaneous hug. We weren't usually affectionate with each other and she stiffened, but then hugged me back.

A muffled crash came from the direction of the spiral staircase and we both looked toward it. I broke into a run, Sophie close behind me, faster than any senior citizen I'd ever seen.

Around and around, up the spiral staircase we ran until we reached the cupola. Dolly had heard the crash too and came puffing up behind us, her huge gold pendant swinging from side to side. Her smoker's breath was ragged as she met up with us, but her great nest of hair was still high and perfect.

Brenda's chair in front of the door was empty, Russ's rifle nowhere to be seen. Damn! The door swung open and we all three ran up the last flight. I could hear the struggle going on in the cupola room. Russ must be trying to escape. Oh, God, this was my fault. If Brenda was hurt, I'd never forgive myself.

I surveyed the room as I reached the top of the stairs. Basil's old armchair was overturned, its torn and dusty cambric tipped up and facing us. Russ and Brenda were struggling on the floor. I could hear her grunts and moans of pain. "I'm here, Brenda!" I yelled. "I won't let him hurt you!" I reached out blindly and grabbed the first thing my hand touched. I pulled the heavy brass kaleidoscope from the basket next to the chair and raised it over my head, preparing to bring it down on Russ.

Brenda sat up, breathing heavily. Russ sat up too, wiping his mouth. Oh. My. God. The image would be burned into my mind for eternity. They'd been making out. At least, I hoped they'd just been making out. "Brenda!" I yelled and shut my eyes.

Brenda stood up and adjusted her clothes. She looked sheepish. "You don't have to pay me."

Russ grinned his toothless smile at me. I'd been holding my breath and I released it with an audible whoosh. The stones inside the kaleidoscope clunked as I lowered my arms. Stones? I gave it another shake. I'd always assumed it was just bits of glass inside there, but now that I thought about it, the sounds they made were thicker and heavier than little chips of glass should be. I held the device up to my eye and pointed it toward the fading sunlight coming from the window. I moved closer and spun the wheel at the end. The pattern inside changed to a bloodred and crystal design. I spun the wheel again and the design was a sparkling blue and green. I stared at the colored fragments for a long moment, then turned around.

"Sophie, what do you know about this kaleidoscope?"

"That old thing? Basil used to come up here every day and mess with it. Spin, spin, spin. It drive me crazy!"

"Do you know where it came from?" I fiddled with the various brass pieces but couldn't figure out how to open the thing up.

"That musta been here when we bought this place. Basil found it somewhere. He used to say, 'Sophie, we're gonna be rich. Sophie, we're gonna be rich,' then do the spin. Over and over. Then he have a heart attack and—pop!—he's gone. And I'm not rich." Her eyes were sad, whether because of the lost husband or the lost fortune, I couldn't say.

I ran my fingers over the device. This time, I found a small catch. I manipulated it and the end chamber hinged open. I located the corresponding catch on the other side and opened that too. The brass cylinder with the eyepiece detached and I laid it on the seat of the chair. Russ and Brenda were standing off to one side, his arm around her possessively. I guess they made . . . Well, nobody could say a cute couple, but a couple who made sense together.

I held the end piece like a cup and looked inside. I

couldn't help letting out a little gasp. Sophie shoved over and leaned over the cup. "What is it?" she demanded, reaching into her apron pocket for her reading glasses. "Looks like marbles." Dolly came over and looked in too. I gave the cup a gentle shake. It was filled with large, translucent, polished stones in various colors of the rainbow. Except these weren't just stones. Unless I was very much mistaken, I was holding what remained of the Spanish crown jewels.

◈ TWENTY-SEVEN ◈

Steps sounded on the stairs behind us. I whipped around, putting the cup behind my back. Inky stood in the doorway, with his arm around Spiro, holding him upright.

"He insisted I help him get up here," Inky explained. Spiro looked like death warmed over and was barely moving under his own power, but he was at long last conscious.

"Where is he?!" he rasped. "I'm going to kill him!"

"Who?" I looked around and then realized, of course, that he meant Russ, who was staring at him malevolently from across the room.

Spiro tried to make a move for Russ, but didn't have the strength to break Inky's hold on him. "Easy, Spiro. He's not worth it."

"He is worth it, damn it!"

Russ's expression darkened in garish contrast to the

yellowish gray bruise covering one side of his face. He pointed to his cheek with a stubby middle finger. "This better not leave a mark." Brenda looked up at the bruise nervously. So there'd been no bar fight keeping him out of work the other day. Spiro hadn't gone willingly. I should have guessed.

I glanced from Spiro to Russ, and back again. There was something I was missing here. Some association that wasn't clear yet.

"My treasure!" Spiro cried in horror as he saw the dismantled kaleidoscope. I still had the cup in my hand. "Where is it?"

"Don't worry, I've got it," I reassured him.

Russ saw his chance and lunged for me. I stepped up on top of the overturned chair and went over the other side, still on my feet and miraculously holding the cup upright. I felt a painful spasm in my calf and knew I'd pulled another muscle.

Inky propped Spiro up against the wall. "Now, stay put! Do as I say!" He crossed the room at warp speed, and put Russ into a headlock. Dolly picked up the gun, which Brenda had stowed over in one of the eight corners of the room, and trained it on her son, not for the first time.

"Now, settle yourself down and shut up," she ordered. "I ain't shot a deer yet this season but I'll settle for you."

"He's always had everything! The best of everything!" Russ spit out, still trapped in the iron circle of Inky's left arm. "Now he's got a bunch of jewels too! It's not fair!"

"Life ain't fair, remember? If you'd gone to community college for restaurant management or up to Wanakena to the forest ranger school like I wanted you to, you'd be making good money by now." She turned to Sophie. "No offense. We've got good jobs here and you treat us real well," she said sincerely. Sophie nodded at her.

"Them jewels should be mine!" Inky tightened his grip. "They're half mine, anyway," Russ choked out.

"What the hell are you talking about?" Dolly asked him, waving the barrel of the gun up and down.

"Them rocks, this house, they're half mine. Basil was my father too."

We all stared at him. Sophie's face was white and stony, her lips compressing into a line so hard it was possible her face might crumble from the pressure. Dolly's face turned scarlet. There was a long moment of silence; then she burst out laughing.

"You idiot!" she managed between guffaws. "Basil wasn't your father!"

Sophie did not relax. It was pretty clear that she had suspected something like this might be true. Now I understood why she had kept Dolly and Russ around all these years, even after we knew he'd been sneaking steaks and bottles of beer and liquor out in the boxes of vegetable trimmings. Maybe having them around was her way of keeping her husband's memory alive. Or more likely, she wanted Russ and Dolly where she could keep an eye on them in case they tried to capitalize on the relationship. She was not taking Dolly's word for it, but she remained silent.

"Oh, come off it, Ma! He must be my father. Look at me and Spiro!"

I looked from Spiro, who appeared to be preparing to throw

up, back to Russ to see whether there was any resemblance. They were about the same height, and both had dark hair and similar hazel eyes. Russ was thirty pounds heavier and ten years Spiro's junior, but hard living had aged him prematurely. All in all, their similarities could easily have been coincidental. I couldn't tell, and I didn't think anybody else could either.

"Russ, your father's dead. You know that." Dolly's first husband, Cliff, who refused to wear anything more rigid than a greasy Yankees ball cap on his head, had died when he hit a tree root hidden by the snow and flipped his four-wheeler thirteen years ago. We'd provided the funeral lunch at no cost.

Russ didn't look convinced. Dolly sighed, then continued. "Russ, how long have I been working here?"

"How the hell should I know?"

"Watch your mouth, mister. Didn't I teach you better than to cuss in front of ladies?" Brenda stood up a little straighter. I doubt she'd been called a lady too many times in her life.

"Well, I've been working here for thirty years. This summer is my anniversary," she added, tipping her head in my direction to make sure I'd heard. We'd have to plan some kind of celebration after Labor Day, or at least a gift. "Now, how old are you?"

"Thirty-three," he answered, and I could see him mentally doing the math, none too quickly, all things considered. He looked up at his mother. "You mean Cliff really was my father, and you weren't banging Basil?"

"I said watch your language! Now, you apologize to Sophie."

"Sorry, Sophie," he said. Inky let go of him but blocked his way to the stairs.

I looked from Sophie to Dolly and back. Dolly hadn't

answered the question at all, but I wasn't going to say anything about it. It was very, very quiet. Sophie finally broke the silence.

"Come downstairs," she ordered. "I made moussaka today. Russ won't get any kind of good food in jail."

EPILOGUE

"So, when's the auction?" Liza asked me over a glass of wine and some shrimp skewers. I bit off a chunk of the delicately spiced crustacean, chewed, and swallowed appreciatively. It was a Wednesday evening, quite warm for September, and Bonaparte Bay was pretty much shut down until the weekend. It would close up for the winter after Columbus Day. Liza's spa business, though, stayed open till Thanksgiving. I reached for my glass and leaned back into the chair.

"After the first of the year. Christie's gave us an estimate of two hundred and fifty thousand. They think half a million wouldn't be out of the ballpark."

She nodded at me. With Jack's help I'd retrieved my table from Devil's Oven Island and managed to get it back to the Bonaparte House unscathed. I had an antique appraiser from DeKalb Junction take a look at it. He offered me a hundred dollars. I declined. Then, just for ha-has, I sent an e-mail and some photos to that PBS television show. An appraiser came barreling up from New York City the next day, and informed us that we had a very fine, early-American table made in Philadelphia in the mid-1700s. We were still trying to document whether Joseph Bonaparte had owned it at his estate in New Jersey. It would have been an antique even then. If we could prove that, the table was practically priceless. The Christie's people were working on that for us now.

"Sophie must be beside herself."

"She's already counting the money, no question about that. But we're likely to be tied up in litigation with the Spanish government and the remaining descendants of the Bonapartes and the Spanish royal family for years. Whether we ever see any money from the jewels is up in the air. And now that Spiro and Inky have decided to buy the Sailor's Rest from Big Dom's long-lost wife, whom he apparently never bothered to divorce, she's afraid she's going to have to support the two of them."

"That doesn't seem likely. Inky has a great head for business."

"I know. Sophie should be happy. They've decided to turn it into a retro nineteen-fifties-style diner, which will attract a totally different clientele than we have at the Bonaparte House. I think they're going to do well." I ate another shrimp. "That's why Spiro got involved with Keith, you know. He wanted to buy a business and a house on the river and start a new life with Inky. He thought he'd be able to pay Keith back once he sold the jewels. But he got in over his head."

"Keith's trial is coming up," she offered, somewhat tentatively. It was kind of her to try to spare me, thinking that I might have still had some feelings for him.

"He wrote me a letter from the county lockup, if you can believe that. Asking me to bail him out."

"I take it you didn't."

"Hell, no. He can rot there for all I care." And I meant it. "The police recovered the bottle of Ouzo he used to knock out Big Dom. It came from the Sailor's Rest. From what Spiro tells me, the day of the murder Spiro, Keith, and Dom were out drinking on a boat, discussing business. They argued, and Keith hit Dom, shot him, and pushed him overboard. Spiro tried to intervene but Keith had already drugged Spiro's Ouzo and he passed out."

"I hear Russ got off with probation," Liza said.

"Well, Inky and Sophie convinced Spiro that he should let it go. Pressing charges for kidnapping would have brought out some pretty unpleasant things about Spiro and the missing money, among other things, and the publicity would be bad for business and for their future together. Of course we fired him, and Dolly told him she'd drive him to jail herself if he ever showed up here again."

"The Sons of Demeter weren't real?"

"The investigation isn't finished, but it looks like Keith just made up the group to draw suspicion away from himself and try to pin it on the Sunshine Acres people. They never found any evidence of illegal drugs being grown there, so it looks like the hippies got off scot-free."

I paused and took a sip of the delicious crisp Pinot Grigio. The stack of papers I'd recovered on my nighttime raid of the commune's barn had been useless. It was simply documentation related to restaurant orders—and Dom's name was crossed off because he wouldn't be needing any more produce.

"Did I tell you I offered to buy out Sophie and Spiro from the restaurant?"

"No!" Liza leaned closer, intrigued. "What did they say?"

"Spiro agreed, of course. He and Inky have the new restaurant, and they've got their eyes on a riverfront cottage they want to rehab, so he wants the money."

"And Sophie?"

"Turned me down."

"I thought she was desperate to get back to Greece full-time? The sale of that table ought to bring enough money for her to retire very comfortably."

"You'd think so. But it seems she's got an iron in the fire here, and she wants to see how it heats up."

Liza had clearly not heard anything about this through the Bay gossip lines. "What do you mean?"

"Remember Hank at Sunshine Acres?"

"Yes, I think so. We get our organic produce from there."

"So do we. I've started buying from them again. There just isn't anyplace else locally to buy that quality of vegetables and dairy. Anyway, he's started coming in to Marina's diner and hanging out, waiting for Sophie to come in. She pretends she's not interested, but I think she likes him. Or she likes the attention. At her age, what does it matter?"

"So what about you? Do you have any irons in the fire?"

I cut my eyes to her. "Jack and I have seen a little bit of each other. I mean, I had to thank him for trying to protect me by following me out to the Devil's Oven that night. And to apologize for Sophie whacking him."

"Come on, Georgie, spill it."

I smiled. "Next time I go to Watertown, I'm seriously considering buying a lace thong. A real one."

AUTHOR'S NOTE

Although the characters and events of *Feta Attraction* are
fictional, there's some real history underlying this story.

When Napoleon Bonaparte was at the height of his
power, he crowned his brother Joseph King of Naples and
Spain. Joseph was deposed after a short time, and he escaped
to America, where he purchased a large tract of land in New
Jersey. He built a lavish estate, almost certainly financed
via the coffers and jewels of the Spanish government that
he raided before he left. He lived extravagantly in the United
States for seventeen years.

Joseph Bonaparte also purchased thousands of acres of
wilderness in Northern New York, near the Canadian border
on the western edge of the Adirondacks. He built some large
homes in that area, including a hunting lodge on the shores
of the lake he called Diana, but which is now known as Lake
Bonaparte. He visited a few times, and installed his mistress,
Annette Savage, and their daughter, Caroline, in the North
Country, far away from his New Jersey estate, once the relationship broke down. Caroline married a local man who

squandered the money Joseph settled on his daughter. Their relationship was long, and very unhappy (and I fully intend to write that story someday).

During the years of Napoleon's defeat and exile to Elba and St. Helena, a number of French expatriates settled along the St. Lawrence River in New York State. According to local legend, a plot was hatched to free Napoleon and hide him out until political events in Europe made his return to power possible. An octagonal stone house was built (known locally as the Cup and Saucer House due to its unusual construction) in Cape Vincent, New York. The house was apparently fitted up nicely for a deposed emperor. It featured movable walls on the upper floor, and was said to contain numerous highly valuable objects, including artwork and a Stradivarius violin. It's unclear where these items ended up. Napoleon died in exile and never made it to New York State, and the house was destroyed by fire decades later.

Evidence is sparse that Joseph Bonaparte was involved with the plot to bring his brother to America, but it seems inconceivable he would not have known about it. For purposes of this story, he did. If you'd like more information about the Bonapartes in America, as well as recipes and other fun stuff, please visit my website at susannahhardy.com.

RECIPES

❖

Recipes to Make You Think
You're on a Greek Island

You don't have to travel to Greece—though I hope you do someday!—to be able to enjoy the flavors of these beautiful islands. Light a candle, put on some bouzouki music (start with the soundtrack from *Zorba the Greek*), and enjoy a night in the Aegean!

Greek Chicken with Lemon and Thyme

Serves two (recipe is easily doubled).

Zest of ½ lemon
Juice of ½ lemon
¼ c. olive oil
1 t. dried thyme, rubbed between your fingers,
or 2 t. fresh thyme leaves

Pinch of sea salt
2 boneless, skinless chicken breasts,
or 6 chicken tenders

Whisk together first 5 ingredients in a shallow bowl. Add chicken, turning to coat in the marinade. Cover with plastic wrap, and refrigerate for at least an hour, basting the chicken with the marinade a couple of times.

Preheat gas or charcoal grill, stovetop grill pan, or countertop electric grill. When it's good and hot, grill the chicken until golden and cooked through. Don't overcook!

◈

Greek-Style Roasted Potatoes

Serves two (recipe is easily doubled).

3 medium potatoes (Yukon Golds are delicious,
but all-purpose spuds are fine too)
1 onion, peeled and sliced
2 T. olive oil
Pinch of sea salt
A few grinds of black pepper
Chopped fresh flat-leaf parsley

Preheat oven to 425 degrees.

Wash and peel potatoes. Cut each potato in half lengthwise, then cut each half into 3 wedges. Dry with a paper towel. Place in a bowl along with the onion slices, and pour the olive oil over the top. Season with sea salt and black pepper and mix to coat the potatoes well.

Line a shallow rimmed baking sheet with foil. (You will not get good results if you use a baking dish with high sides.) Spread the potato mixture in a single layer on the baking sheet.

Bake for 35 minutes, or until potatoes have a nice, crispy golden crust. Check on the potatoes once or twice during the baking process to be sure they're browning evenly and the onions are not burning. Give them a stir if necessary. Sprinkle with chopped flat-leaf parsley.

◈

Tomato Salad with Cucumber and Feta

Serves two (recipe is easily doubled).

1 pint grape or cherry tomatoes
½ medium cucumber, peeled and seeded
Handful of fresh basil
4 oz. feta cheese, cubed or crumbled
1 or 2 T. olive oil, depending on how
juicy your tomatoes are
Sea salt and fresh cracked pepper to taste

Halve tomatoes and place in a pretty serving bowl. Cut seeded cucumber in half lengthwise, then into chunks approximately the same size as the tomato halves. Make a chiffonade of the basil by stacking the leaves and rolling them into a tube, then slicing through the tube to create fragrant ribbons. Add to the tomatoes and cucumbers, along with the cubed or crumbled feta. Drizzle the salad with olive oil and sprinkle with salt and pepper. Toss gently so as not to break up the cheese too much. Serve at room temperature for best flavor.

◈

Chicken Marengo

While not historically a Greek dish, Chicken Marengo echoes the flavors of the Mediterranean. Napoleon is said to have requested Chicken Marengo the night before every battle. Whether that's true or not, there are many interpretations of the recipe, all no doubt delicious. Here's my Greek-style version, which can be cooked in a slow cooker or on top of the stove:

Serves six.

1 large onion, peeled, halved, and sliced
2 large cloves garlic, crushed
2 T. olive oil
2 c. cleaned, sliced white button mushrooms
½ t. dried oregano, rubbed between your fingers
½ t. dried thyme, rubbed between your fingers
½ c. dry white wine or chicken broth

2 T. Metaxa 7 Star (a delectable Greek liqueur)
1 28-oz. can good quality, low-salt crushed tomatoes
½ c. pitted, sliced Kalamata olives
6 boneless, skinless, meaty chicken thighs
18 medium-sized shrimp, peeled and deveined
6 eggs
Handful of chopped, fresh flat-leaf (Italian) parsley

In large Dutch oven, sauté onions and garlic in olive oil just until fragrant. Add mushrooms and cook for 3 minutes more. Add spices, wine or broth, and Metaxa, then stir in tomatoes and sliced olives.

If you are using a slow cooker (recommended for busy people!), transfer half the mixture to the crock, place chicken thighs on top, and cover with remaining sauce mixture. Cook on high for one hour, then turn to low and cook several hours or until chicken is tender (slow cookers vary).

If you are cooking on the stove, place chicken breasts into sauce mixture and spoon sauce over the meat. Cover, and cook on low for approximately an hour and a quarter or until chicken is tender. Add salt and pepper to taste.

Just before serving, add shrimp to mixture in slow cooker or Dutch oven and cook several minutes, just until pink.

Using a nonstick skillet, fry 6 eggs over easy (in batches, if necessary) in additional olive oil.

Place one chicken thigh on each plate and ladle sauce over it, making sure each plate gets its share of shrimp. Top each serving with a fried egg. Serve with crusty bread to soak up the juices. Any leftover sauce is delicious the next day over pasta or rice.

Cherry Ouzotini

1 oz. Ouzo (an anise-flavored Greek liqueur)
1 oz. citrus-flavored vodka
4 oz. orange juice
½ oz. maraschino cherry juice (more if
you like a sweeter drink)
Splash of seltzer or lemon-lime soda

Place Ouzo, vodka, and orange and cherry juices into a cock-tail shaker with ice. Shake it, shake it, baby! Pour into martini glass (there'll be some left over for a second drink), add a splash of seltzer or soda, then garnish with orange slice, maraschino cherry, and a mint leaf. Enjoy!

For more recipes, visit the author's website:
susannahhardy.com